THE SWIMMING CLUB

Rachel McLean writes thrillers that make your pulse race and your brain tick. A proud indie author who manages her own publishing company, she has sold millions of copies digitally and hundreds of thousands in print, regularly topping the bestseller lists. She is the author of the Dorset Crime novels and five spin-off crime series, with beloved characters appearing in multiple series. In 2021, she won the Kindle Storyteller Award with *The Corfe Castle Murders*. She divides her time between Birmingham and Dorset and lives with her wife, three children and two cats Cagney and Lacey.

Millie Ravensworth is the pen name of two authors who have been writing entertaining novels together for more than ten years. The Millie Ravensworth books focus on their shared love of crime stories and charming characters who readers love spending time with.

ALSO BY RACHEL MCLEAN AND
MILLIE RAVENSWORTH

The Jurassic Coast Mystery series
The Swimming Club
The Empty Easel
The Shattered Bauble

The London Cosy Mystery series
Death at Westminster
Death in the West End
Death at Tower Bridge
Death on the Thames
Death at St Paul's Cathedral
Death at Abbey Road

RACHEL McLEAN
MiLLiE RAVENSWORTH

THE SWIMMING CLUB

A JURASSIC COAST MYSTERY

Copyright © 2025 by Rachel McLean and Millie Ravensworth

All rights reserved.

No part of this book may be reproduced in any form or by any electronic or mechanical means, including information storage and retrieval systems, without written permission from the author, except for the use of brief quotations in a book review.

This is a work of fiction. Names, characters, businesses, places, events and incidents are either the products of the author's imagination or used in a fictitious manner. Any resemblance to actual persons, living or dead, or actual events is purely coincidental.

Ackroyd Publishing

ackroydpublishing.com

Printed and bound in the UK by CPI Group (Uk) Ltd, Croydon CR0 4YY

CHAPTER ONE

"Oh!"

Annie Abbott hesitated as the cold water of Lyme Regis Bay reached her waistline.

By now, she should have got used to this, but every morning she came down here, it took her by surprise.

The dreaded 'oh' zone, as she called it.

She squeezed her eyes shut and waded a little further out. She could do this. In fact, once she was fully immersed, it would be bliss.

"Swim!" came a voice from up ahead. Her friend – acquaintance maybe, Annie wasn't sure – Rosamund, never the slightest bit fazed by the water temperature.

"You can do it, Annie!" Another voice from behind: her friend Helen, still in the shallows but always encouraging.

Rosamund turned away and swam out towards the buoys, oblivious to Annie's pain and carving a smooth crawl through the waters of the bay.

Go for it, Annie told herself. *Do it*.

Annie grinned, or it may have been a grimace, she wasn't

entirely sure, and ducked down to bring her shoulders under the water.

"Oh!"

There it was again. The cold-water shock, but not quite as bad this time.

She smiled. *Now* she had it. The perfect way to begin a morning in her beloved hometown, even with the initial pain. This would make her feel alive for the rest of the day. Not that it took much to make Annie Abbott feel alive.

She swam out past the end of the harbour wall, waving to other swimmers as she went and racing Helen, who'd somehow overtaken her and was almost out as far as Rosamund now.

Annie pulled in regular breaths, timing her strokes with the habit of someone who'd done this for a while – not the decades of some of the other women here, but long enough. At last, she was with the other two.

"Well done," called Rosamund. "Every time I imagine you're going to chicken out and go back onto the beach."

Helen barked out a laugh. "Our Annie, never!" She threw Annie a wink. "You're made of sterner stuff than that."

Perfect.

She swam on, almost to the line of orange buoys that were always their goal, and tipped onto her back to float and enjoy the early summer sunshine in her face.

She pulled in a deep breath and felt her body relax.

A splash interrupted her calm: Rosamund, approaching with precise, powerful strokes. She paused, stretched her long neck and peered towards the shore. "I see she's sticking it out."

"Who?"

"That odd young woman with the silly name."

CHAPTER ONE

Rosamund turned in the water, all elegance and grace as usual. "See you back on the beach."

Annie allowed herself a few more minutes' floating – it really was bliss, with the bright shapes of the beach in the distance and the waves bobbing her up and down – then headed for shore.

When she arrived, Rosamund was standing by the harbour wall, hopping on one leg.

"You alright, love?" Annie said.

Rosamund shook her head. She was wincing and blood was pouring from her left foot.

"Oh. That's not good."

Helen had an arm out to support Rosamund. "That's it, darling. You're doing swimmingly. No pun intended."

Rosamund let out a gasp.

"What happened?" Annie asked.

Helen turned to her. "Not sure. She can barely speak."

"Trod on something." Rosamund's lips were pale and tight. "Bloody hurts."

Annie had never heard Rosamund swear before.

Rosamund managed to hop further onto the beach. Annie crouched down behind her and peered under her foot. *Ouch.*

"You've stepped on a razor clam."

A piece of straight, broken shell was embedded lengthwise in the sole of Rosamund's foot.

"That must hurt like buggery," Annie said.

Rosamund gasped. "It does."

Slowly, the four of them moved up the beach to the promenade, Helen on one side, Annie on the other, and young Figgy flapping about behind.

At the steps, Rosamund leaned on the railings, looked down at her foot, and groaned.

Annie peered at it. Should she pull the thing out? It was hardly a mortal wound, but it was possible the jagged shell was plugging the injury. Maybe pulling it out would make things worse.

Rosamund eyed her. "You're not pulling it out," she said.

"Probably wise. But you're going to have to go to the hospital."

Annie turned to Figgy, who'd fetched a towel to drape over Rosamund's shoulders. "Go to the Kiosk. See if they have a first aid kit."

"Don't tell Cameron," grunted Rosamund as the young woman ran off. Her twenty-year-old son worked at the Kiosk. Figgy nodded.

"Where's your car?" Annie asked her.

"Cobb Gate," said Helen. "Her usual spot."

Rosamund shook her head. "I can't drive with this in my foot."

Annie raised her eyebrows at Helen.

"I can't drive it," Helen said. "It's an automatic. I've watched her. It's like flying a spaceship."

"You are *not* crashing my car," grunted Rosamund.

"I don't want to."

A woman in an orange baseball cap and apron emerged from the Kiosk carrying a green first aid case. She took one look at the foot and said, "Hospital."

"Yes," said Annie. "We're just debating who can operate Rosamund's car."

The woman shook her head. "My car's just there. I'll run you to the medical centre. You got another towel? I don't want blood on my foot mats."

CHAPTER ONE

With one of Annie's towels cradled under Rosamund's foot to catch the blood, the group moved over to a Peugeot parked on the promenade. Helen got into the back with Rosamund.

"Keys," said Annie, holding out her hand to Rosamund. "We need to move your car. I'll drive it. Figgy will supervise."

"Thanks, ladies," said Rosamund with a weak smile. "Keys are in my lime green tote, on the wall down there."

Annie gave her a reassuring smile. "They'll soon fix you right up, lovely. We'll take care of your things for you."

The Peugeot pulled away.

"Right," said Annie. "Let's fly this spaceship."

"You're sure you can do it?" Figgy asked. She'd been quiet throughout the whole incident and seemed almost scared of Rosamund.

"I can give it my best shot," Annie said. "Don't have much choice, do I?"

Figgy nodded and followed her to the Cobb Gate car park, which was at the eastern end of the promenade.

"I think parking's only free at the Cobb Gate before eight, so we might need to get a wiggle on. Don't want to anger the parking gods."

They retrieved Rosamund's bag and strolled along the Marine Parade towards the wedge of car parking at the Cobb Gate.

In front of the Kiosk, a wary customer moved away from the counter, cradling her purchase and glaring at a seagull circling above.

"Bloody thieves, those gulls," Annie noted.

"They do put up warning signs," said Figgy, pointing one out.

"And some people still try to get refunds if they've been targeted."

"Oh, I know," said Figgy. "Cameron told me."

Annie narrowed her eyes at the younger woman. "So this Cameron...?"

Figgy was blushing.

Annie winked. "Ah, just friends, then?"

Figgy dropped her gaze, smiling. "I don't know."

Young love was a wonderful thing. Horrible, stressful and awkward, but wonderful, nonetheless.

"Well," said Annie, "I hope Cameron gives the refund-hunters short shrift. It's not like anyone can control the seagulls, is it?"

Figgy nodded. "There's one that comes round my caravan. I swear it can tell the time; it knows all my routines."

Annie wondered what sort of routine might interest a seagull. Did it watch her alarm clock, waiting until she was due to wake up, then do the job itself?

"Bin day can be hard work," said Figgy, putting an end to Annie's speculation.

"I bet it's a proper nuisance."

Figgy frowned. "It's like it's my nemesis, but also my pet."

"Complicated, then?"

A laugh. "Oh, yes."

They reached the car park, an area below the main road up and out of town, where a dozen or so cars could park in a circle.

"D'you know which one's Rosamund's?" Figgy asked.

"It'll be something swanky, I'll bet." Annie fished the keys out of the tote bag and pressed the fob. "Looks like it's an Audi."

Figgy pointed. "Over there."

It was indeed swanky. Annie and Figgy walked over to an SUV the steel grey of a rain-heavy sky.

"Oh," said Figgy.

"What?"

Figgy was peering inside. "Is someone in there? Rosamund never said..." She frowned at Annie.

Annie followed her gaze. In the front passenger seat, shadowed by the high stone wall above, was a man.

"Well, this might be a bit awkward," she said. "I guess this is Rosamund's hubby."

"You know him?"

Annie blew out her cheeks. "I don't even know what his name is. She doesn't talk about him much."

"What do we do?"

"We do what we came here to do. At least we can tell him what's happened to Rosamund."

She tapped on the tinted window, but the man didn't respond. Now that she was up close, she could see he was asleep.

She tapped harder.

"Don't wake him," hissed Figgy.

"We have to wake him."

"D'you think he's ill?"

"He might be drunk," mouthed Annie, trying not to sound judgmental. "Maybe he needs a bit of a prod."

She eased open the door so that she could reach in and shake the man's shoulder, but his weight shifted sideways. She found herself having to catch hold of him before he toppled out of the car.

It was only then, as she shouldered him back into an

upright position, that she noticed the wound on the top of his head.

"Oh, hell!" She backed away from the man and the open door, grasping for her young friend's hand. "Figgy, what's...?"

Figgy had her free hand pressed to her mouth. She looked back at Annie, reflecting her fear back at her.

"Is he...?" she whispered.

Annie nodded. "I think you're right. Oh my God Figgy, Rosamund's got her dead husband in her car."

CHAPTER TWO

DC Tina Abbott stood in the doorway of what had once been her and her husband Mike's bedroom, watching him pushing something into the wall. It looked like he was trying to patch up a section that had crumbled.

"Are you sure you're doing that right?" she asked.

He turned to her. His face fell.

"T," he said. "I was hoping you wouldn't see."

She smiled, walking up to him and putting an arm around his waist. He turned to her and gave her stomach a rub. Only a matter of days now until the baby was due.

"It's OK," she said. "You don't have to hide it from me."

"I can't believe what a hash I've made of all this." He gestured around the room.

She grabbed his hand and kissed the back of it. "I'm sure I wouldn't have done any better. But I *am* going to have to move out for a bit."

"I know." He sighed. "I envy you."

"Really? Going to Lyme Regis where my mum can go

into full-on supergranny mode while she waits for this baby to come out?"

"She's not that bad."

"She *is* that bad."

"She does it because she loves you, you know."

"Oh, I know that. But I just wish she would rein it in sometimes. Last week she bought a set of Barbie princesses for this one." She patted her stomach. "I mean, she hasn't even been born yet."

"And you haven't told your mum she's a she."

"No. But I must have let it slip at some point, because Mum's house is becoming pinker and pinker every time I go over there."

Mike stifled a laugh. "Sorry, but it is funny. Annie Abbott wants to be a good granny, and for her, that means buying stuff for her grandkids."

Tina raised an eyebrow. One of the reasons Mike was doing this DIY, a project that had gone wrong in ways she preferred not to think about, was to create more storage space for their son Louis, who acquired a new toy every time they went to Lyme Regis.

"She does. Anyway, I'm heading off now. Louis is ready and waiting with a picture book and his favourite teddy. Are you sure you don't mind us disappearing when things are so close?"

"You'll be back before your due date, won't you?"

She nodded. "Definitely. There's no way I'm letting my mum pretend she's a midwife."

"Or a doula."

Tina pulled a face. "Don't even think about it. Did I tell you what she did when Naomi was in labour with Poppy?" Naomi was Tina's sister.

CHAPTER TWO

"You told me a fair few things."

"I don't think I told you about the singing. Mum reckoned that if she stood outside the delivery room and sang happy songs, Naomi would experience less pain."

Mike laughed. "Where did she get that idea from? Her cranky friend at the gallery?"

"Helen Cruickshank? Probably. Certainly not the one who looks like she's got a broom up her you-know-what. Rosamund."

"Oh, they're harmless," Mike said.

"I wouldn't bet on it. And if Dougie had had his way, he'd have arrested Mum right outside the delivery room."

Mike grinned. "PC Dougie Anderson, never off duty." Dougie was Naomi's husband and a PC in Lyme Regis police.

"You and I both know what that's like," Tina said. "At least with me away for a few days, you won't have to worry about getting home on time."

He cocked his head. "I *like* getting home on time."

"You know what I mean. You can clear up some paperwork before your paternity leave."

He curled his lip. "Paperwork. The scourge of any police detective."

"And you're marvellous at it, love." She kissed him then picked up the last of her bags. "I'll see you at the weekend, yes? You'll come over to give me some moral support."

"I thought you weren't even staying at your mum's?"

"Oh, I'm staying at Naomi's. But Mum is livid about it. I'm not sure if I've given myself a quieter life or not."

"It'll be fun. A bit of R&R by the sea while I sort out this wall." He looked at it, his body slumping. "I'm so sorry about this."

Mike was attempting to divide the larger of the two bedrooms in their tiny Sandford house into two, so that Daisy could have her own room when she came back from the hospital. It hadn't gone well so far.

"You'll get it sorted. I trust you." She rubbed his arm and headed down the stairs.

As she reached the front door, she heard her husband's voice call down the stairs.

"Make sure those friends of your mum's don't get up to any trouble!"

She chuckled. They may be a strange bunch, but they were, as Mike said, harmless.

"I will!" she called back.

CHAPTER THREE

ANNIE SHUT the door and took a breath.

Figgy was right. There was a dead body in Rosamund's car.

This wasn't the sort of thing she expected to find after a morning swim. It wasn't the sort of thing she expected to find at any time.

She opened the door for another look.

Yes. There was a dead man in there.

She closed it again. "I don't understand."

Figgy shrugged. "Me neither."

Annie opened the door and double-checked. Yes, definitely a man. She closed it again.

"What are you doing?" Figgy asked. "You're just wafting it."

"I'm not *wafting* it. I'm stunned."

She looked around. Lyme Regis was a town of early risers, and there were other vehicles parked in the car park, people moving around. But no one was looking their way. No one had a clue what they'd just uncovered.

"Hop into the back seat," she said.

"What? It's folded down."

"We need to gather our thoughts. Let's put it back up."

Figgy's eyes were wide. "We're getting in the car with... with *him*?"

The two of them pushed the seat up and climbed into the back of Rosamund's car.

"I don't understand," whispered Figgy.

"I don't either, but we probably don't need to whisper."

They stared at each other.

"He might not actually be dead," said Figgy.

"True."

"We should check for a pulse."

"Good point," Annie replied. "Where's the best place to, er, do that?"

"Neck." Figgy held her fingers up to her own neck.

Annie steeled herself. She liked to think of herself as good in an emergency. She wasn't squeamish, but this... This was outside her comfort zone.

The man in the front seat wore a suit. Not a tidy one. His hair – where it wasn't matted with blood – was loose and uncombed. From back here, the way he lolled in his seat made it look like he was just catching forty winks.

Annie reached forward. "'Scuse me, Mr Winters." She pressed her fingers into the man's neck.

Nothing. Not even a flutter.

"No." She turned to Figgy. "Nothing. In fact he feels a bit... well..."

"A bit well?"

"A bit, well, dead."

"How does someone feel dead?"

Annie shrugged. "I don't know. D'you want to feel him?"

"I do not."

The two of them stared at each other for a moment.

"Listen," said Annie. "I'm just going to come right out and say this. Because I reckon that we're both thinking the same thing."

Figgy was shaking. "*I'm* thinking that we voluntarily decided to sit in a car with a dead man." She ducked down, glancing behind her. "And there's someone watching."

Annie looked past her towards the steps leading up beside the car park. A spiky-haired man was standing in the second step, peering in their direction. He wore a khaki fishing vest and had a fabric satchel slung across his chest.

"Oh, hell," Annie said. "Do you think he saw?"

"Saw what?" Figgy was bent down so low she was practically lying across the back seat.

"Saw us wrestling with a dead man."

The spiky-haired man wrinkled his nose, turned away and trotted up the steps. He didn't look back.

Annie put a hand to her heart. "I think we got away with it," she said. "He's gone."

"You're sure?"

Annie nodded. She looked at the man in the front seat. "As I was saying, before spiky-haired wotsisname so rudely interrupted us. I'm thinking Rosamund must have known her husband was here when she parked her car this morning."

"*What?*" said Figgy.

Annie pursed her lips. "I'm assuming it's her husband. Yeah? And he's dead. So, she must have known that."

"No." Figgy frowned. "Why would she do that? Are you saying she killed him? And then told us where her keys were?"

Annie bit her lip. "I mean, we don't know what happened, do we?"

"So should we call the police?"

Annie was torn. She knew and trusted the police, they were family, after all. But Rosamund was a friend. You didn't just find a body and immediately call the police. Well, obviously that *was* what you did, but this was an unusual situation.

"I think," she said, "that we should get Rosamund's side of the story before we involve anyone else. It seems only fair."

"Yeah? You think?"

"I mean, it's not like he's going anywhere, is it?"

"Are you joking? Is that a joke?"

Annie put a hand on Figgy's arm. "I'm not joking, Figgy. I'm just saying that we need to discuss this with Rosamund. We take the car to her—"

"We're disturbing a crime scene."

"It's more like taking the crime scene with us, isn't it?"

Figgy peered over at the man. "We need to check it's him. That it's Mr Rosamund."

Annie nodded. The girl was right. "We could check his wallet," she said.

"*We* could..." echoed Figgy.

Annie snorted. *If you want something doing...*

"I'll get into the driver's seat," she said. "We need to move this bad boy in the next few minutes anyway." She frowned. "And by bad boy, I mean the car, not the erm—"

"Yeah. Yeah. I know."

Annie sat alongside the corpse, then took out her phone and snapped a couple of pictures. "There we go."

"What are they for?"

"Identification purposes."

"I mean... OK."

Annie showed her the pictures.

Figgy checked them. "Take some close-ups of his face, then check his pockets."

Annie reached over to the man's jacket. Men's jackets had so many pockets, lucky so-and-sos. She checked the outer patch pockets: empty, bar some crumbs. There was an inner left pocket with something bulky inside. She slid it out.

"Cigarettes."

"Does Mr Rosamund smoke?"

"No idea. I don't recognise the brand." Annie looked at the classy-looking gold wrapping. Old-fashioned. She took a photo of the packet, then slid it back in place. She checked the other inside pockets, and his trouser pockets, too. All empty.

"Nope, that's it. Mr Rosamund was travelling light apart from his, erm..." Annie flicked through her photo library to check. "Furongwang cigarettes."

"Buckle him in if we're all done," said Figgy, fastening her own seatbelt in the back.

"Buckle him in? It's not like he's going to get hurt."

Figgy pulled a face. "It's a fancy modern car. It probably won't even let you drive away if it thinks the passengers aren't secured."

Annie remembered that Figgy was a bit of a geek. A *lot* of a geek. "Right you are." She grimaced. "I don't believe I'm doing this."

CHAPTER FOUR

Helen sat in the back of the kiosk woman's Peugeot, clutching Rosamund's hand as they sped up the hill away from the beach. Rosamund was pale, muttering to herself.

The woman turned to glance at them. "My name's Pat," she said. "I'll take you to the medical centre on Uplyme Road. They've got an urgent care service."

Helen nodded. At least that wasn't far.

They made their way up Cobb Road, repeatedly stopping for cars coming the other way. Every time the car slowed, Rosamund grunted.

Don't be sick, Helen thought. *Don't be sick*. The woman – Pat – had been concerned enough about her car to protect its mats with towels. What would she be like with vomit?

At last they reached the medical centre.

"Here we are," Pat said as she pulled up right outside the doors. "I can't stop, sorry – too busy at the kiosk – but I hope you get on OK."

"Thanks," Helen said. "This was very kind of you."

Pat shrugged. "Least I could do." She got out of the car

CHAPTER FOUR

and came round to open the back door. Helen climbed out and between the two of them, they helped Rosamund out.

"Ouch," Rosamund said as her foot made contact with the ground.

"You need a wheelchair," Pat said. She helped Rosamund to a low wall, where she and Helen helped her sit, then hurried back to her car and drove off.

Helen looked around her. Had they picked up any of Rosamund's things before coming up here? Any of her own things?

No, they hadn't.

All she'd had with her was her swimming gear. She never took valuables to the beach when she was swimming, she knew her girlfriend Harper would let her in when she got home. But she was very fond of her dry robe. She'd bought it on Etsy from a woman who made custom ones with swirling patterns and vivid colours. It complemented her bronze-coloured kaftan and her floppy wicker sunhat.

It's fine, she told herself. *Annie will have it all in hand.* Figgy, too. She hadn't spoken to Figgy much – the younger woman seemed painfully shy – but she seemed the sensible type.

And besides, Rosamund's foot was more important. Helen could only hope that someone here would be able to remove the clam and do whatever was needed to prevent infection.

Rosamund was slumped on the wall, her foot raised in front of her.

"Can you lean on me, to get inside?" Helen asked.

Rosamund shook her head. She'd started crying.

"Oh, hell," Helen said. "I'm sorry, Rosamund, darling."

"I can't believe this is happening," Rosamund sobbed. "On top of everything else."

"Everything else?"

"David. My husband. He's... I don't want to talk about it." Rosamund covered her face with her hands. "Can you see if they'll bring a wheelchair? Please?"

"Of course," Helen said. "Marvellous idea." She sped through the front doors of the medical centre. There were four people sitting in the waiting room and a woman behind the reception desk.

"Hello," she said, aware that she was garbling her words. "My friend's had an accident on the beach. She trod on a razor clam."

The woman frowned. "Is she still there?"

Helen gestured towards the doors. "She's here. We got a lift. But she can't walk. Can you bring a wheelchair?"

"Of course." The woman, whose name badge said *Janet*, stood up. She disappeared through a doorway then re-emerged with a wheelchair, which she wheeled out next to Helen.

"Show the way," she said.

Helen could have kissed her, she was so grateful. "Follow me."

Rosamund was still on the wall, sobbing openly now. When she saw Helen and Janet, she wiped her face with her sleeve, which was already crusted with blood.

She pointed to her foot. "It hurts so much. I hope there isn't nerve damage."

"Let's get you inside," Janet said, "so a doctor can take a look. Don't worry, you're in good hands now."

Helen swallowed. *Oh, thank goodness.* She wasn't good

CHAPTER FOUR

in an emergency, and now that she was no longer the person in charge, she felt like she might faint herself.

As Rosamund was wheeled inside, Helen's phone rang: Annie.

"Annie," she said. "I'm at the medical centre with Rosamund. They haven't seen her yet, but—"

"Has she said anything about her husband?" Annie interrupted.

"I'm sorry?"

"I don't know his name. Mr Winters, I suppose. Has she said anything about him?"

Helen frowned. "She... well, she did mention him. But she said she didn't want to talk about it."

"Oh, hell." Annie's voice went quiet; she was covering the phone, talking to someone with her. Figgy?

"Have you managed to move her car?" Helen said.

"We have. Long story. But we're going to come and find you. We need to talk."

"You'll be wanting to know how Rosamund's foot is, I imagine." Helen was puzzled as to why her friend hadn't asked. This wasn't like Annie.

"Oh yes," Annie said. "That, too. But there's something else. We'll explain when we get there."

CHAPTER FIVE

Annie started Rosamund's car and pulled away, imagining she was captaining an ocean liner. A smooth, stately ride, although somewhat spoiled by the corpse riding shotgun.

She made her way up the hill, squeezing the car along Silver Street. It was a two-way street, but not wide enough for two cars the size of Rosamund's to pass each other.

Annie looked in the rear-view mirror at Figgy, who was staring out of the back window. "Bold choice of Rosamund's to have such a big car in Lyme Regis," she said, driving cautiously so as not to draw attention. Figgy grunted, swallowing repeatedly. *Poor kid*.

"Did you know what she was like?" Figgy asked.

"What who was like?"

Figgy closed her eyes; anything to avoid looking at the dead man in the front seat. They'd wedged him with some towels, doing their best to avoid direct contact. Fortunately, he was staying upright.

CHAPTER FIVE

Should they be doing this? After finding a dead body, the right thing to do was call the police. Annie didn't need to have three police officers in the family to know that. But if this was Rosamund's husband, and she'd killed him...

Rosamund didn't speak about her husband much. But Annie had heard rumours. What if he was violent? What if she'd acted in self-defence?

There was something about Rosamund: her toned physique, her Nordic blonde hair and blue eyes, perhaps even her chilly surname, that made her seem cold and robotic, maybe even loveless. But even all that didn't make Annie think she was a killer.

Rosamund should have a chance to explain herself before Annie brought Tina's lot in.

"Rosamund, of course," Figgy said. "Did you know she was a killer?"

Annie shook her head. "We *don't* know she's a killer. We don't even know who this fella is." She gestured towards him, careful not to touch. "And if it is her husband, and he..."

"I know." Figgy sniffed. "If he hurt her, then maybe she did it out of self-defence."

"Or maybe she didn't do it at all," Annie said. "Maybe he killed himself."

"What, sitting there in the car?"

Annie shrugged. "I don't know, do I?"

"I thought your daughter was police?"

Annie looked in the rear-view mirror. Since when was Figgy so argumentative?

"She is," she replied. "But that doesn't make me an expert."

Figgy nodded. "She doesn't approve of me."

"Who? Tina?"

Since when did Tina know Figgy? Annie glanced in the mirror; she supposed they weren't far apart in age. Possibly the exact same age.

Figgy wrinkled her nose. "No. Rosamund. I'm pretty sure she doesn't approve of me getting friendly with her son. I've got brown skin, and I live in a caravan."

"Rosamund's no racist," Annie said. "And yours is no ordinary caravan. One of the best spots in town, Monmouth beach."

"It's still a caravan."

"I thought you were proud of your home? Of the memories of your nan?"

"I am," Figgy grunted. "But Rosamund..."

"You think Rosamund's judging you?"

Figgy shrugged.

"That's just mothers for you. We're protective. When my Tina told me she was pregnant with Louis—"

"We're here," Figgy said, cutting Annie off.

"Ah yes," she said. *At last.*

She took the right turn to the medical centre and parked in the car park round the side, putting the passenger side next to a hedge so people wouldn't see their passenger. She pushed the driver's door open, glad to get out of the car.

Figgy was climbing out of the back seat, dusting herself off as if the man had been sitting on her lap.

"Let's give Rosamund a chance to explain herself," Annie said. "Helen can tell us if she's said anything."

"She was delirious when she left the beach."

Annie shrugged. "Either way, she's our friend. We talk to her, then we call the police."

Figgy folded her arms across her chest. "Fine. As long as we won't get blamed."

"We won't, Figgy love. Don't worry."

"So how are we going to get Rosamund to talk?" Figgy asked.

Annie pursed her lips. "Don't know. Let's cross that bridge when we come to it."

CHAPTER SIX

Figgy sighed, and they went inside the building. Janet on reception was someone Annie knew by sight; she flashed her a smile. "You've got Rosamund Winters in? I'm taking care of some arrangements for her. Need a very quick word."

"Some arrangements?" murmured Figgy.

"Oh, hi Annie," Janet replied. "She can't be disturbed right now, you'll need to wait."

"She's going to be facing one hell of a fine if I wait," replied Annie. "She had to drop everything, and you know how strict the parking is down at Cobb Gate. I just need to get her car keys."

The receptionist huffed and picked up a phone. A moment later she put it down. "Treatment Room Three, but you must keep it brief."

Annie exchanged a look with Figgy. They hurried to the treatment room, closing the door behind them.

Rosamund reclined on a bed, a cloth draped over her foot. Helen sat on a chair nearby.

"Hello, darlings," said Helen. "Can you believe we're still waiting for the doctor?"

"Not strictly true," muttered Rosamund. "I've had some painkillers and a local anaesthetic already."

"But no actual doctor." Helen drummed her fingers on the chair. "I need to open the gallery at nine."

"Yes, good. Glad you're being taken care of, Rosamund," said Annie. "There's something important that Figgy and I need to ask you about. We went to fetch your car."

Rosamund hitched herself up onto her elbows. "What's the matter?" she asked, concern passing over her face. "Did you crash it or something?"

"No. The car's fine. Well, it's fine in terms of being intact." Annie looked at Figgy.

"Annie's a great driver, she drove us up here very safely," Figgy confirmed.

"Thanks, Figgy." Annie scrutinised Rosamund's face. "As I say, we drove your car here. We were in it."

"I assumed you might be," said Rosamund.

"We were..." Annie waved her arms around, unsure how to express what she wanted to say. "We were inside it."

Rosamund frowned. "Did you get sand on the seats?"

"No," said Annie. "Not that we're aware of."

"Actually, I think we did," Figgy interjected. "I had sand on my thighs."

Rosamund looked relieved. "That's fine," she said.

"I don't think Figgy's sandy thighs are the issue here," said Annie. "We were inside your car, Rosamund. *Inside*."

"This is like some sort of obscure Victorian parlour game," said Helen. "Are we *all* inside Rosamund's car?"

"No."

"Are you having some sort of mental episode?"

"I am not, Helen," said Annie. "We were inside and got to look all around the inside. Because we were *in it*."

Rosamund remained stony-faced.

"We saw everything," said Figgy. "It's time to confess."

Rosamund's eyebrows shot up. "Oh!"

"Oh, indeed," said Figgy.

"Oh, indeedy-do," added Annie.

"And that's it, is it?" said Rosamund. "You're going to judge me? Right now, when I'm at a low point?"

Annie frowned. "We're not here to judge. We're here to help. Tell us all about it."

"Look, I know it's bad for me, and I know what they say about the link with heart attacks."

Annie looked at her. "Heart attacks?"

Rosamund fixed her with a glare. "It's one energy drink. I don't think it's going to kill me. It's just that I've had trouble sleeping lately."

"Energy drink?" asked Figgy.

Rosamund nodded. "In the cup holder, right?"

Annie looked at Figgy. Figgy looked back at Annie.

Helen stood up. "Excuse us a second, Rosamund," she said. "I'm going to have a word with our friends outside."

Helen might have been smaller than either Annie or Figgy, but she ushered them out with unstoppable momentum.

Once in the corridor, with the door closed behind them, Helen gave the two of them a fierce look.

"What are you two blethering on about?"

"The body," Figgy hissed.

"*What* body?"

"Helen," said Annie, "Rosamund's car wasn't empty when we found it. Her husband was inside."

"Yes?"

"And he was dead."

"Dead," agreed Figgy.

Helen blinked. "Do you mind repeating that? Because it sounded like you just said the body of Rosamund's husband was in her car."

Annie nodded. "Yes. There's a dead man in the passenger seat. He's been murdered."

"Head wound," said Figgy, pointing in the general direction of the car park. "We brought him with us."

Helen gave them an incredulous look. "Why?"

Annie shrugged. "Well, I guess she had her reasons. Husbands and wives kill each other all the time, don't they? I might have killed mine at some point if he hadn't rudely kicked the bucket first. Helen, has Rosamund said anything to you about him?"

Helen frowned. "She did mention him on the way over, but she was delirious. And she hardly said anything."

"She's lying," Figgy said.

"Hang on, you two," Helen said. "Are you really saying you drove here with him in the passenger seat?"

Annie looked back at Helen. Figgy bit her lip. All of a sudden, Annie realised what a stupid idea that had been.

"Why?" hissed Helen, her tone incredulous. "Why on earth did you bring him with you? Why haven't you called the police?"

Annie sniffed. "We thought it would be best to give Rosamund the chance to explain first. And... and we thought we were being watched."

"By a man with spiky hair and a waistcoat with lots of pockets," Figgy said.

"A fishing jacket," Annie corrected.

Helen shook her head. "What? That's Jason Mordaunt you're talking about. Local journalist, master of hatchet jobs."

"What kind of hatchet jobs?" asked Annie, her stomach clenching.

"Oh, complaining that the shops in Lyme are ripping off customers. Comparing café sandwich prices with Tesco meal deals. He's got it in for Clifford Muldoon, the artist who paints the Cobb. I can tell you, I'm privileged to be able to sell Clifford's artwork."

"So you think he'll do a hatchet job on us, if he saw us with a dead body?" Annie asked.

Helen looked at her. "I think Rosamund's got more to worry about in this matter, don't you?"

"Yes," Annie admitted.

Helen cocked her head. "Although you have tampered with a crime scene."

"That's what I said," said Figgy.

"But Rosamund is refusing to admit it," Annie pointed out.

"Maybe because she didn't know he was in there!" Helen hissed.

Annie shook her head. "It's pretty flippin' obvious he was in there. He's there in the front seat with blood all over his head."

Helen's eyes widened.

"Maybe it's like that film with thingy in it," said Figgy. "The angry British guy. He commits a murder and then gets so confused he forgets he even did it. She did say she was having trouble sleeping."

"Drinking Red Bulls..." added Helen.

"I think it was one of those Monster energy drinks, actually," said Figgy.

CHAPTER SIX

Helen pulled in a long breath. "Drinking energy drinks doesn't make you lose your memory, does it? Show me this man." She made to move to the exit.

Annie stopped her with a wave of the hand. "I took a photo."

"Oh, taking photos of dead husbands. The prosecution are going to have a field day with you."

Annie brought up the photos. She flicked past the cigarettes and close-ups until she reached the best image of the man's whole body.

Helen blinked. "This isn't Rosamund's husband."

"What?" said Annie.

"He was in the car," added Figgy.

"It must be him," said Annie, suddenly unsure of herself.

Helen looked at her, her gaze sharp.

"*This,*" she said, gesturing at the photo on Annie's phone. "This isn't Rosamund's husband."

CHAPTER SEVEN

"You know this person?" Annie asked Helen, her eyes still on the photo of the dead man.

Helen nodded. "It's Marco."

Figgy and Annie glanced at each other.

Helen tutted. "What? Neither of you know Marco Callington? He's the guy with the fossil shop next door to me."

Annie could picture the fossil shop. It was one of several in Lyme Regis that traded on the town's reputation as the jewel in the crown of the Jurassic Coast. Fossils could be found in plentiful supply on Charmouth beach, but there were shops that built on the excitement by selling tours, books, trinkets and other paraphernalia. Not to mention other fossils from halfway across the world.

"Marco?" Annie said. "No, can't picture him."

She scowled at her feet, trying to work out what to do next.

The receptionist appeared, making her jump.

"Dr MacKenzie will be with Mrs Winters shortly. You *will* need to leave while she takes care of Mrs Winters's

CHAPTER SEVEN

foot." She opened the door to Rosamund's room and then looked back. "Will someone be able to drive her home in a couple of hours?"

Annie nodded. "Yes, of course." She waved through the door at Rosamund. "Back to pick you up in a bit, Rosamund!"

Rosamund nodded and waved back.

Annie, Figgy, and Helen walked out through reception and to the car park.

"So the question now is, what on earth do we actually do with Marco?" said Annie.

"Why is that even a question?" asked Helen. "Dead bodies are not our business. You have police in your family, don't you, Annie? Get them to do the necessary." She flapped a dismissive hand.

"Yes. I mean, that's the problem," said Annie. "We've messed about with a crime scene. Not just a bit, but a lot. That makes us... what does it make us? Accessories?"

"That can't be right," Figgy said, her eyes wide. "Maybe we should put the corpse back where we found it."

"In the car park? In the car?"

Figgy didn't look sure. "Well, somewhere appropriate."

They reached the car. Helen used both hands to shield her eyes as she peered through the passenger window.

"Well, this just doesn't make sense," said Helen.

"I don't know about making sense," said Annie. "It is what it is. The corpse is here. Look. Quite plainly visible."

"Just..." Helen closed her eyes and took a breath. "Just tell me what happened."

"There's not much to tell," said Figgy. "We were at the beach with you. You and Rosamund went off in the lady's car and then we came over to Rosamund's car and..."

"Boom! Body in the front seat!" said Annie. "Just sat there, plain as day."

"But that doesn't make sense," said Helen.

"You've said that already. Is this what artists do, Helen? Do they imagine the world as they want it to be? Because if you could imagine this body somewhere else, that might be helpful."

"I just can't see the sequence of events."

Figgy sighed. "Beach. Car. Open car door."

"Boom. Body," said Annie.

"So, what do we assume happened *before* that? Did Rosamund invite Marco into her car, clobber him over the head and then think 'oh, I think I'll pop to the beach for a swim'? Does she even know Marco? Do they move in the same social circles?"

"These are not the questions the police are going to be asking," said Annie. "They're less fussed about what social strata the murderer and victim belonged to and more inclined to ask: 'What is this man's body doing in your car, Mrs Winters?'"

"Well, that's what I'm wondering," said Helen. "Odious chap, he was."

"Should we be speaking like that?" said Figgy. "About the dead, I mean."

"Best time to talk about people, in my opinion," Helen observed. "His shop was a bargain basement tourist trap. Of all the shops targeted by that buffoon of a journalist's articles, Marco's was the one that actually deserved it. Shoddy fossils. Era-inappropriate toys."

Annie wrinkled her nose. "Era-inappropriate toys?"

"I saw a plastic dimetrodon in the window display.

Permian creature if ever there was one, and the coastline here throws up fossils from no earlier than the Triassic."

Annie suppressed a laugh. "OK, OK. Can I be really, really clear here? Really one hundred percent crystal clear? Neither me, the police, nor sweet baby Jesus cares what kinds of dinosaurs this poor dead man had in his shop—"

"The dimetrodon was not technically a dinosaur," said Helen.

"What we care about is that there is – and I can't believe I have to remind you of this – what we care about is that there is a dead man sat in this car right now and we really, really need to do something about that."

The other two women nodded. A second later, Figgy turned to Helen.

"What's a dimetrodon?" she whispered.

"It's like a big chonky crocodile but with a spiny sail all along its back," Helen muttered.

"Oh, yes. I've seen pictures of them."

Annie rolled her eyes. "We are all going to prison."

CHAPTER EIGHT

"We don't have to go to prison if we move the body somewhere more appropriate," said Figgy.

Annie frowned. "Like where? What would be a more appropriate place for a dead body?"

"I know," said Helen. "He leaves the key for the back door of the shop in a little nook he thinks is secret. We could let ourselves in and put him in there."

"In his shop?"

"What could be more natural?"

Helen gave a *ta-da* gesture, as if she were describing the best way to arrange flowers.

Figgy raised a hand. "I agree. Put him back in his own environment and tip off the police with an anonymous call."

"Good," said Annie. "Get in, everyone."

Figgy looked doubtful about getting back in the car with the corpse.

"Come on," said Annie. "In you all get, we can't draw attention to ourselves like this."

Figgy and Helen climbed into the back, but Helen leaned forward again.

"It's fascinating to see someone in death, don't you think?" she said. "It reveals the differences that our conscious mind makes to our appearance. Where we tense our muscles, the way our posture asserts itself."

Annie glanced at Marco, but of course she had no frame of reference. She didn't know what the 'before' picture looked like.

"Does anything about his appearance look unusual to you?" she asked Helen. "Posture aside."

Helen shook her head. "Don't think so. That dreadful suit was very much his regular uniform. Now, do you know how to get to the back of my shop? We need to go round the houses a bit via Monmouth Street. I'll point it out when we get close, so we can be discreet."

Annie drove Rosamund's car back into town, slowly getting used to the huge vehicle. She followed Helen's directions to the back of the shops, heading down smaller and smaller alleys until they'd wrapped themselves in a complex spiral.

"I'd suggest that we all step out and make sure we know where we're going, before we disturb him," said Helen. "If we're fortunate, we might figure out an easy way to move him, because that's not going to be straightforward."

Annie shrugged: *makes sense*. "Lead the way."

Behind the shop was an area of rough shale bounded by tumbledown walls and a scrubby hedge. A few other cars were parked there, and a cluster of wheelie bins stood by a gate.

They hurried after Helen, who was already waiting at the back door of the fossil shop. Like so many doorways in

Lyme, it was made from ancient, crooked wood, painted with umpteen layers of black paint. Helen reached up to a large groove above the door frame and felt for the key.

"Will there be customers in there?" hissed Annie.

"Not if the front door's still locked. Come on."

They followed Helen inside. The first room was something like a storeroom crossed with a kitchen. Annie grimaced at the dirty mugs piled on the side. They would need a soak to get them clean.

"We should be careful not to touch anything," said Figgy. "When the police come, we can't have our fingerprints all over the place."

Annie walked on, holding her hands in front of her. Helen nudged a door with her shoulder, and they found themselves inside the shop.

It was familiar, although Annie hadn't been inside for ages. It was a shop that specialised in uncovering fun surprises in darkened corners. Hidden nooks with baskets full of gemstones had always held appeal for her girls when they were young. She smiled at the thought that her grandchildren would soon be enjoying them. The higher shelves, out of reach of toddlers' hands, held the expensive polished fossils and chunks of agate. In between were other treasures, although 'treasure' was a relative term. Some of the stuff for sale included plastic dinosaur eggs, excavate-your-own-fossil kits and plaster casting kits for any dinosaur footprints a person might stumble across.

"OK," said Helen, "so we bring him in here."

Annie and Figgy nodded.

"Just lay him on the floor?" said Figgy.

"That could work," agreed Annie.

There was a big fossil, an ammonite, on the shop counter.

CHAPTER EIGHT

It rested on a piece of paper on which someone had scrawled the words: *How much is this worth to you?*

"Maybe he was murdered by someone clonking him over the head with a big fossil like this," Annie suggested.

"Are we speculating," said Helen, "or trying to invent a new crime scene?"

Figgy was gesturing back towards the storeroom. "There was one of them upright trolley things in that back room. Maybe we could use that to move him?"

"Sack truck," said Helen. "Yes. That'll work."

They retraced their steps and grabbed the sack truck. Figgy pulled her sleeves down over her hands to form gloves while Annie cleared away the paper and plastic packing material scrunched up around its base.

It was a bumpy ride for the sack truck over the grey shale, but it still seemed like their best bet for moving a corpse. Annie watched Figgy as she steered it over the uneven ground.

Helen, up ahead, stopped suddenly. "Well, this is odd."

Annie almost crashed into her. "What's wrong?"

Helen waved an arm at Rosamund's car.

"He's gone," she said.

"Don't be daft," said Annie. She took a step forward.

"See?" said Helen. "Gone. The passenger seat's empty."

CHAPTER NINE

Annie looked between her two friends. "How can he have just disappeared?"

It wasn't as if she actually expected an answer. There was no sane or sensible reason for the body of Marco Callington to have vanished from the car.

"Well," said Helen, licking her lips. "Did you definitely check that he was dead?"

"What?" said Figgy.

"If he was just unconscious, maybe he walked away."

Figgy shook her head. "No, we all saw him. He didn't walk away. There's some other explanation."

Helen raised an eyebrow. "And do you know what that explanation might be?"

Figgy held up a hand to count ideas off on her fingers. "OK. Some of these are more likely than others."

"Yes?" prompted Helen.

"One. We might have hallucinated this."

"All three of us?" Annie asked.

"I am very suggestible. Or two, it was a ghost."

"Annie took his photo," said Helen. "Pretty sure ghosts don't show up in photos."

Annie nodded, feeling in her pocket for her phone. Could she have imagined it all?

"Yeah. Not a ghost." Figgy counted off another finger. "Three. Glitch in the matrix. That's another possibility."

"Erm," said Annie, "run through that one for us, Figgy, will you, love?"

"Well, it depends on whether you believe it's possible that we're all living in a computer simulation."

Annie could see Helen frowning. She resisted the urge to smirk. "It seems like a bit of an outside possibility. What else is there?"

"Four. He fell out of the car, or someone else moved him." Figgy finished her finger count with a flourish.

All three of them looked at the ground beside the car, where Marco might have fallen if the door had been opened. As one, they ducked down to see if he'd rolled beneath the car.

The ground beneath the car was bare. No dead body.

They exchanged shrugs.

"I guess we don't know," said Annie.

"Well, that's confusing," said Helen.

"Yes, but... it *does* mean we don't have a body to deal with."

Annie looked at her co-conspirators. Helen appeared merely irritated, while something that looked very much like relief had come over Figgy's face.

"Which means we're in the clear," said Figgy.

Helen crouched and looked under the Audi again. "But he just walked off. A dead man."

There was a bashing and a clanging from one of the back

yards. Helen looked up. "That'll be Harper starting up in her workshop."

"There you go then," said Annie. "A new day dawns. Our little problem has gone away."

Helen nodded and turned toward the gate leading to the rear of her shop. "There'll be people outside waiting to get in."

"There will," said Annie, although she wondered if there really was a queue of art lovers waiting outside the gallery at opening time, ready to part with the sort of money that Helen charged. She imagined that the majority of Helen's business was conducted at evening soirées, where free glasses of prosecco would increase people's enthusiasm and loosen their purse strings. It was a world that Annie found incomprehensible.

"I need to go and do some work, too," said Figgy, already sidling away.

Figgy's work was just as incomprehensible. It involved computers, and although Figgy's mastery of technology was a very casual thing, Annie secretly thought of it as a superpower.

"We all have things to attend to." Annie had the family coming round, which was exciting. "I need to go and buy some emergency gherkins."

"Tina's got cravings, has she?" Helen asked.

Annie nodded. "Should we reconvene when it's time to take Rosamund home from the medical centre?"

There was a chorus of agreement. Annie could see the others burned with curiosity just as she did, as much about Rosamund's swanky house as about what had just happened. As far as she knew, none of them had ever been invited round, so this was a perfect opportunity to try to understand their friend a little better.

"And that's it?" said Helen. "We're either going to put this down to us living in a dream world—"

"A simulation," Figgy corrected her.

"—or that someone took him? And we're happy with that?"

Annie put a hand on her friend's shoulder. "I don't think we're happy with any of this, Helen. This started off as a perfectly lovely day. It's not even lunchtime and it's all a horrid mess."

"But I want it to make sense!"

"I thought you were an artist."

"Art dealer."

"Same thing. This is going to be one of those weird mysteries of life like what is love and where do lost socks go."

"And why dogs tilt their heads when you talk to them," added Figgy.

"That," said Annie. "Just accept that this is one of those mysteries. We had a body. We didn't want a body. Now there is no body."

"The universe is helping us," said Figgy. "The power of manifestation."

"How can you be so calm about this?" Helen asked the younger woman.

Figgy gave a nervous smile. "I'm terrified. If the police catch us I'm going to tell them two old ladies made me do it."

"What two old...?" Helen scowled. "But it doesn't make sense."

Annie raised her hands. "There's no body. It's gone. We could even, possibly, pretend it never happened."

"You want us to just forget it?" asked Helen.

"Like that time a Spanish waiter with devilish hips turned my head in Torremolinos, I am going to act like it never happened, and if I'm very lucky, just completely forget it ever did."

"I'm very happy to do that," said Figgy, blinking and nodding.

Helen frowned, visibly rolling the idea around in her head. "We forget about it and just get on with our lives." She looked at the other two women. "Alright."

CHAPTER TEN

DC Tina Abbott heaved herself out of the passenger side of the car. Her sister, Naomi, was by the rear door, getting Tina's little boy Louis out. Naomi's daughter Poppy was already skipping up the driveway to her grandma's house. Skipping was currently Poppy's thing.

Tina leaned on the car roof and took some deep breaths before walking up to the house.

Eight months pregnant with her second child and getting out of a car was enough to leave her breathless.

Tina had been on maternity leave from Dorset Police for a week. It would have been a relaxing week if not for Mike's disastrous attempt to put up some shelves, which had caused a complete collapse of the plasterwork in not one, but two bedrooms of their house in Sandford. Naomi had been kind enough to put her and Louis up while Mike tried to rectify things.

"You watch," said Tina. "I bet Mum'll try to convince me to move into her place over lunch."

"You've had that conversation," said Naomi.

"And we will have it again," Tina replied.

Six-year-old Poppy was too short to reach the doorbell, but Annie was already there, door open and arms open wide to hug her granddaughter.

Annie's house on Anning Road was a former council house. A boxy three-bedroomed property with a large and varied front garden. Annie blew a raspberry kiss on Poppy's cheek and then reached out to take Louis in her arms. Louis patted her face and giggled as she gave him the same treatment.

"Come in, you two," said Annie. "Lunch is ready. I bought gherkins."

As Annie led the children down the hallway to the dining room, Naomi looked at her sister.

"You might be right. She's softening you up with gherkins, and then she's going to ask you."

Tina smiled. "But I do love a gherkin."

As she stepped through the hallway, Tina spotted a slip of paper on the telephone table. She turned it round to look at it. Was she nosy because she was a police detective? Or had she always been like this?

It was a receipt from a local baby shop for a *Winnie the Pooh* baby bath. Tina groaned and went through to join the others.

What constituted lunch at Tina's mum's house hadn't changed in thirty years. These days Tina might find falafels and hummus and onion bhajis among the savoury buffet items on the table, but for the most part, it was the same vast array of sandwiches, pork pies, potato salad and chips she'd grown up with. All beige.

Louis and Poppy tucked in, knowing that after lunch there was Granny Annie's back garden to play in, a much-loved wilderness full of secret spots and far more children's outdoor toys than any fifty-something woman should own.

Annie fussed around them all, getting cups of squash for the children and tea for her two daughters. Annie always fussed, but Tina thought she was more highly strung than usual. There was a frantic, almost anxious edge to her movements.

Once she had finished chewing her second gherkin (because at eight months pregnant, talking, eating and breathing at the same time was impossible), Tina asked, "Busy morning, Mum?"

Annie's head whipped round. "What?"

"Your morning. Busy?"

"Er, yes. Well, no. The usual." Her mum was blushing. She cleared her throat. "Well, actually, one of my swimming gals cut her foot on a razor clam. Had to go to the medical centre."

"She all right?" asked Naomi.

"I think so. I've got her car parked out front now."

Tina recalled seeing an Audi SUV, 2023 plates, parked out there. It stood out on this street.

She looked at her mum. "And I thought sea swimming was a relatively safe activity."

Annie was still flustered. What was wrong with her? "Most of us don't tread on razor clams. And then I had to go shopping."

Tina cocked her head. "A baby bath?"

Annie gave her an innocent look. "Actually, I bought that at the weekend."

"You do know we've still got Louis's stuff?"

"Well, you know. New baby, new bath."

"That's not a thing." Tina sighed and stopped herself

reaching for a third gherkin. "I don't want you spending your money on things we don't need."

"It's what your dad would've wanted," said Annie.

Tina sighed again. "I thought we'd agreed that you can't use him to back up your arguments. And I reckon he'd have sided with me on this one."

"He always did," agreed Naomi.

"I certainly don't need to be bombarded with new baby clothes and changing mats and stuff," said Tina.

Annie attempted a light laugh. "Bombard? Me?"

Naomi laughed.

"You think this is funny?" Tina said.

Naomi grinned. "I'm not the one getting love-bombed by Mum."

Annie put a kiss on Naomi's head. "Oh, don't you worry, my flower. I can love-bomb you, too, just watch me. Who wants jelly?"

Poppy gave a yell of delight. Louis, realising there was something to get excited about, joined in.

"Green stuff first," said Tina, plonking a couple of halved cherry tomatoes from her bag on Poppy's plate and another on Louis's. The children made short work of them.

"Tomatoes are red, Aunty T," Poppy noted, tomato juice dripping from her chin.

Tina heard her phone buzz in her handbag. She pulled it out: a message from her husband, Mike.

You heard about this body they've found in Lyme? Potential murder, says DS Strunk.

She sent back a message asking for details.

"Your Dougie mentioned anything about a body found in the town?" she asked Naomi.

Naomi's husband Douglas Anderson was a police

constable in the town. Annie had a police officer for a daughter and two police officers for sons-in-law. Tina had no idea what quirk had brought that out in the family.

"Er, no," said Naomi. "*We* send each other normal messages. Like when bin night is and whether we've run out of milk or not."

Tina went to Douglas's contact in her phone and called him.

"Tina," he said. "Wondered how long it would take you. Enjoying your maternity leave?"

"Yeah, yeah," she replied, ignoring Naomi's smirk. "I was—"

"Only me and Wendy just made a bet. About how long it would be before we heard from you. I won."

PC Wendy Sharman was Dougie's colleague. Tina didn't like the idea of being laughed at by the two of them.

"Dougie," she said. "What's this I hear about a body?"

Naomi gave her a deep frown and tilted her head towards the children.

"Local resident just found the man," Dougie said. "In a wheelie bin of all places, in a car park behind Monmouth Street."

"Suspicious death?"

"Well, I can't see how he got in there naturally."

Tina took a deep breath. "I'll come over."

"I thought you were on maternity leave."

"I'm in the town. Be another hour before CID gets there." She ended the call.

Naomi was blinking at her. "You're eight months pregnant."

"I can stand upright. My brain still functions. Key skills for any detective."

Tina stood just as Annie returned from the kitchen.

"You don't mind looking after these two while Naomi drives me into town, do you?" Tina asked her.

"I'm driving you?" said Naomi.

Annie gave Tina a questioning look. Tina glanced at the children, but they were playing a silly game with the tomato pips on Louis's plate.

"A man's body's been found in a wheelie bin near Monmouth Street," she said. "Possible murder."

"Oh," said Annie. The bowls of jelly wobbled in her hands.

Had she turned pale?

"Oh," Annie said. "Of course. If you must…"

CHAPTER ELEVEN

It was less than half a mile from Annie's house to Monmouth Street, but Tina would be taking the lift even if it was just a roll down the hill and a right at St Michael's Church.

"This'll do." She unclipped her seatbelt.

"You know the way Mum can't help sticking her nose into our business?" said Naomi.

Tina recognised the tone. "Yeah, yeah. At least it's a positive quality in a copper."

She waved Naomi off and walked down the side road between the houses.

PC Wendy Sharman stood behind a taped-off section of the narrow street. Tina stepped past a bystander with a dog and lifted the tape to go through.

"Looking well, DC Abbott." Wendy's gaze flicked to Tina's bump.

"Feeling fat, PC Sharman."

Wendy smiled. "How's it going, Tina?"

"Oh, it's... it's going, thanks, Wendy. I'll be glad when I'm not the size of a whale."

"I bet." Wendy pointed. "Dougie's down there with Sergeant Connor."

Tina walked on. The scrubby patch of land at the bottom served as a car park for the hodgepodge of houses and shops that backed onto this area. Properties some distance away had little alleys that led out into this space. Four cars were parked here, and a collection of wheelie bins stood by the back wall of a house.

Local police had cordoned off all entrances to the area. Sergeant Jim Connor stood at the edge of the cordon. He had been in the police force for decades and had been the town sergeant when Tina was a little girl.

"Afternoon, Sarge."

"Ah, hello, Tina." He frowned at her belly. "You not on maternity leave?"

"Thought I'd get a head start. CID won't be here for another half hour."

"Right you are. We've secured the site. Apart from checking his pulse to make sure the poor man was dead, we haven't disturbed him."

He gestured at the dusty earth and impacted gravel. "Apart from the necessary footsteps we've made, I don't know if your lot will find any decent footprints or tyre prints."

"Tyre prints?"

Sergeant Connor shrugged. "Way I see it, if you've got a body in a wheelie bin, either person or persons unknown dragged or carried him here, or he was brought here by car."

"Which bin is it?"

CHAPTER ELEVEN

The sarge closed one eye and pointed out a big black bin. Tina examined the ground around it.

"Two further options," she said.

"Oh, yes?"

"The deceased was brought here in the wheelie bin."

"It belongs to one of the neighbouring houses. The owner of the bin found him. Must've been quite a shock for her."

Tina wrinkled her nose. His point didn't invalidate her theory.

"Second possibility," she continued. "It was self-inflicted."

"Self-inflicted? There's a man head-down in a wheelie bin."

She shrugged. "Head-down makes more sense. The guy's drunk. Comes down here in the night. Maybe feels dodgy and decides to throw up in a wheelie bin. He overreaches, topples in and..."

The sarge stepped back, eyebrows raised. "Bit unlikely, if you don't mind me saying."

"I can't think of any likely scenarios when it comes to bodies in wheelie bins. Do we have any indication of when the body went in there?"

He consulted his notebook. "The owner of the bin last checked it on bin day, last Thursday."

"Big window."

"I'm no pathologist, but I don't reckon he's been there since last Thursday. And there's no smell of alcohol on him."

"Have you ID'd him yet?"

"Not possible from the way he's lying."

She scanned the surrounding houses. There were no CCTV cameras in sight, but more than twenty windows overlooked the spot, from varying distances. What were the chances that someone at one of those windows had seen something?

"We should start canvassing neighbours," she said. "Ask if anyone heard or saw anything, see if anyone's got CCTV pointing out over this yard."

"Dougie's made a start on that. He's with the initial caller in number eight over there. Reckon she needed a strong brew to calm her nerves."

Tina nodded. If this death was anything other than a tragic, stupid accident, Forensics would need to inspect the entire area. But the priority would be identifying the body. Once they did that, they could talk to his family.

A thought crossed her mind.

"Sarge?"

"Yes?"

"If he's upside down in a wheelie bin, how did you take his pulse?"

"The feet," he replied.

"What?"

"The feet. You've got a pulse in your foot. My Jacqueline's a chiropodist. That's how they take a pulse. She showed me."

"Ah. Didn't know that." *You learn a new thing every day.*

CHAPTER TWELVE

As soon as Naomi returned from running Tina into town, Annie hurried out of her house, jiggling a set of car keys.

"Gotta go. Poppy and Louis are just inside."

"Go?" Naomi frowned.

Annie pointed at the Audi on the side of the road. "Just had a text from Rosamund. She needs someone to drive her home."

This was true, but it hid a deeper lie. While Naomi was out, Annie had been pacing back and forth wondering what in God's name she was going to do. First there was the body in the car, then there wasn't a body, and now, there very much was a body again.

And, based on what Tina had said before she'd left for town, it was somehow in a wheelie bin in that car park off Monmouth Street.

Yes, Rosamund had messaged to be picked up, but if Annie had been entirely truthful, she'd have added something along the lines of: "Oh, and your mum's going to go to prison for messing about with a dead body."

"OK," said Naomi. "I might take the kids home with me."

"Yes, yes. Do that. Take some of the sausage rolls with you." Annie looked at her daughter, wondering if those would be her final words to Naomi before she was hauled away to prison. She gave her daughter a fierce hug before getting into the car.

Before she'd reached the end of her road, she called Helen Cruickshank on speakerphone and dropped the phone onto the passenger seat.

"Hello," said Helen, picking up.

"Helen, they've found the body."

"Annie," Helen said in a weird, upbeat voice, "you'll never guess what's happened. The police have just been here. Your Naomi's Dougie. They say they've found a body in the car park out back. Can you believe it?"

Annie glanced at the phone. "Oh, you know."

"Harper and I were wondering who it could possibly be and who might do such a thing. I'm going to—" There was a sound of a door closing, and then Helen's voice shifted to a harsh whisper. "Yes! They've found him. In a wheelie bin! The police have been asking if we've seen anything or know who it might be."

"And what did you tell them?"

"What do you think? I played dumb. I went swimming this morning, don't you know, and then came here to open up. They're up at Solomon's shop now, asking the same questions."

"Did you learn anything from them? What do they know?"

"What do you expect them to tell me? All I know is they've not yet slapped me in irons, dear, so they don't know it's us yet."

"Good, good," said Annie, wondering exactly what *good* looked like. "Well, I'm going to the medical centre to collect Rosamund and take her home."

"And I'm going to stay here and play happy little shopkeepers. Which involves lying to Harper, something else I'm not happy about."

"Needs must. I'll call you back."

As Annie drove along Woodmead Road towards the medical centre, she debated whether to call Figgy. The young woman deserved to know the truth, but if she'd gone home to her static caravan beyond the Cobb then she was well out of harm's way.

The need for honesty won out. The moment Annie told her, Figgy gave a high-pitched yelp of alarm.

"Listen," Annie said. "We stick with the story. I'm going to go get Rosamund now and take her home. Maybe she'll open up a bit about what she did."

"I hope so." Figgy's voice shook.

"Don't worry, Figgy. She'll tell us."

There was a grunt.

"Figgy?" Annie said. "Hold it together love, please."

She ended the call and parked outside the medical centre. Rosamund was in the waiting area, dressed and with her injured foot bandaged and elevated.

"There you are," said Annie, pasting on the most authentic smile she could muster.

"All done." Rosamund's mouth was set in a firm line. "Nearly messed my foot up good and proper."

"What did the doctors say?"

"When I finally saw one, I was told I'm lucky not to have done myself some serious nerve or tendon damage. I've got to keep off it for a few days." She grabbed the crutch that leaned on a wall beside her. "As if life wasn't tough enough already."

Yes, thought Annie. *You'd stood on a razor clam, and you had a murder victim in the front of your car.*

"We should get you home. A cup of tea, get you settled, and you can tell me all about it."

Rosamund grunted. The steel in her cool blue eyes softened. "You've been really helpful today. Thank you."

Annie nodded grimly. "Yup. Helpful. That's me. Let's have you up."

She put her arm under Rosamund's to help her up. Rosamund fumbled with the crutch and together they wobbled out to the car park, where Figgy was waiting for them, doubled over and out of breath like she'd just sprinted all the way up from the caravan park.

"Hey... Rosamund," she panted. "How's the foot?"

"Sore," said Rosamund.

Annie gave Figgy a pointed look. "All friends, helping each other."

Figgy panted, clutching her chest and wheezing. She was young, but she wasn't built for running.

She gave Annie a look and then switched her gaze to Rosamund, blinking. "And you can tell us all about it."

CHAPTER THIRTEEN

ROSAMUND LIVED in a fancy detached house on the corner of Somers Road. Any house with solid wooden gates in front and a wide gravel drive beyond was automatically posh in Annie's eyes. Figgy hopped out to open the gates.

Rosamund had sat in the front passenger seat all the way here. Right where the corpse of Marco Callington had so recently sat. And she hadn't batted an eyelid.

Annie helped her inside. Figgy scowled as Annie passed her and pointed up. There was a pair of CCTV cameras on the wall, one, looking out towards the gate, the other, directed down at the door. Both had what looked like pillowcases draped over them, hiding their lenses.

Annie cocked her head. "Security cameras not working, Rosamund?"

"Broken," said Rosamund. "Need to get someone out to replace them."

Annie shrugged and helped her into the house. The décor was an expensive wood-based minimalism. There was no clutter in the hallway, no mountain of shoes or jumble of coats or the pile of mail Annie had expected. The theme continued through to the living room, which was like a show room out of an interior design magazine, an unlived-in work of perfection apart from a large space on the wall where there were two picture hooks but no picture.

"This is nice," Annie lied.

She'd imagined Rosamund's life as a luxurious, perfect, empty thing. *Not far off*.

"Thank you for seeing me in," said Rosamund. "I won't keep you any longer."

"It's OK," said Figgy. "I'll go put the kettle on. You two can sit. And chat."

"Really..." Rosamund began.

"It's no trouble." Figgy tugged at the collar of her T-shirt. "It's warm in here, isn't it?"

Annie thought Figgy might still be hot from her run to the medical centre but no, she was right. The house was very warm. Annie reached over and felt the radiator, sleek and barely noticeable under a floating shelf. It was piping hot. On a warm May afternoon.

"Heating could do with turning down," she said.

"I like it warm," replied Rosamund.

From what seemed like a distance, Figgy made clattering noises.

"Have you told your husband – I want to say Greg—"

"David," Rosamund corrected.

"David. Told him about your foot?"

"He's away with work. London. He's not back this week."

Annie swallowed. "You know, when I first approached your car from the beach, I thought I saw someone sitting in it."

"Oh?"

CHAPTER THIRTEEN

"Someone sitting in the front passenger seat of your car."

"Yes? And was there?"

Annie held Rosamund's gaze. "I don't know. Was there?"

Rosamund frowned. "Sorry, was there someone sitting in my car or not?"

"I wondered if, perhaps," said Annie, "you left your car unlocked and someone could have got in."

"I don't think I left my car unlocked. It's not the kind of thing I'd do."

"No? So your car would have been locked the whole time you were down at the Cobb Gate car park?"

Rosamund's frown deepened. "Are you saying that you found my car unlocked?"

"I don't know. I pressed the dooberry several times."

"Dooberry?"

"The plipper." Annie mimed working a key fob.

"But there wasn't someone in my car."

Annie leaned back and gave what she considered her 'French' shrug.

"Are you trying to admit something to me, Annie?" said Rosamund.

"Or *you* might want to admit something to me..."

Rosamund's frown had become a disbelieving stare. She huffed and propelled herself up from the leather sofa.

"I can do it, whatever it is," said Annie.

"I'm fine!" Rosamund hobbled with her crutch to the window, which she unlatched and flung wide. "It's stuffy in here."

"It *is* warm," said Annie. "We could turn the radiators down."

"I like it warm!" Rosamund snapped. "And breezy!"

There was another clatter of cups from the kitchen.

"Is she breaking things?" asked Rosamund.

"Let me go see," said Annie. "One lump or two?"

Rosamund simply stared at her.

"In your tea," said Annie.

"Green tea. Nothing in it."

That sounded like the most miserable tea on earth, but this wasn't Annie's house, and Rosamund could have her tea just how she wanted it.

In the kitchen, Figgy was fighting with a boiling water tap. "How's it going in there?" she whispered.

"She's a cool cucumber and a tough nut to crack," said Annie. "Won't admit to anything."

Figgy twisted the boiling water tap and pushed down. A steaming column of water shot out. Figgy tried to insert a cup under it without sending water everywhere.

As she did this, the rear kitchen door opened and Rosamund's son walked in. Cameron was tall and a little gangly, like all the nuts and bolts that should have made him into an adult hadn't been properly tightened. His hair was a floppy blob on top of his head.

He called out "Mum!" and then noticed the strange women in his kitchen.

He narrowed his eyes and pointed at Figgy. "Two scoops of vanilla honeycomb crunch."

"That's me!" Figgy's delighted smile was the girliest thing Annie had seen outside of a teen romcom.

"Your mum's done herself a bit of a mischief," said Annie, pointing in the direction of the living room. "We're helping by making tea."

"I really don't need tea," said Rosamund, hobbling in.

Cameron stared at her bandaged foot. "Mum, what have you done now?"

Rosamund gave him a look. "*Now*, he says."

Cameron went to her and held her by the shoulders. Rosamund was tall, but Cameron loomed over her.

"I really don't need tea," she said, her voice weary.

Annie nodded. Rosamund's boy was home. Trying to winkle any evidence out of her had been difficult enough already. In front of family, it would be impossible.

"Time for us to go then," she said.

"I just got the thing working," said Figgy, pointing at the hot water tap, but Annie pulled her towards the door.

"You have been most kind," said Rosamund, pursuing them to the door and closing it behind them without another word.

Standing on the wide driveway, Annie and Figgy looked at each other.

"So what did you find out?" said Figgy.

Annie had encountered very few corpses in her life and was still shaken by the one she'd found that morning, especially when it had been just sitting there in the front of a car like it was going on a day out. And the whole mess made no more sense than before. She shook her head, silent.

"Pick up any clues?" said Figgy.

"There are no clues!" Annie replied. "This isn't *Scooby Doo* and you're not thingy, the one who solves the mysteries."

"Velma Dinkley," Figgy replied, her eyes brightening.

"Right, her."

They let themselves out through the gate and walked down to Uplyme Road.

"I always saw myself as a bit of a Velma," said Figgy. "Except not gay."

"Velma? Gay?"

Figgy nodded.

"Good for her," said Annie. She sighed. "But no clues, no. Rosamund is making out like it never happened. I say we go back to Plan A and do the same."

"Shame," said Figgy. "I'd have quite enjoyed solving a mystery."

CHAPTER FOURTEEN

Detectives from Dorset Police's Major Crimes Investigations Team had appeared in Lyme Regis late in the afternoon, including Tina's colleagues, DS Nathan Strunk and DI Hannah Patterson. DS Strunk, who was now experimenting with a neatly trimmed beard after hearing DCI Lesley Clarke describe him as baby-faced, had expressed surprise that Tina had come down to the crime scene in the dusty car park. He had suggested she should be at home resting.

DI Patterson had been both blunter and more accepting of her presence.

"As long as you stay out of the way, an extra pair of eyes can't hurt."

Gav from Forensics had put a tent over the bin and the body and had gone to work. Several hours later he and his colleague had gathered enough photographs and materials to be satisfied that the body could be removed from the bin.

Tina went over with the DI and DS to look at the man. The injury on his head was large and obvious.

"You don't get an injury like that falling into a wheelie bin," said the DI.

"Nope," agreed the DS.

"Murder, then." The DI sighed. "I'll let DCI Clarke know. We'll need to get a pathologist in. And Devon Police will want to stick their nose in and all."

Lyme Regis sat right on the border between Dorset and Devon. While no police detective wanted an extra case on their desk, cross-border cases often brought out the territorial side of local police forces. DI Patterson had worked both sides of the border, and Tina had seen her exhibit that territorial behaviour.

"No ID on the body. No phone. Nothing. He's all dressed up with nowhere to go." The DI looked at Tina. "You're local, or your family is. You recognise him?"

Tina shook her head. "We can ask the local police."

The DI nodded. "Get them in here or show them a photo and..." She stopped herself. "Sorry, Tina. You're on maternity leave."

"I'm fine." Tina's ankles were aching, but she wasn't about to admit that.

"I'll ask the local police," said the DS. "And we'll see if anyone's missing from the local houses."

DI Patterson nodded. She could be difficult; liable to change her mind, and her mood, on a whim, But Tina was getting used to her.

Tina and the DS stepped outside the tent.

"You should go home," he said.

"I will." She hissed at the pain in her ankles.

"How's your Mike getting on with repairing the house?"

"Um. Getting there."

CHAPTER FOURTEEN

He smiled. He'd heard the stories, she was sure. Handy Andy, they called Mike in Winfrith.

"You all right getting home?"

She nodded. "I'll ask my sister to collect me. But if you get an ID on this guy, you let me know."

He nodded, then shook his head.

"You've not quite got to grips with this maternity leave malarkey, have you?"

CHAPTER FIFTEEN

Bright and early the following morning, Annie took her neighbour's dog Dex for a walk.

Dex was a playful boxer dog. He was also a good listener. In many ways, Dex encapsulated all of her favourite attributes in a man.

Annie and Dex strode down the hill towards town. Walking a dog was like having some sort of VIP access-all-areas pass. She could wander wherever she liked, and no questions would be asked as to what she might be doing.

"Good boy, Dex!" she said. "We'll go and find young Figgy, shall we?"

She let him lead the way, choosing the path according to the whims of his doggy nose. She didn't mind which route they took, as most of the roads and paths flowed down towards the sea.

Dex pulled towards the beach.

"Not where we're headed today, pal. Along the promenade we go, and you can look at the waves from up here."

She enjoyed the warm sunshine as they made their way

CHAPTER FIFTEEN

along the Marine Parade, past the beach and onwards past the Cobb.

Figgy lived in a static caravan right on the edge of Monmouth beach, past the immaculate bowling green. It was an enviable spot. Figgy's caravan was bounded by a low white picket fence with a tiny gate. Gravel borders formed a path around it, and Annie led Dex around to the main door.

"Hello!" shouted Annie as she knocked on the door. "It's Annie."

Figgy opened the door. She looked at Annie and then down at Dex.

"You like dogs?" Annie asked. If the answer was no, her options might be limited.

"Yup," said Figgy. "You'd better come in before Kevin sees him, though."

Annie hustled Dex inside, wondering who Kevin was. A strict landlord? Or perhaps a jealous boyfriend?

"What kind of dog is he?" asked Figgy, settling onto a bench seat in the huge bay window.

Annie sat opposite, transfixed by the view. The shoreline filled the window, like a seaside paradise on the very widest wide-screen television.

"What a place to live, Figgy! Amazing view! Dex is a boxer. Handsome devil, isn't he?"

Figgy reached down to ruffle Dex's ears. "He is."

"Listen, Figgy, I hope I'm not disturbing you." Annie glanced at the open laptop on the table.

She'd never been properly inside the caravan before and was surprised by how fusty and old-fashioned it was. As far as she knew, Figgy lived here alone, yet it had the air of a space that had been decorated by a much older person. The heavy, damask seat cushions and swirly-patterned Axminster carpet seemed at odds with the sleek laptop and the air fryer.

Figgy shrugged. "Only a bit. I don't get many visitors. I suppose I'd better make a cup of tea."

Annie smiled her thanks and watched as Figgy put the kettle on and pulled a packet of teabags out of a cupboard. The young woman surreptitiously checked the date on them; she hadn't been joking about not getting visitors.

"Have you come to talk about the police finding Marco's body?" Figgy asked, her back to Annie. "Where was he?"

"He was in a bin, would you believe? I was going to mention it in our swimming WhatsApp group, but I couldn't think of a way to say it in code."

"A bin? Wow." Figgy turned to her. "That can't have happened by accident, can it?"

"No. No, it can't." Annie looked down at Dex, now curled up at her feet.

Figgy slid back into the seat opposite Annie, handing her a mug of tea while she sipped from a glass of water.

"Do the police know that we were, um, involved?" she asked.

"Lord, no!" said Annie. "And we weren't. Involved, I mean. I say we just keep our heads down and forget the whole business. Apart from one small possible follow-up action, that is."

Figgy raised her eyebrows, just as there was a knock at the door of the caravan.

Dex raised his head.

Figgy frowned as she rose to answer. "Did you ask the others to come here?"

"No," said Annie, twisting in her seat to see who was there.

CHAPTER FIFTEEN

"Can I help you?" Figgy asked, opening the door.

It was the journalist Annie had seen at the beach, Jason Mordaunt. A Land Rover was pulled up outside behind him, an old one, but it looked like it had been restored. The sea breeze ruffled Jason's spiky hair, but he smiled at Figgy.

"You're Figgy Edmunds? I heard that you've been having some interesting interactions with a seagull?"

Figgy stared back at him. "Have you?"

"I wondered if you might be prepared to talk to me about it."

"Um, yes?" Figgy glanced at Annie. "I've actually got a visitor right now, so can you come back another time?"

"Oh, please don't turn him away on my account," said Annie. "I'd love to hear about your seagull friend." She gave Dex a glance. "And Dex here will remain on his best behaviour, won't you lad?"

Dex looked up at her and yawned.

"That's decided then," Figgy said, gesturing for Jason to come in. "Sit at the table and I'll make you a cup of tea."

He did as he was told, watching her. Annie wondered if he also suspected he was about to get a cup of possibly out-of-date tea. It tasted alright, though.

Jason flicked through a notebook, then settled on a blank page.

"I'm surprised you favour pen and paper," Annie said. "I thought the whole world had gone digital."

He smiled. "It's reliable. Reliable and always to hand." He tapped the little pocket he'd pulled it from.

Figgy brought his tea and sat down. "What d'you want to know?"

"The seagull – does it have a name?"

"Kevin," said Figgy. "D'you want to see him?"

"Er, yes?" Jason peered around, as if he might have overlooked a seagull in the room.

Figgy went to a cupboard and pulled out a packet of Mr Kipling Fondant Fancies. She put them on the table and turned to Annie and Jason. "You can have one if you want, but first..."

She pushed the packet towards the large picture window. Within ten seconds a huge seagull had landed on the outside, its eyes focused on the packet, screeching loudly as it flapped its enormous wings. Its beak scraped the outside of the window.

"Good grief!" said Annie. She put a restraining hand on Dex's collar. The dog was dozing, but it didn't hurt to be careful.

"Very nice." Jason brought up his camera to take some pictures.

"I need to let him have some cake now, or we'll get no peace," said Figgy. She removed a fondant fancy from the box.

She pushed a side window open and placed the fondant fancy onto a shelf below it. The seagull swooped down and grabbed it, pulling its head back and swallowing the thing whole, it seemed. Anie put a hand on her chest, hoping the bird wouldn't choke.

Kevin returned to the windowsill and put his head to the glass, eyeing Annie. She pulled back. Dex gave a little grunt and turned over, one foot slapping against her thigh. *Thank Goodness*.

"Is that shelf there specially to feed the birds?" Jason asked.

Figgy was still grinning at the seagull. "Birds? No. It's just for Kevin. He can get quite possessive."

Kevin gave Figgy something Annie could have sworn was a wink and then flew off.

Jason nodded and scribbled notes in tiny, precise handwriting. "Can you tell me how you know which of the gulls is Kevin? Don't they all look alike?"

"Only in the same way humans do," said Figgy. "Once you've got to know him... he has a look. It sets him apart."

"A look?"

"A look in his eyes. He's mischievous. Ha! One time he brought me the keys to the bowls club. I think it was his way of saying thank you for all the cakes."

Jason was writing, nodding. "Your relationship with Kevin is generally a positive one, then?"

Figgy shook her head. "Not always. He can be awful. In the winter he gets desperate and tries to come in. He managed it once and it took me a week to get the place straight again. He's a big guy."

Annie tried to picture a rampaging seagull inside this small, neat space. She shuddered.

"Do you have any hints and tips for those people who have run-ins with seagulls in Lyme Regis?" asked Jason.

Figgy screwed up her face, thinking. "It's easy to forget they can see you when you can't see them. When you eat a snack out in the open, you're inviting them in. So you need to keep your food covered up."

"That's good advice, Figgy," said Annie.

Jason put his notebook back in his pocket. "This will be such a nice public interest story. You know what it needs, though?"

Figgy shook her head.

"I can picture a fabulous photo." Jason looked away into the distance. "We get you outside and we somehow rig you up with seagull snacks along your arms and shoulders. Maybe your head, too. Then when Kevin and his friends descend, we get the money shot. You surrounded by gulls, screaming for their food."

Figgy's expression darkened.

"That sounds a bit... dangerous," suggested Annie.

"You could wear a hat?" Jason offered.

"My therapist wants me to identify my personal boundaries," said Figgy. "Identify them and stick to them. I didn't know that this was a boundary I needed until now. No. There won't be any photos like that." She smiled at Jason. "But thanks for helping me find a new boundary."

"You're welcome," said Jason. "I think I have everything I need. Thanks for the tea."

CHAPTER SIXTEEN

"Well, that was peculiar." Annie watched Figgy close the door behind the journalist.

"Which bit?"

Annie blew out her cheeks. "All of it, to be honest. Hey, you were very assertive with your boundaries there. Good job."

"Thanks." Figgy nodded. "It helps me to articulate what's going on in my head sometimes. I suffer from agoraphobia. That's the main reason I'm seeing the therapist."

"Oh, I see." Annie frowned. Agoraphobia was the fear of being outside, wasn't it? She'd seen Figgy outside lots of times. And that big bay window wouldn't help.

Figgy smiled. "It's more complex than just being afraid of going outside. It's more like being extremely anxious in crowded places or somewhere I can't easily escape from. Joining you all for the morning swimming sessions was a deliberate choice. It's been really helpful."

"I'm pleased to hear it, Figgy. Good for you." Annie

waved a hand around the caravan. "Have you always lived here?"

"It's my grandma's old place. Been here for seven years now." She looked down. "Grandma's been dead eighteen months."

"Sorry for your loss, Figgy. I bet you miss her. My husband died not long ago and... and it hurts, doesn't it?"

"We still have the Shipping Forecast." Figgy gave her a warm smile.

"You do?" Annie wasn't following.

"It was one of her rituals. Now it's mine. It somehow helps, like she's still around when it's on."

"Well, that sounds thoroughly wholesome." Annie had never seen the attraction of the iconic BBC broadcast. Was it the hypnotic lull of the voice, the lists of areas and the conditions expected? Was it the names of those areas, like Viking and Dogger, both familiar and exotic? Maybe Figgy would explain it to her one day, but not when they had a mystery to solve.

Annie sat back in her seat and inclined her head towards Figgy's laptop. "Computers and whatnot. You're a bit of a whizz."

Figgy shrugged.

Annie wasn't sure how to phrase the next question. "Now, if I ask you something that's ever-so-slightly... questionable, would you give it some thought?"

Figgy frowned. "Depends what it is."

"Just don't dismiss it out of hand, that's all I ask. Knee-jerk reactions sometimes stop us considering interesting possibilities."

"OK. I'll think about it."

"The thought that's been in my head since that unfortunate business with Marco is this. How did he come to be in Rosamund's car? If we could solve that mystery, we'd all sleep a little easier, wouldn't we?"

Figgy gave a light shrug.

Annie pressed on. "Would it be possible for a person who was good with computers to access CCTV cameras that help us crack that mystery? Imagine if we could get actual footage of what happened."

"It doesn't work like that, Annie." Figgy shook her head. "I don't know how much you know about computers, but just because a person has basic mastery of modern technology, that doesn't make them a hacker. They're different skillsets."

"Oh." Annie had suspected as much, but liked to assume all things were possible until they proved otherwise.

"Although..." Figgy chewed on her lip and stared at the ceiling. "There's a chance someone down there's not properly secured their Wi-Fi. I could take a quick look, just in case."

"That would be great!" Annie looked over at the laptop, wondering if Figgy would do it now.

"The thing is, I'll need to go there," said Figgy. "I won't be able to see the local Wi-Fi networks from here."

"Well come on, then! No time like the present."

Figgy sighed and picked up her laptop. Dex sensed that they were on the move and jumped up, ready for action.

As Figgy locked her front door, they spotted the journalist, Jason, some distance away. He was taking photographs of a pair of dog walkers further along the beach.

"What are the neighbours like here?" Annie asked, with a nod to the other caravans. It was a sparse cluster of vans, not like the densely packed holiday parks she knew from further along the coast.

"Mostly they were friends of my gran. I guess they're all older people, really. There was a woman just across there, Mrs Delacroix, she was on the same ward when my grandmother died. Both of them... cancer... the same time."

"How dreadful," said Annie. "But at the same time, it would be a comfort to be there with a friend."

"I guess so," said Figgy. "I didn't think of it like that. I hope so."

The two of them walked back along the Marine Parade towards the Cobb Gate, where Rosamund's car had been parked the day before. They found a section of low wall to sit on, and Figgy opened her laptop.

Annie remained silent while Figgy worked. Dex tugged briefly at the lead then settled down. Annie gazed out over the beach, watching individuals and families enjoying the sea and the sand. The swimmers were there for their own personal challenges, as well as the social side of things, but family groups formed a nucleus around a rug or a windbreak where they could dig, rest or play, depending on the age of the children.

"Ooh, I might have something," said Figgy.

"Yes?" Annie leaned over.

Figgy shunted the screen sideways so they could both see it. "Here. You can see Rosamund's car."

Annie stared. It was a clear shot, angled down from the Marine Theatre over the beach, with a view of around a third of the car park.

Figgy pointed at the timestamp in the corner of the screen. "We can rewind and see when Rosamund arrived, see."

Annie watched as the view changed. Rosamund pulled

into the parking space. She climbed out and walked away towards the beach.

"Such a shame we can't see inside the passenger seat," Annie said. She was staring hard at the screen, but the glass remained opaque.

"Yeah, I know. But we can look at this view for the whole time the car was parked and see if anyone else comes near the vehicle."

Figgy tapped the screen, and the footage sped up. People walked at comically fast speeds on the beach and around the car park, but Rosamund's car remained untouched until Annie and Figgy turned up to move it.

"Amazing job, Figgy," said Annie. "I can't believe you actually hacked into the CCTV."

"It turns out I didn't need to do anything shady. This is a public webcam."

Annie looked around. "A public webcam? Well, I never. I wonder who looks at things like that." She'd be taking a look herself, later on. Who knew such a thing was possible?

Figgy nodded. "So we've got proof that the body was in Rosamund's car when she parked up. Nobody went near her car between her parking it and us going there to move it."

"You're right," said Annie. "And that casts an interesting light on what Rosamund told us." She beamed at her young friend. "Well done, Figgy!"

CHAPTER SEVENTEEN

TINA OPENED her phone to find a text from DS Strunk.

Got an ID on the body, Marco Callington. Ran a shop called Jurassic Fossils. Know him?

Tina didn't know a Marco Callington, but she did know the fossil shop. Half an hour later, she was down in the heart of the town, where the narrow road curved towards the sea front. Jurassic Fossils sat on Bridge Street, right around the corner from The Cruickshank Gallery art shop. PC Wendy Sharman was on duty outside the shop, and let Tina enter.

"CSI have just finished up," she said. "Should be all right to go in."

The DS stood in the centre of the shop with Sergeant Connor. He grunted at Tina's entrance. "Me telling you the guy's name as a courtesy wasn't an invitation to come down."

"Second pair of eyes," she said.

He stuck out his bottom lip. "Nothing to see here. No sign of a struggle. No murder weapon. CSI are happy that the flat upstairs is clean, too."

"No murder weapon?"

CHAPTER SEVENTEEN

He shook his head. "Pathologist'll get round to a post-mortem in a day or two. A messy head injury, whatever it was."

There was a rickety looking stool by the counter. A godsend. Tina sat down and cradled her bump.

Her mum and dad had brought her to this shop when she and Naomi were younger. She remembered the display cases on the walls with their ammonites and belemnite fossils, pride of Lyme. There was a museum full of them across the road and a statue to Mary Anning, Georgian-era fossil hunter and palaeontologist, just along the coast path. The town made a mint from fossil hunting.

Tina looked at the huge Tyrannosaurus Rex skull hanging from the ceiling. She didn't remember it being there when she was a girl – or any local connection with T-Rex fossils. There was a whole aisle of colourful dinosaur toys and some large fossils and geodes that definitely weren't local. The whole shop was gaudier and tackier than she remembered it being.

"How did you ID him?" she asked. Presumably a friend or neighbour had reported him missing.

"Fingerprints," said the sarge. "We picked him up for affray a few years back. I was the arresting officer. Road rage incident." He wrinkled his nose.

No one had missed Marco Callington. No family or friends had come forward, concerned about him. This shop, overflowing with merchandise, had a chaotic air to it. Shelves were over-stuffed. Faded cardboard boxes of toys crowded together. The display cases containing the more expensive fossils – not local ones, that was certain – were dusty. Tina could only imagine what his flat upstairs might be like.

"This used to be a nice shop," said the sarge.

She laughed. "Just what I was thinking."

"No love lost between him and his neighbours in the shops either side."

"Not probable motive, though," said the DS, before Tina could ask. "Running a tacky fossil shop is not murder motive material."

"What's this?" she asked, gesturing towards the glass-topped counter behind her.

Next to the ancient till was a large, well-defined ammonite fossil embedded in a lump of rock. It sat on a square of folded paper which bore the handwritten words: *How much is this worth to you?*

It was a surprisingly large ammonite. A brilliant find if it was local. Someone had brought it in for valuation, she guessed.

"Is the fossil business particularly cut-throat?" she wondered aloud.

"Killed over an expensive fossil?" said the sarge.

The DS tapped a display cabinet. "The price tags on these. Twelve hundred pounds for this one."

"Marked up for the tourists," said Sergeant Connor. "But the stock here is worth something. I don't know fossils, but I reckon you could bag up a bunch of the best pieces and it would be quite a haul."

Tina picked up the ammonite on the counter. It was lighter than she expected. If the murder was a burglary gone wrong, then there would be more obvious signs.

"We'll get that lot bagged up as evidence anyway," said the DS. He pointed out to the rear of the shop. "Back door leads to a yard, then a narrow private passage out to the car park where his body was found. Leading hypothesis is that

CHAPTER SEVENTEEN

he was killed out there by the bins. If he was killed here, then CSIs can't find any sign of that. Come look."

Tina pushed herself off the stool and followed him, glad to be given a role as a sounding board.

The rear of the shop was even more cluttered than the front. In a back room with a kettle and a sink in one corner, boxes of old stock were piled up. DS Strunk gestured to an empty spot.

"We found a little push-along parcel thingy."

"Sack truck," said the sarge.

"Right. It had dusty tyres and had clearly been taken out back. Nothing unusual there, but we're having it dusted for prints."

Tina nodded. She wandered over to the mounds of torn plastic and cardboard from the old stock, drawn to a sheet written in a foreign script. She picked it up to look at it.

"What's that?" asked the DS.

"Import label," she said. "From China."

"It's where they make all the toys, isn't it?" said Sergeant Connor.

She nodded; he was right. But this label wasn't for a consignment of toys. In between the chunks of text that she guessed was Mandarin or Cantonese or something, the listings in a Western alphabet suggested something else.

"Imported fossils." She grunted. "Runs a fossil shop right by a world-famous fossil beach, and he felt the need to import his fossils."

"I guess he knew his business," said the DS.

"Can't say I like it," said the sarge.

Tina chewed her lip. "Well, either personally or professionally, someone hated him enough to murder him, didn't they?"

CHAPTER EIGHTEEN

Annie made her way over to Helen's art shop. The Cruickshank Gallery sat on the inside curve of the road that swept round opposite the museum. The narrow pavements could get congested during busy times, but Annie paused to look at the window displays.

Helen had a talent for drawing the eye towards the artwork. There were plenty of seaside views, catering for those who wanted to take home a view of the Cobb, or a seagull sitting on a beach hut. There were blocks of pastel-painted wood displaying chunks of driftwood and clusters of shells, continuing the beach theme.

Annie pushed open the door and went inside.

Helen was unwrapping a large frame covered in brown paper and bubble wrap. She glanced up. "Do you have fingernails?"

Annie held up her hands. "They're not fancy but they do the job. What do you need?"

Helen pointed at the tape around the package. "I daren't

use scissors in case I damage the painting, but this is driving me mad."

Annie found the end and pulled it loose. "There you go. I came in to see how you're doing."

"Me?" Helen looked at her with wide eyes. "Once I get this thing on the wall, I'll be a whole lot better, but I'm generally fine. How about you? I imagine you've heard what the police discovered?"

Annie looked around the shop. It wasn't a large space, but she wanted to be sure they were alone. "I did. In a bin?"

Helen nodded. "It's a proper circus out the back. I can show you in a minute."

Annie held the canvas upright as Helen unwound the packaging material. In a few moments, the painting was free. Helen clapped her hands in delight.

"This is interesting," said Annie. Was it upside-down? It was abstract, she knew that much, but beyond that...

"Isn't it just?" Helen said. "It's going to form the most intriguing centrepiece for this wall. We've had it in here once before, you know, and now I have the privilege of selling it again."

Annie helped her hang it, and the two of them stepped back to take a proper look.

It was a riot of deep colours. The seaside views tended to deploy the same palette of bleached-out blues and greens, so this provided some much-needed relief.

"It's called *Viscera*," said Helen. She pulled a face. "I might leave the label off for now, given everything that's going on. You know..."

Helen always seemed so fearless, but this business with the body had brought out a nervous side in her.

"Ooh yes." Annie looked at the painting again. The livid

reds and purples did have a hint of the butcher's shop about them.

"Tea?" Helen asked. "With a spot of snooping out the back, obviously."

Annie nodded.

The room at the back would have offered a panoramic view of the parking area, but like so many of the older buildings it had only one window, a small square about seven feet off the ground.

"I'll pop a cup over to Harper," Helen said. "Do come and say hello."

Helen handed Annie a mug that featured a hand-painted pansy. She took a tall, fluted china mug with a delicate handle for herself, and then picked up a giant mug that held more than both of the others put together. "She gets pretty thirsty in the workshop."

The two of them stepped out through the back door. The paved back yard behind the shop was bordered by fences and filled with piles of scrap metal and equipment that formed the construction material for Harper's larger creations. Annie stepped past a giant bird sculpture made of industrial parts and peered over the fence. In the scrubby car park behind she could see a white tent inside a cordoned-off area.

"I believe they've removed the body," said Helen. "Come on."

To one side of the yard was a stone building that abutted the main gallery space. A former outhouse, now it was an entirely separate area, with its own entrance.

Annie tripped over some metal and rubble as she moved away from the fence. Helen tutted.

"My love is excellent at gathering materials. Less good at

binning them," she said. "Tea, Harper!" she called, as she opened the door.

Inside the shed, a low buzzing noise eased to a halt. Annie's eyes took a moment to adjust to the interior gloom. Harper stepped forward to take the mug, removing her welding mask.

"Thanks, babe."

Annie smiled at that 'babe'. Helen suited the word, with her crinkly elfin smile and whimsical, pantomime clothing. Harper, round-faced and with a scattering of freckles, was about ten years younger than Helen. But in spite of their obvious differences, the couple seemed happy.

"What is it you're making, Harper?" Annie asked.

"Dragonfly," said Harper, slurping tea. "I have to make ten dragonflies for every passion project. It's like a rule."

"It's not a rule as such, darling," said Helen, touching her arm. "More of a guideline. Dragonflies are so easy to sell," she explained, turning to Annie and spotting the confusion on her face. "Everyone wants them. It doesn't matter if they're small ones made out of old cutlery or large ones made out of fan blades, they are a perennial favourite. It's such a boost to make sales, isn't it, darling?"

"Yep," said Harper. She reached further into the shed, picked up a small dragonfly, and dropped it into Annie's hand.

"Oh, I say, this is lovely!" said Annie. The cutlery was still visible, the maker's stamps clear on the knife blade wings. Little feet had been formed from the tines of forks.

She handed it back to Harper. "So what are your passion projects?"

Harper shrugged. "They tend to be bigger. The last one was a racing chariot. Made from car parts and garden tools."

"Nice," said Annie. "Where did that end up?"

"Garden installation."

"It's so much harder to find homes for the larger pieces," said Helen. "Sometimes it can take longer to place them than it does to build them. Hence the dragonflies."

"Hence the dragonflies," echoed Harper.

"We also agreed you would do something about the rubbish outside," said Helen.

Harper eyed her. "I think you said something about the materials outside, babe. But we agreed this is my domain." She turned to Annie. "She acts like she's the tidy one. Ask her who pairs the socks in the laundry."

Annie looked between them. She wasn't going to get involved.

"Socks don't need pairing," said Helen. "If an identical pair comes together again by accident, that's simply universal serendipity."

Harper grunted and sipped her tea. "I'll have a sort through the rubbish outside this afternoon."

"It's all I ever asked."

Harper laughed. "Such lies." She gave Annie a wink. "I have never known a more demanding woman."

CHAPTER NINETEEN

HELEN LED Annie back inside the gallery.

"Something I wanted to ask you, Helen," Annie said. "Rosamund was here that morning we all went swimming, yes?"

"She was," replied Helen. "She came to bring me some pictures she's looking to sell. They're over in the office still, we need to agree a price." She frowned. "It can be tricky when it's art we sold in the first place. People remember the price tag and assume we'll pay them more than we can afford. It's the mark-ups, you know."

"She bought them from here in the first place, you mean?" Annie asked.

Helen nodded. "Yes, so I know they'll sell. We just need to work out a price that works for both of us."

"Any idea why she's selling them?"

"Didn't ask. People have their reasons. Could be a change of décor or a change of heart. Who knows?"

The door chimed as someone entered the gallery.

"Solomon," said Helen with a smile. "Do you know Annie?"

Solomon Matheson from the children's shop two doors down nodded at Annie. "She's a very good customer."

"Of course," said Helen. "The grandchildren. I know how you like to treat them."

"It is my duty as a grandparent," Annie said. "Although their mums are becoming a little mutinous about it all. I've had to hide some of my latest purchases."

Solomon gave Annie a smile just long enough to be polite, then turned to Helen, clearly bursting with the need to talk about the body. "It's Marco, did you hear? The dead body."

"I did hear," replied Helen, with a glance at Annie. "Marco's the one with the fossil shop next door, in between this place and Solomon's."

"Oh, I see," said Annie. Her voice was too bright, she realised at once.

"I mean, it's early days," said Solomon, "but goodness me, it'll shake things up a bit, won't it?"

Annie nodded along, not quite sure how Marco's death would shake things up.

Solomon looked at Helen. "I mean, you've always wanted that space yourself, haven't you?"

"It's a nicely positioned spot, there's no doubt about it," said Helen, tugging at a spiral of hair. "Be perfect if I were to expand sideways."

Annie's eyebrows shot up. Were they really discussing who might take over Marco's shop already? It felt cold, but then, she wasn't a businessperson.

"I would never speak ill of the dead," continued Solomon.

"No, of course," said Helen.

"But that Transit van that used to pull up right outside! I don't know how it didn't cause an accident."

"Double yellow lines." Helen shook her head. "Some people think they're above such things."

"Mind you," said Solomon, lowering his voice. "I heard that Marco sacked the window cleaner. Claimed business was too slow to warrant one."

Annie frowned. "It's always busy in there, you can't move for people."

"Ah, but it's no good being packed out if people aren't buying," said Solomon.

"I see," she said. "What is it that makes the difference, in your opinion?"

"One has to form a relationship with the customer. Make a connection," he told her. "For example, I know enough about you and your delightful grandchildren that I can make recommendations to you, and because it's personal, I won't just look like a pushy salesman. I'll look like a friend with some great ideas. For instance, has young Poppy ever tried pressing flowers?"

"Oh?" Annie's interest was piqued. "I don't think so."

"Pop in and I'll show you the new flower press I've got in. Might be just the thing you need," he said with a wink.

"You are incorrigible!" said Helen, poking Solomon with a finger.

Solomon shrugged. "I'm just illustrating my point. A little care goes a long way. Unlike the gruff demeanour we came to associate with our deceased colleague from next door. You heard he was involved in a bit of a to-do at the weekend?"

"No," said Helen. "What kind of a to-do?"

"At the café bar, Breaststrokes, down at the front. He was in a full-blown argument with someone on Friday night. Sounds awful."

Helen pulled a wide-eyed face at Annie. Annie nodded. Had Marco annoyed someone enough for them to kill him?

"Who was it he was arguing with?" she asked.

"I didn't hear that part," said Solomon. "But I'm sure it'll come to light, there must have been plenty of witnesses."

CHAPTER TWENTY

AFTER FINISHING her cup of tea in Helen's gallery, Annie called in two doors down at Solomon's shop.

He emerged from behind the counter. "Ah hello! You've come to see the flower press."

Solomon's shop was filled with anything a small child might need or want. Annie liked to tell herself everything she bought was a necessity, but she knew the stock catered for grandparents and parents exactly like her.

If it was wholesome and appealing, Solomon sold it. There were cute hand-knitted outfits crafted by an unseen army of knitters. Wooden toys harking back to a simpler time. Musical instruments and other toys combining fun with education. Solomon sold plenty to tourist grandparents keen for something to take back home, but Annie was a self-confessed sucker for all of it.

She worried that when Poppy turned eight in two years, she'd need to look elsewhere for gifts, but at that age, her granddaughter would start to form more fixed ideas about what she wanted.

"Here you go." He lifted a large wooden box from a shelf. "It's a good size, look. Most of the ones sold for kids are too small. You want to be able to fit a snapdragon in there. Kids love snapdragons, the way they can open and close their mouths."

Annie nodded, recalling vague memories of pressing flowers as a child. Trying to cram a flower into a puny little press the size of a postage stamp was frustrating.

"It looks perfect, thank you. If I take something for Poppy, I'll need to buy something for Louis as well. To be fair."

"Let me see..." Solomon cast his gaze over the shelves. "How about a pull-along duck? It has big floppy feet and looks very funny."

He lifted one down and took it out of the box to show her. It had over-sized feet that slapped the ground as its wheels rotated.

"Well that's a hoot!" Annie grinned. "Sold to the doting grandma."

She followed Solomon to the counter. It wouldn't be long before she had a third grandchild, and she was enjoying this part of being a grandparent more than she'd have believed possible. She would indulge those gorgeous babies, even if their mums didn't approve.

She carried her purchases back home and opened up the spare wardrobe. It no longer contained clothes, now she'd finally cleared out Paul's things, eighteen months after his death. She felt that using it for grandchildren's treats would be something he'd approve of.

It was crowded with bits and pieces she'd picked up recently, but that was fine. When she got Poppy and Louis to herself, she could sneak them some of these gifts. Tina and Naomi didn't need to know, did they? She looked out of the window, already identifying some of the flowers she thought Poppy might like to press.

CHAPTER TWENTY-ONE

TINA ARRIVED at the Lyme Regis Emergency Services Centre, where the police took up the lion's share of the office space. She'd persuaded Dougie, who'd given her a lift, to go via the bakery for some freshly baked cookies.

"Are you trying to curry favour by bringing snacks?" asked Dougie as they went inside.

"They're double choc chip," she replied.

"Yep, that's gonna work."

They walked through to the spacious office that was currently serving as an incident room. DS Strunk and DI Patterson were both in there, along with Wendy.

Sergeant Connor was handing out a round of teas. He gave Tina a look. "I'll fetch another mug, then."

Tina put the cookies down on a table. "What do we have?"

"Nathan was just about to walk us through a briefing," said the DI with a thin smile. "I guess you'd like to join us?"

Tina settled into a chair and took a cookie. The baby had

CHAPTER TWENTY-ONE

been moving around less these past few days, probably because space was getting tight. The skin of her stomach must be stretched to the limit now. It had turned her into a chair connoisseur, valuing a supportive chair in a way she'd never have considered before. These wheeled office chairs scored badly, mainly because they had no arms, but she perched uncomfortably and kept silent, because when it came to a choice between a comfy seat and boredom or a bad chair and a murder investigation, then it wasn't really a choice at all.

"Right," said DS Strunk, standing at the board. He tapped it with his pen. "The name of our deceased is Marco Callington. We know he owned and operated the shop Jurassic Fossils and lived alone in the flat above. Apprehended for a road rage incident three years ago. His body was discovered by Margaret Forsyth, whose house backs onto the yard behind. He was in her wheelie bin, which she hadn't accessed since the previous Thursday. CSIs are processing the bin for fingerprints." He sniffed, looked around the team, and continued. "Initial hypothesis is that our victim died from blunt force trauma to the head. We'll know more after the post-mortem, because there are signs of irritation around the eyes that don't have an obvious explanation. We know the body was moved, so we're treating both the inside of the shop and the area around the bins as crime scenes."

"Did Marco have any relatives?" asked Dougie.

"He had no emergency contacts in his phone. We're seeing if anything turns up in his flat, but so far there are no signs of any significant relationships in his life."

"That road rage incident, do we know what happened?" asked Tina.

"Jim? What do you remember?" asked the DS, looking at the sarge.

Sergeant Collins addressed the room. "It was high season, which as we all know gets a bit barmy around town. Parking on that bend by the fossil shop causes massive disruption, which is why we jump on it if we spot it. Anyway, Marco was taking a delivery from a van that had pulled up. A driver in a car behind became frustrated with the hold-up, exited his vehicle and approached the van. There was a heated exchange between Marco, the delivery driver and the driver who'd approached, and during the exchange, Marco hit the guy's wing mirror with one of those little fossil hammers and shattered it. There was a bit of pushing and shoving between the three of them. I believe Marco eventually paid for a new wing mirror and the CPS dropped the assault charge."

"We should take a look at wing mirror guy," said Tina.

The sarge nodded. "He was a tourist, as I remember. From somewhere in the Midlands."

"How about the murder weapon?" she asked. "Do we know what it was?"

"There was a fossil on the counter when we arrived," said the DS. "No blood stains, but forensics will confirm. CSIs are processing anything else that seems like a candidate from inside the shop and the flat, but at the moment we don't think we have the murder weapon."

The DI nodded. "Let's run through some actions, shall we? If Marco had a temper, we should dig into that. Let's organise some door-to-door interviews, see if we can find any further examples of him getting into altercations. Finding the weapon is key. Dougie, can you see what that list of murder weapon candidates looks like? Work up some ideas for where else we might look."

"Yep."

"And do we know when the post-mortem is scheduled?" she asked.

"Day after tomorrow," said DS Strunk.

The DI nodded. "I'm heading back over to Bournemouth, but we'll stay in touch. Nathan, you're on point for the team here, yeah?"

He nodded. "Yes, boss."

"And Tina? Remember you're on maternity leave. An extra pair of eyes is good, but take it easy, yeah?"

Tina patted her stomach. "No door-to-door for me in this state."

CHAPTER TWENTY-TWO

As full summer approached, each day brought more tourists to Lyme Regis. But the early morning, that colourful time after dawn, was reserved for the swimmers, the dog walkers, and the gulls.

Annie swam out a good distance, accelerating to the fastest speed her wobbly style would allow. She'd had a curry the night before, double helpings. She was under no illusions about the capacity of her exercise regime to eradicate a big pile of mutton jalfrezi, but she reckoned that if she observed an extra bout of high-energy penitence, it might even things up a little.

Slightly out of breath, she floated on the waves and looked over towards the Cobb. The artist, Clifford Muldoon, had set up his easel and paintbox on its very end, ready to paint. The grey-haired man could be seen out there most days, and his seascapes and landscapes sold for thousands of pounds in Helen's gallery. Quite a life.

The swimming twins, Sally and Peg, their identical pale

CHAPTER TWENTY-TWO

heads covered with swimming caps, one pink, one yellow, came paddling by.

"Morning, Annie," said one.

"Nice day for it," said the other.

They paddled on. Their style was slow and unhurried, but if Annie was still swimming about in her late seventies or possibly early eighties, she'd be more than grateful.

Back on the beach, she trod carefully over the bands of pebbles, feeling the cool wind and warm sun prickle the beads of water on her arms and shoulders. Helen and Figgy were there, drying off, while Rosamund tried to stand on one leg as she put down her things in preparation for going in.

Annie doubted the wisdom of going back into the sea with an injury, but Rosamund, her foot inside a plastic bag taped firmly to her leg, was set on it.

"No, no. I get it," said Helen. "You've got to get back in the sea. Get back on that horse, so to speak."

She gesticulated with her hand, fingers crooked as though holding an imaginary cigarette. Annie thought it would be a fancy French cigarette, not some common British brand or... She tried to remember that brand of cigarettes Marco had on him. Fumerang? Rummywang? A brand she'd never seen before.

Figgy cleared her throat. The young woman was lovely company, but she struggled with the flow of conversation.

"What is it, Figgy love?" Annie asked.

"Have you seen the front page of the *Lyme Echo*?"

"Can't say I have."

"Sensationalist claptrap with no loyalty to local businesses," sniffed Helen.

Figgy reached into her bag and pulled out one of several copies. She held it out for them all to see.

"Local Woman Lives with Abusive Seagull," Annie read.

The front page of the local rag had a picture of Figgy standing in the doorway of her caravan, giving the camera a puzzled look, with one hand raised. A picture of a seagull appeared in an inset just above her hand, as though she was holding it.

Annie peered closer. She needed reading glasses.

"He gets very desperate and tries to come inside, said Miss Newton (22) who lives in a caravan near Lyme Regis beach," she read.

"It's good to highlight the problem we sometimes have with the gulls," said Figgy. "Although he's technically wrong to call Kevin a seagull."

"Really?" said Helen.

"None of the gull species are called seagulls and they don't all live by the sea."

"An article like that, you'll get nutters sniffing round," said Helen.

"You can't call people with mental health problems nutters," said Figgy.

Helen looked at her. "Didn't say they had mental health problems. Said they were nutters."

Rosamund gave a grunt of laughter. "What kind of world do we live in," she said, "where a seagull makes it onto the front page, on the day after an actual murder in Lyme Regis? You've heard about the man they found in the wheelie bin, haven't you?"

Annie, Figgy and Helen stared at Rosamund. Annie's throat felt dry, and a chill ran over her that had little to do with still being wet.

"Um. Um, yes," she said. "Chap called Marco something, wasn't it?"

Rosamund nodded. "A grisly murder. A killer still on the loose. Now that's what I call news."

She turned, and using the sea wall as support, hobbled down to the waves.

The three of them silently watched her go.

"That's quite an act," said Helen.

"What do you mean?" asked Figgy.

Helen waved her invisible cigarette towards Rosamund. "If she did kill him, she's playing it very cool."

"I think Rosamund is a woman very much in control of her emotions," said Annie.

"A sociopath," said Helen.

"I didn't say that."

Figgy folded her newspaper. "I think if I'd killed someone, I wouldn't be able to lie about it. I'd have to confess straight away."

"I think you would, young Figglington," agreed Annie. "And that says something very complimentary about you."

There was a grind of shutters. Along the promenade, someone was opening up the Breaststrokes café bar for the morning.

"Whether or not Rosamund killed him," said Annie, "there's nothing to stop us doing a little more snooping of our own."

Helen followed her gaze. "Solomon did say that Marco was heard having a blazing row with someone there last week."

"The phrase he used was a 'to-do'," said Annie.

"Exactly," said Helen. "A blazing row. We could pop along and ask some questions."

"Buy ourselves a morning coffee, have a genial chat with the waiting staff."

"Aren't we going to the Kiosk?" asked Figgy, alarmed.

Annie rolled her eyes and explained to Helen, "Two scoops of vanilla honeycomb crunch here likes to get her daily fix of Cameron Winters."

"Annie!" said Figgy.

"It's true. She's going to ask him out before the weekend."

"I am not. Who told you that?"

"No one. I'm just saying you should. Velma from *Scooby Doo* would be brave enough to ask someone out." She turned to Helen. "Did you know Velma from *Scooby Doo* was a lesbian?"

"Gay icon," said Helen. "Fancied her myself for a while." She picked up her bags.

Annie fastened up her dry robe. "Come on, gang. Let's go ask some searching questions."

CHAPTER TWENTY-THREE

Annie had never really taken to Breaststrokes. It had a prime position on the promenade and was popular with visitors, but somehow it felt more like a Mediterranean nightclub than a Lyme Regis café. The fact that its name made it sound like a lap dancing club didn't help.

Breaststrokes was open, but there weren't any customers yet. A guy with a ponytail was putting out the cushions on some chunky wicker seating. A middle-aged woman stood behind the bar.

Annie gave an eyebrow waggle and a side nod to Helen and Figgy, and they made their way over.

"Not quite open yet, love." The woman had shades of a London accent and, Annie could imagine her yelling 'Time!' in an East End boozer.

"We'd just like some coffees," Annie said.

"Mocha for me," said Figgy. "I don't like strong coffee."

"When we're open." The woman brought up a tray of glasses and put it on the end of the counter. "You lot don't usually come in here."

"Us lot?" said Helen.

"You three. And your swimming mates. You've got a little club going."

"It's not really a club," said Annie.

"The Lyme Regis Women's Swimming Club," added Figgy, with a cheeky grin and wide eyes.

"We're not a club," insisted Annie.

Helen looked at Figgy. "Why's it the women's swimming club?"

"Because we're women," said Figgy.

"Aren't men allowed to join?"

"Yes," said Figgy just as Annie said, "No."

Helen raised an eyebrow. "Why not?"

"Because it's not a club!" said Annie. "We don't need to have a club to have a good time together."

"So, why come here today?" asked the woman.

Annie searched for a clever conversation opener but had nothing.

"You know that man they found dead in a wheelie bin the other day?" she said, instead.

The woman gave them a calculating look. "You're not journalists. And you're not cops."

"We're not," said Helen. "But Marco was my next-door neighbour."

The woman pulled a face. "Friends?"

"I wouldn't go so far as that."

"No."

"You knew him, too?" asked Annie.

The woman tilted her head. "After a fashion. He was due to buy this place."

"Breaststrokes? This bar?"

"Café bar." The woman cleared her throat. "It's my

CHAPTER TWENTY-THREE

name above the door. Barbara Spiro, licensee and manager. You can call me Babs."

"Nice to meet you, Babs," Annie said.

"And if he'd bought it, he'd have been my new manager."

Ouch. "I get the sense you weren't a fan."

"You get a feel for people in this business. I saw how he ran his so-called fossil shop on the front. Messy, cheap. Always looking for a quick profit."

"Absolutely disgusting," agreed Helen.

"He's dead," said Figgy. "We should be kind."

"He can't hear us, love," said Babs.

"I tell you," said Helen, "if I had that place, I'd knock right through from the gallery, expand sideways, and turn it into a shop the town could be proud of. No cheap imported toy dinosaurs. Art one side, fossils the other."

"We heard he was in here the other night," said Annie.

Babs shrugged. "He'd been in here a lot."

"But he was arguing."

Babs smiled. "Are you just here for a bit of gossip?"

Annie twisted her lips. "What if we are?"

Babs's smile widened. "Coffees, you say?"

"Mocha for me," repeated Figgy.

"Latte for me and Annie," said Helen.

Babs set to work at the big Italian machine behind the bar.

"He was in here," she said over the hiss of the steam. "He kept coming in, like I say. Wanting to check the books or reinspect the building. He should have signed the contract a week or more ago but there was some financial hold up. I don't honestly care who owns the bricks and mortar as long as they let me run this place in peace."

"The argument..." prompted Annie.

"I'm getting to it. He'd been drinking. Half a dozen bottled beers. He did that. He was with a woman. Blonde woman. I've seen her around town. She was nursing a glass of wine while he knocked back the beers."

"And that's who he argued with?"

"I was busy serving customers. We might be open all day, but this place comes alive at night. Get the eighties party mix on the PA and the people keep drinking and dancing."

"Oh, yes. Very Club Tropicana," said Annie, looking round at the potted palm trees.

"And then out of the blue I can hear her yelling at him. Not regular husband-and-wife spiteful whispers. This was more 'I'm bellowing for all the world to hear' stuff." Babs threw her head back and pretended to bellow. "'Do you think I'm at all interested in that?' she yelled. 'What? Because I'm single? Why don't you just curl up and die?' Something to that effect, although with juicier language. A full minute it went on, and then she tossed the remains of her wine in his face and stormed out."

"A right ding-dong," said Annie.

"But who was she?" asked Figgy.

Babs presented them all with their coffees. "No idea. I've seen her around town, but she's not a regular here."

Annie tutted and wrapped her fingers around the latte.

"Of course," said Babs, "if you were really interested, you could check the bar CCTV footage."

"Really?" said Helen.

Babs raised her eyebrows.

"Why would you let us do that?" asked Figgy.

"You seem a fine bunch of ladies. And it's not like it's against the law, is it?"

"Isn't it?" said Annie.

"They're my cameras, taking perfectly ordinary video in a public space. I can share that with whomever I like."

"You're a very nice woman, Babs Spiro," said Annie.

"That'll be twelve quid for the coffees, plus the price of a large cappuccino for a gander at my CCTV footage."

"And you're an astute businesswoman."

Babs cocked her head.

"Maybe you should buy the bar yourself," said Annie.

"Where would I find the money for that? Besides, another buyer leapt in with a new offer last week."

Annie perked up. "A new buyer? And a higher offer?"

"A tad lower, actually," said Babs. "But old Marco Callington is dead now and it's no skin off my nose. I'll still be the manager, whoever owns the place."

"And who would that new buyer be?"

"Gillian Hewish. Big in property round here. Don't know if you know her."

Annie felt her blood run cold.

"That's your cousin Gillian, isn't it, Annie?" said Helen.

"It is," said Annie through gritted teeth.

CHAPTER TWENTY-FOUR

Annie had imagined the four of them squeezing into a small, secret room with a wall of screens to watch the bar CCTV. She was disappointed to discover it was just a program on Babs the manager's laptop. Babs signed in and opened it up.

There were five cameras, and as Figgy took control of the laptop, she cycled through all of them.

"What time on Friday was it?" she asked.

"Oh, now you're asking." Babs frowned. "It was getting dark. Any time after nine."

Figgy zoomed up and down a timeline at the bottom of the screen.

"You've used this software before, have you?" Helen asked her.

"No, but it's pretty intuitive."

They sipped their coffees while Figgy played.

"Nine pm up to eleven," Figgy muttered. "Two hours. Five cameras. That's ten hours of footage."

"A bit of binge watching," said Babs.

CHAPTER TWENTY-FOUR

Figgy clicked on the menu. "I can export the files."

"Be my guest."

Figgy looked at the side of the laptop, made a hum of appreciation, then fiddled with her phone, took out the storage card and slid it into the side of the laptop.

"You going to put ten hours on that?" said Helen.

"Won't be more than a few gig," Figgy assured her.

In what seemed the blink of an eye, it was done. The little card went back inside Figgy's phone and Figgy turned the laptop round to present it to Babs once more.

"Thank you, love," Babs said. "And be sure to come to the grand re-opening of the café bar."

As Annie reached the bottom of her cup, there came a loud shout from outside.

"You! Yes, you! Get back here at once!" a voice yelled. "I saw what you did! Don't think I didn't!"

The three women swivelled in their seats. Out on the promenade, Solomon Matheson, who ran the shop two doors up from Helen, was bellowing at someone out of sight, red-faced with rage.

"Come here and pick this up!" he yelled.

The person he was yelling at obviously called something in reply, because he shouted back, "Yes, it is! Because I saw it come out of your dog's bum!"

A young man with a tiny terrier on a lead came into view, and Solomon continued to berate him while he nervously bent down and scooped up what was evidently some dog poo into a little plastic bag. The man hurried off, but not before shouting a few choice words back at Solomon. The shopkeeper spluttered, turned round to see who had witnessed the altercation, and assuming it had passed unnoticed, straightened his jacket and marched on.

"And to think that man runs a children's shop," said Annie.

"But dog mess is a proper scourge, isn't it?" said Helen.

"Yes, but there's ways of talking to people, aren't there?" Annie drained the last dregs from her cup and turned to Figgy. "So, we've got all the video footage there?"

"I can look at it on my laptop."

"Back to yours, then?"

Figgy looked between Annie and Helen. "The three of us? It's not a big caravan."

"She's calling you fat, Helen," said Annie.

"No, I'm not," said Figgy. Annie thought Helen was positively waifish, and if anything, could have done with a few more sausage rolls and doughnuts. "Of course you can come back to mine."

The three of them, hair still stiff and salty from the sea, walked westward along the front, past the harbour, the Cobb and the bowling green.

"A caravan indeed," said Helen, admiring the small structure that sat almost on the beach. "I lived in a caravan once. I lie. It was a gîte in the Dordogne."

Figgy let them in.

"But this," said Helen, "this is something else."

Where Annie had simply noted the Axminster carpet and the heavy fabrics, Helen was positively transported.

"Please tell me your grandma hasn't changed a thing in forty years."

"My grandma didn't change a thing in forty years," said Figgy dutifully.

While Figgy sorted out her laptop, Helen studied the seascape prints on the wall.

"Kitsch and worthless but wonderful nonetheless," she

said. "Your whole home is like a piece of curated art. What's this?" Helen reached for an elderly wood-boxed FM radio on a nearby shelf.

"Don't touch that!" said Figgy with surprising sharpness.

Helen's hand froze.

"It's tuned in," said Figgy.

"I can see that."

"It has to be tuned in."

Helen crouched to peer at the dial. "Radio Four."

"The Shipping Forecast. I listen to the Shipping Forecast."

Figgy had her laptop open, and a range of files arrayed on the screen.

"Let's look at this," she said. "I can open several windows at once."

The three women gathered on a plush banquette seat with the laptop on the table before them. Figgy had four videos running simultaneously.

"Aren't the people moving quickly?" said Helen.

"Double speed for now," Figgy explained.

They watched people come and go, along the promenade outside, at the bar, sitting, standing, drinking with comedic speed. Ten minutes in they were interrupted by a loud squawk and a battering against the window.

"Oh, my word!" gulped Helen.

"Meet Kevin the seagull," said Annie. "Now a front-page celebrity in the local newspaper."

As Kevin paced angrily along the windowsill, Helen got up to inspect him. She approached in a low crouch, spreading her arms low and wide. Was she mimicking a bird's wings?

"Are you trying to commune with him, dear?" said Annie.

"I'm fascinated." Helen cocked her head. "You say he always comes here?"

"Constantly," said Figgy. "There's some fondant fancies on the table there if you want to give him one."

Helen glanced at the packet of iced cakes. She took one out, pink with white stripes. She unwrapped the paper cup. Kevin's beady yellow eyes latched onto it.

"Hmmm," said Helen, and took a big bite of cake.

Annie wasn't sure if seagulls did surprise. There was certainly some sort of change in its expression.

"He gets angry if I don't feed him," said Figgy.

"But the more you feed him, the more he comes back," said Helen. "Blackmailers are like that. Never satisfied, not until you deal with them."

"I hope you're not suggesting Figgy does away with—" Annie said but was interrupted by Figgy tapping urgently on her arm.

"Look! Look!"

Helen stuffed the other half of the fondant fancy in her mouth and hurried to sit down and join them.

Figgy paused the videos, moved them back a bit and pressed play.

Moving from view in one camera to the next, Marco Callington walked towards the bar, dressed in a dark suit. He turned, expelling a lungful of cigarette smoke before entering. Then he spoke to Babs Spiro, who poured him a tall glass of lager.

"Is there no sound on this thing?" asked Helen.

"No," said Figgy. "It's picture only."

CHAPTER TWENTY-FOUR

Marco took his beer and approached a woman at a table. She already had a glass of wine in front of her.

Annie felt her jaw drop open.

"Is that...?" Figgy whispered.

Annie's breath had caught in her throat. "It is," she said.

On the screen, Marco Callington sat down across the table from Rosamund Winters.

CHAPTER TWENTY-FIVE

ANNIE, Figgy, and Helen watched the CCTV footage of Marco and Rosamund.

Annie itched to hear what was being said. But there was no sound.

"She doesn't like him," said Helen.

"How can you tell?" Figgy asked.

"Body language. Look, he's open and expressive, arms out. He's taking up half the table by himself. But look at her, one arm crossed over her chest, her knees angled away."

"She's bored of him," Annie said.

"He was a boring man," said Helen. "So many are. Orbiting their own self-interested planets."

"Not all men," said Annie. "And look. She's had enough of him."

Over the course of several minutes of conversation, most of it coming from Marco, Rosamund had become visibly irritated.

And then she suddenly exploded with fury. Her mouth was wide, shouting now. Her arms had become animated.

"To hell with you, Marco," said Helen in a pretend voice, dubbing over the conversation. "I hate you."

"'Do you think I'm interested in that?' the lady said," added Figgy. "And something about 'because I'm single'."

"But she's not single," said Annie. "Rosamund is married."

"She's out at a bar without her husband," said Figgy.

"Women are allowed out on their own," said Helen.

Figgy shook her head. "But Babs told us the woman said something about being single."

"Her husband's away for work a lot. Maybe while the cat's away..."

On screen, there was a violent arm movement. Rosamund had flung her wine in Marco's face. As he spluttered, she got up and stormed out.

"Nice dress," said Annie. "Cocktail dress, would you say?"

"She's got the legs for it," Helen commented.

Annie tutted. "Married women don't wear cocktail dresses that short when they're out alone."

"Are we policing what another woman wears?" asked Figgy.

Helen grunted in agreement.

"I'm just saying it as I see it," Annie said. "Even if I had the figure for it, I'd only be wearing that dress if I was in company. Or if I was *seeking* company."

Figgy rewound the video.

"I might need a cuppa to think this one over," said Annie. "Mind if I put a brew on, Figgy?"

"I'll do it." Figgy stood and opened the window to give a sulking Kevin his cake before putting the kettle on.

"That bird needs to be dealt with more harshly," said Helen.

"You sound like you want to wring its neck," Annie commented.

Helen laughed. "And bring down a curse upon me and the crew? Bad luck to kill a seagull."

"I think you're thinking of albatrosses."

"Same difference, just a matter of scale."

Annie smiled as she watched Figgy drop tea bags into a pot, something you didn't often see young people do. The pot was of green glazed earthenware, and looked like it might have come straight from a wartime village hall or an old-style church coffee morning.

Marco's death was one hell of a mystery. Baffling. And every moment they kept what they knew to themselves, the guiltier Annie felt.

"So, what do we know so far?" she asked.

Helen raised an eyebrow. "So far?"

"About this whole business. What do we know?"

"From the beginning?"

"Should I take notes?" asked Figgy, placing the teapot on the coffee table.

"Only if you're willing to eat the evidence when the police come knocking," Helen said. She stood and paced, not that there was much room for pacing in the caravan. "First thing. You two found Marco's body in the front passenger seat of Rosamund's honking great car."

"We did," said Annie. "And we know it was there when she arrived, because we've already looked at the CCTV from the street and no one got in or out of the car from the moment Rosamund left, up to us arriving and finding the body."

CHAPTER TWENTY-FIVE

Helen nodded. "So, Rosamund drove the body to the beach. Which is madness."

"Utter madness."

"He'd been hit over the head," said Figgy. "That icky wound."

"Still wet," added Annie. "It's not like he'd been dead for days."

"And then when we took him back to his shop, he somehow got out of the car and into the wheelie bin."

"And I'm just going to say it," said Helen. "He was definitely dead. He didn't get out and walk."

"Unless he was a zombie," suggested Figgy.

Annie eyed her. "Bit of an outside chance there, Figgy."

Helen sighed. "Makes as much sense as anything else."

CHAPTER TWENTY-SIX

Figgy put mugs on the coffee table and presented a jug of milk. Annie picked up the teapot, gave it a swirl and poured three cups.

"That's what happened after he died," she said. "What about before that? Who had the motive to kill him?"

Helen laughed. "Everyone."

"So, he was generally disliked. He ran a fossil shop that didn't, shall we say, match the character of the town."

"Grubby, horrid, tacky thing," Helen muttered. "Selling cheap, nasty imported tat at top prices to unwary tourists."

"Particularly disliked among local business owners."

"And that man next door but one has a serious temper problem," said Figgy.

"Solomon Matheson?" said Helen, surprised.

"You heard him shout at that dog owner."

"Doesn't make him a murderer."

"Maybe he sees potential in the shop next door."

"Are we really going to accuse my long-standing friend of murder?" said Helen.

CHAPTER TWENTY-SIX

"Are we really convinced it was our mutual long-standing friend, Rosamund?" asked Annie.

Helen turned to her. "His body was in her car! And she was seen arguing with him in Breaststrokes."

"And that just doesn't make sense. What were they doing there?"

"The bar manager said he was looking to buy the place," said Figgy.

Annie grunted.

"Except it looks like Annie's cousin Gillian is stepping in to buy it," said Helen.

Annie gave another grunt then caught Figgy's eye. "Gillian and I are not on the best of terms."

"Oh?"

"Gillian Hewish owns Hewish Developments," said Helen. "Also trading as Hewish Homes. You'll have seen the signs about."

Figgy pursed her lips. "Oh, the holiday homes."

"And the new homes and the cottages being converted into flats. Not unlike those of the late Marco Callington, Gillian Hewish's business practices are not viewed favourably by a number of locals."

"My cousin's ripping the guts out of the town in order to turn a profit," hissed Annie. "And because of her and her kind, God help any local who hopes to find affordable housing in this town."

"So, if she wanted to buy the bar but Marco got there first...?" suggested Figgy.

"Oh, now *she's* a murder suspect, too?" said Annie.

"Someone murdered him, didn't they?"

"You've accused practically everyone except Kevin the seagull there," said Annie. "My cousin, Gillian. Solomon at the baby clothes shop."

"But neither of them actually had Marco's corpse sitting in the front seat of their car," said Helen. "Or was seen arguing with him in that bar."

Annie licked her lips. "And that landlord lady said that Rosamund mentioned being single, even though she's married."

Helen chuckled. "Not the first woman to seek a bit of fun away from home."

"We didn't see any sign of him at her home," said Figgy. "In fact..."

"What?" asked Helen.

"Her house was weird."

"In what way?"

"It *was* weird," agreed Annie. "She had covers on the security cameras outside her house, like they were draped over them."

"And she had the heating turned up really high," added Figgy.

"Really high," said Annie. "But then she opened the windows. It didn't make any sense."

Helen shrugged. "So, she's got secrets. She's hiding something."

"Of course, we could take things a step further if we wanted to," said Annie, raising her eyebrows at the others. "In for a penny, in for a pound."

Helen rolled her eyes. "I think what you actually mean is that you're taking us all down your rabbit hole with you. Remember, I live with an artist. I know what obsession looks like."

Annie looked at her friends, thinking of her penchant for buying baby paraphernalia. Figgy had the Shipping Forecast,

CHAPTER TWENTY-SIX

and the seagull and the fondant fancies. And Rosamund... What did Rosamund have?

But this... this was just healthy curiosity. Not obsession.

"To be fair," said Helen, "I think we all do. I was merely pointing out what it is we're doing. You won't catch me stopping people from following their dreams." She crossed her legs with a flourish that exposed a froth of coloured petticoats. "Come on, Annie, what's next?"

"I thought we might go and stake out Rosamund's house. See what she's doing with herself. We've all observed how cool she plays things when she's in company. She might let her guard slip when she's home alone."

"We know that Cameron's at the Kiosk for the rest of the day," said Figgy with a nod.

Annie and Helen exchanged a smile.

"What? We go there often enough that I know his working hours."

"You sure he's not going to be home?" said Helen.

"You could pop down to the Kiosk and ask him," said Annie with a grin. "You know, just to check."

"I... I could," said Figgy.

Annie laughed. Figgy reddened.

"Do we need a vehicle?" asked Helen. "For a stakeout?"

"Probably," said Annie.

"Mine's closest, at the back of the gallery," Helen said.

"Well, I think I might need to pop home and get changed. This dry robe is lovely, but I don't think a swimming cossie and dry robe are the ideal getup for a stakeout."

"My shop at, shall we say, noon?" suggested Helen.

The others nodded.

"And Figgy's going to go chat up young Cameron, aren't you?" added Annie.

CHAPTER TWENTY-SEVEN

Figgy approached the Kiosk on the seafront.

She'd been here plenty of times for post-swim drinks and ice creams. But this time, she was here to speak to Cameron.

Yes, she'd spoken to Cameron before, but that had been to get something to eat. Talking to Cameron had always been part of the process, but on those occasions, it had been drink *and* talk to Cameron, or ice cream *and* talk to Cameron.

But this time it was talk to Cameron *and* ice cream. A reversal of priorities. She'd put on her best dress, the black one with the pleated skirt and red cherry pattern. As she walked, she wished she hadn't. Too obvious.

Her stomach flipped as she approached. She berated herself. She was twenty-two years old, not some lovestruck teenager.

She emboldened herself by imagining how she would tell her therapist Xandrea about this during their next session.

That's right, Xandrea, she'd say. *Walked right up to him and made small talk, like a normal human being.*

CHAPTER TWENTY-SEVEN

Cameron was behind the counter. There were no other customers. He was already looking at her.

"The usual?"

"Er, no." She didn't want ice cream. Well, she did. She often wanted ice cream. There was always room for ice cream.

But she was on a mission. She had to meet with two old ladies and join them on a stakeout. This was not the time for ice cream.

But now that she'd said no, what did she actually want? Cameron was looking at her. Gentle, easy-going Cameron, all six-foot-something of him. Tall but not imposing, not threatening. Patient Cameron.

She dithered over whether to backtrack and go for the ice cream. Or maybe order a coffee or another drink. But every millisecond she hesitated, the weirder things got.

There was a squawk and shriek and a yell behind her. On the beach, a grey-haired man leapt up from his deckchair and stared at the seagull flapping away with what appeared to be a whole slice of carrot cake in its mouth.

Cameron tutted.

"Circle of life," said Figgy.

He frowned, then pointed. "You were in the paper."

She pulled a face. "I just mentioned that I have a seagull who pesters me for food."

"It read like you share your place with him."

She shook her head. "I'm not a lunatic."

He shrugged. "You've got one of the caravans down the far end of the beach, then?"

"It was my grandma's really. Before she died."

He nodded. "Sounds idyllic. Er, I mean the caravan thing, not the dead grandma thing. Damn. Sorry."

"That's OK. I'm not sure about idyllic."

"A place of your own, though, right? I mean, I assume you... I don't see you with anyone else and... Not that I'm spying on customers. I meant you look like the kind of person who lives by themselves."

Figgy laughed, wondering whether her awkwardness had somehow transferred itself to Cameron. "Wow. Like a mad old cat lady. Or that one covered in cobwebs in the Charles Dickens book."

"Miss Havisham."

"Yes. Her. Very good."

"English Lit A-level. Now it sounds like I'm bragging. No, I didn't mean..." He closed his eyes and tilted his head as if doing a mental reset. "What I did mean was that it was cool you having your own place. By the sea, close to nature. I also meant that I assumed you were a strong and independent woman. Which is cool."

"Ah, right."

"I don't know how I'll ever get a place of my own."

"We all have to move on eventually."

He smiled. "I don't think that's even crossed my mum's mind. She might want me to go to uni, but only so I can come straight back. She's so... well, you saw what she did to her foot."

"I don't think you being here or not would have stopped her treading on a shell."

He grunted in agreement. "I'm sorry. We got distracted. You didn't want an ice cream?"

She pulled in a breath. "No, I will take one. Single scoop. I've got a place to be." She reminded herself that she was going to spy on his mum's house. On *his* house. "A work thing."

CHAPTER TWENTY-SEVEN

"I thought you worked in IT, like from home."

She raised an eyebrow. "You pay attention."

"I'm interested."

"It's a work meeting," she lied. "And then I'm done for the day. You... you working late?"

"Here till five."

"Good, good. I mean, it's good that you're getting hours."

He handed her an ice cream. She tapped her card. And then she walked away. Simple as that. She'd engaged him, she'd asked him her question, in a kind of cool and off-hand manner, and he'd answered. Smooth as silk.

She felt like the cat that had got the cream – ice cream in her case – and the feeling stayed with her all the way to the end of the prom and the side road, where Helen and Annie stood by the side of a small white car.

"He's at work until five," Figgy said, failing to suppress a grin.

Annie winked. "Good work, double-o Figgy."

They all climbed into the car. Annie took the back seat so that Figgy could sit in the front. It was a tight fit. Figgy was glad she'd finished the ice cream.

"What kind of a car is this?" Figgy asked.

"It's a Fiat Cinquecento," Helen told her.

"What a lovely name."

"Is that the same thing as a Fiat 500?" asked Annie.

"It sounds so much better in Italian, don't you think?" Helen said as she turned opposite St Michael's Church.

They made their way up the Sidmouth Road to Rosamund's house.

"Where should we park?" Helen asked as they approached.

"Good question." Annie leaned forward for a better

view. "She's got those tall hedges all around the place. We won't see anything at all unless we park right opposite her drive. Is that too obvious?"

"I have an idea," said Helen. "Let me park up and I'll show you."

Helen parked directly opposite the end of Rosamund's drive, then leaned over into the back. "Can you pass me that please, Annie?" She pointed at a reflective sunshade.

Annie passed it over.

"See this? This gives us the privacy we need, and it just looks as if we're annoying tourists who've parked up here for the day to avoid paying for parking in the town." Helen used the sucker cups on the sunshade to stick it onto the side windows that faced Rosamund's house.

"I hate to rain on your parade, my love," said Annie, "but it also means we can't see anything."

"I'm not done!" Helen reached into one of the huge pockets of her skirt and pulled out a pair of nail scissors. She cut a little slot in the reflective sunshade. "This is my viewing slot. You'll both need to cut your own, and then we can peek out without being observed."

"Flipping heck, that's genius," said Annie, holding out her hand for the scissors.

Figgy laughed. Today was turning out well. "It's like being in a shiny cocoon," she said.

CHAPTER TWENTY-EIGHT

HALF AN HOUR LATER, it was feeling close inside Helen's car.

"I could use some air," said Annie.

"Fan on the parcel shelf," replied Helen, her eyes fixed on her viewing slot.

Annie turned to see an honest-to-goodness folding fan. She'd have expected nothing less from a Victorian time traveller, which was what Helen appeared to be. She flicked it open and stirred the air.

There were a few shouts when Rosamund was spotted walking past a window, but otherwise the time passed slowly.

"We've not seen her husband at all, have we?" Annie asked the others as she fanned the air. "If he was in the house, we'd have seen him by now, surely?"

"Yeah, that's true," said Figgy. "Wouldn't there be another car there as well?"

"Probably," agreed Helen. "Ooh, while I remember..." she delved into her pockets "...I had a chance to do a little painting while I waited for you two. Acrylics dry so fast."

Helen's pockets were wondrous things, and Annie often wondered how she came to have so many. She wore multi-layered skirts, and there was always a pocket, or several, tucked away in there. She rummaged in them now.

"I think you're going to enjoy them, Figgy." Helen made a small crowing noise of victory and her hand emerged, clutching a pile of pebbles that she deposited in Figgy's lap with a stony clatter. Figgy turned them over in her hands. Annie pushed herself forward from the back to examine the objects.

Each was painted to resemble a snack. There was a large flat one, a convincing replica of a cinnamon swirl, another that looked like a birds-eye view of a burger and several cupcakes.

"It's where art meets science," Helen explained. "If you want to discourage the gulls from raiding your snacks, they must un-learn the behaviour. They need to experience some negative results from their plundering ways, and these stones are just the thing, no?"

"Just the thing?" Annie asked. "I mean, it's a hell of a leap you've made there, Helen."

"It's not a new idea. You wouldn't believe the number of people who've asked for strawberry painted stones in the gallery. Gardeners swear by them for keeping birds off their crops."

"How many?" Figgy asked.

"Sorry?"

"You said we wouldn't believe how many people asked you for strawberry painted stones. How many is it?"

Helen huffed. "Well, I don't know. At least two. I did think about stocking them if I could find a source."

Annie cradled the cinnamon swirl stone in her hand.

"Well, I think it's a marvellous idea, I really do. Do you think you might try them out on Kevin, Figgy?"

"I might. I don't want him to hurt his beak, though."

"Pfft," said Helen. "Seagulls are pretty tough. If they can bash their way into a crab, they'll survive pecking a rock, surely?"

"Do they bash crabs open?" Annie asked, mildly horrified.

"I don't know about that," Helen admitted, then fell silent, shushed by Figgy, who was flapping her hands.

"She's coming out!"

Annie closed the fan and pressed her face to the side of the car. Rosamund was at the front door, standing in the doorway. She was wafting the door itself back and forth, as if she, too, was trying to cool down.

"You think she's still got the heating on?" asked Helen. "It must cost her a fortune to run it like that in the summer."

"She doesn't even seem to be enjoying it," said Annie. "Oh, she's on the move."

They all watched as Rosamund carried a bin liner across the front of the house towards the area that housed the dustbins. What was peculiar was the way she moved, edging along and hugging the front of the building.

"What on earth is she doing?" Helen asked. "She looks like the world's worst burglar, sneaking rubbish out of her own house."

"I wish we had binoculars," said Figgy, "because I think there's a CCTV camera on that part of the building she just squeezed past. It's like she was trying not to let it see her."

"Where d'you mean?" Annie asked.

"Up there, in the apex of the roof of that garage or whatever."

Annie squinted. "Yeah, can't tell. There's something up there. Binoculars would be good."

Rosamund dumped the bag of rubbish into the bin and then repeated the same eccentric manoeuvres in reverse as she returned to the front door. She wafted the door back and forth a few more times before disappearing inside again.

"Well, that was peculiar," said Annie. "What do we think we've learned from this experience?"

"Bring drinks and snacks on a stakeout?" Figgy suggested.

"Loo breaks are a must, too," said Helen. "I think I might go for a bush wee. I'm going to nip round to one of these back gardens. Back in a jiffy."

"Or," said Annie, "we could call it a day. We've learned that Rosamund's behaving oddly, which is useful."

She didn't want to plead with Helen not to wee in someone's garden, but at the same time, she didn't want to get caught up in the awkwardness that might arise if she was spotted.

"Righto, let's do that," said Helen, removing the sunshade from the window and starting the engine. "Buckle in, ladies, and we'll head back into town."

CHAPTER TWENTY-NINE

TINA SAT in a deckchair on Lyme Regis beach, one of the old-fashioned wooden folding ones. She was aware that when she decided it was time to get out, she'd need to either roll out of it like a beached seal or call for the help of a random passer-by. Alternatively, she could just stay there forever, which felt pretty appealing.

Louis was playing in the sand with a bucket and spade. His mastery of the sandcastle was coming on, and he was focused on building a whole line of fortifications along the sand in front of her.

A shadow crossed over her. She looked up, shielding her eyes from the sun.

"I thought it was you," said DS Nathan Strunk.

"Not some other massively pregnant woman then?" she said. "There's a few of us about."

He tilted his head towards the Kiosk not twenty feet away. "Want a coffee?"

She shook her head. "Tea. Just a small one or I'll need a pee."

He smiled. "I'm sure you used to be prim and proper."

"Motherhood has robbed me of all dignity."

While Nathan got the drinks, she re-read the copy of the *Lyme Echo* she'd picked up. Louis banged his spade on the top of his upturned bucket and turned out his next sandcastle.

The DS returned with two cups.

"You seen this?" she asked, holding out the paper with one hand as she took the cup with the other.

"'Local Cub Scouts Collect 300 Odd Socks for Charity'?" he read.

"Below that."

He looked. "'Tourist Traps Leave Holidaymakers Out of Pocket.'"

"Apparently, there's a whole series of articles on the shops and businesses in the town. They seem keen to highlight places they consider to be a rip-off. Jurassic Fossils does *not* come out of it covered in glory."

The DS sat on the deckchair beside her and scanned the article. "'Cheap imported fossils', 'fake fossils', 'more of a toy shop than a fossil shop'." He looked at the byline. "Written by one Jason Mordaunt. Reckon the man had it in for Marco?"

Tina grunted. "He probably thinks this is searing investigative journalism. This from the man who gave us the 'Woman Scared By Seagull' headline the other day."

"Could be worth questioning him, though." He sipped his coffee and winced at the heat. "Now that I've found you, I wondered if you wanted filling in on the case so far."

"Of course I bloody do," Tina said, glancing over at her son with an apologetic shrug.

"Of course. Well, forensics from the scene haven't turned

up anything new. There are blood droplets in the car park area. All Marco's. Every resident, including the shopkeepers round the front, has been questioned. Most of the businesses weren't open during the window we're looking at—"

"What is that window? Do we know when he died?"

"Mere hours before we found him. Pathologist hasn't given a precise time."

"Of course."

"But he probably died after five in the morning. His body was moved after he died. We knew that already. So the location and the circumstances of death are unclear. The head wound is the cause of death. Bleeding on the brain, followed by unconsciousness and death. The murder weapon was an unevenly shaped heavy object, like a rock."

"Or a fossil," Tina suggested.

"Or a fossil," he agreed. "So, yes, we've been bagging and tagging every rock in that shop for analysis. Which reminds me..."

"Yes?"

"That fossil on the counter."

She nodded. "The 'How much is this worth to you?' fossil?"

"Right. Well, whoever wrote the message either didn't know their fossils, or the message meant something else. It's made of resin."

"You mean it's 3D printed?"

"Maybe. But it's not a real fossil. Just a pretty paperweight. There's a whole box of them out back. Imported from China."

Tina held onto her tea, knowing not to drink it until it had cooled down. "Just like the guy says in the newspaper article. Selling knock-off fossils, which isn't a crime unless you're trying to pass them off as the genuine article. That's more of a trades description kind of thing."

"Yeah, so the shop itself is a bit of dead end." The DS sipped his coffee cautiously. "But Marco Callington's finances are a bit more interesting."

"Ooh, go on."

"The fossil racket was clearly working. He had considerable savings. Plenty of money in and out. Interestingly, he withdrew five thousand pounds from the bank in cash, three days before he was killed."

"That *is* interesting."

"Right? Large cash withdrawals always interest me. Second only to large cash deposits. We've got no clue what he was using that money for. Not yet. But another thing was that he was due to exchange on the purchase of a bar called Breaststrokes around the same time." He shifted forward in his deckchair and gestured along the promenade to his right. "Beachfront bar."

"I know the one," said Tina, who had drunk (and *been* drunk) in there in the past.

"The exchange of contracts didn't happen and someone else swooped in."

"You're building up to the juicy part, I can tell."

"A local property developer called Gillian Hewish."

It was a good thing Tina hadn't started drinking her tea, or she might have spat it out. "Oh... Oh, I see."

He eyed her. "A little bird tells me you know her."

"What? Aunt Gillian? Well, not technically my aunt. Some sort of second cousin once removed. Yes, I know her." She narrowed her eyes at him. "You didn't just come to buy me a drink."

"We're going to interview her when we get a chance. Wouldn't mind some insights from you."

She narrowed her eyes. "Think my Aunt Gillian might have murdered Marco to get her hands on Breaststrokes?"

The DS gave her a look. "Think it's possible?"

"If you asked my mum, she'd say Gillian was capable of that and more. But, no."

"No?"

"Aunt Gillian has money. Property, money, influence. In my experience, people like that don't need to kill anyone to get what they want."

He nodded.

Tina gestured to the row of sandcastles in front of them. "Imagine the town of Lyme Regis. They say that every fifth house belongs to Hewish Homes. When you've got influence like that, you don't need to resort to murder."

CHAPTER THIRTY

THE NEXT DAY, Annie made her way down to Figgy's caravan with Dex leading the way. Dex was a fast learner and keen to see Figgy again.

"Kettle's on," said Figgy as she opened the door. "Hello, Dex!"

Annie smiled and settled onto the seat by the window, Dex at her feet while Figgy boiled the kettle.

"Helen's snack stones working?" she asked. She could see some of them on the outside windowsill.

"You'll see soon," Figgy replied.

Right on cue, a huge seagull descended onto a lurid pink cupcake-painted stone, opening its beak wide as it swooped down. It scrabbled for a moment with the unexpected weight and then screamed in rage, taking off empty-handed.

"Good Lord!" said Annie.

"Yep," said Figgy. "It's quite distracting. I might have to move them. It happens every five minutes or so."

Annie raised her eyebrows. "Who knew that Helen was

onto something? Maybe she should paint a few more and see who else wants to hear the rage of the seagulls?"

"Rage of the seagulls. Sounds like an indie album," said Figgy with a smile as she sat down. "Actually, about Helen..."

"Yes?"

"Should we consider..." She bit her lip, hesitating.

"What?" Annie blinked at her. "Should we consider that Helen, our Helen, perhaps had a motive for killing Marco Callington? Is that what you were going to say?"

Figgy cast her gaze down. "Sorry."

"No, don't be sorry," Annie said. "It's a thought. They were neighbours. She didn't like him. Not one bit, that much is clear."

"And maybe she wanted his shop."

Annie gave a slow nod.

"Did she want it badly enough to kill him, though?" Figgy asked.

Annie shrugged. "She's a canny businesswoman. Must have driven her mad seeing the premises being used in a way that she didn't approve of. She seems to have strong ideas about it."

"She does. Although Helen has strong ideas about lots of things. It doesn't mean she'd kill for them."

"Yes," said Annie. "It's a back-burner idea, but we should keep it in mind."

Figgy's laptop was in its usual place on the table. Annie's visit had presumably disrupted her work, although she didn't seem too bothered.

"You have those magical powers of making the internet obey you," Annie observed, with a nod to the laptop.

Figgy laughed. "It's not magic."

"Very well, then, let's just say that your mastery is greater than mine. What's the chance of you finding out more about Rosamund's husband, eh?"

Figgy frowned. "But we know the dead man wasn't Rosamund's husband."

Annie cocked her head.

"Oh! Oh yes!" Figgy's hands flew to her face. "Of course, you're thinking Marco might not be the only murder victim."

"It has to be a possibility, doesn't it?"

Figgy went over to her laptop. "What do we know about him?"

Annie considered. "Very little. He's called David. That's it. David Winters."

Figgy spent a few minutes tapping at her laptop. "Not sure what we want to find out. And there's lots of David Winters out there."

Annie reached down to tickle Dex's ears, aware that what she was about to say would cause a reaction. "Actually, I can think of a way that we could get the complete lowdown on the Winters family."

"Yeah? What?" Figgy sat back in her chair and looked at Annie.

"Cameron," said Annie. "You and he seem to have some – what should we call it? – chemistry. We could use that."

Figgy drew back. "Use that how?"

"You and he should take things up a notch. You could ask him out on a date."

Figgy's mouth dropped open. "Ask him?"

"Out on a date. Yes. Why not? You're on good speaking terms now."

Annie watched while Figgy's face tried out a variety of expressions. Once she'd moved on from the initial shock, there was definitely interest in the idea. "I'm not really sure how I would do that."

Annie smiled at her. "OK, shall we try roleplay? I'll be Cameron. I'm serving in the Kiosk, and you've chosen a time when it's just the two of you there." She stood and wiped an imaginary counter in front of her.

Figgy looked unsure, but eventually she too stood and walked over to Annie. "Hi, Cameron."

"Two scoops of vanilla honeycomb crunch?" Annie asked, picking up an imaginary scoop.

Figgy giggled. "Yes, please."

Annie handed over the ice cream with a wide smile.

"And..." Figgy began, her voice tight. "Cameron, would you like to go for a drink when you get off work?"

"Would I ever!" roared Annie. She calmed herself. "I mean, yes, I'd love to. Great job, Figgy. You nailed it. All you have to do is repeat that with the real Cameron."

"When?"

Annie turned towards the door. "No time like the present. I'll even pay for the ice cream if you like."

CHAPTER THIRTY-ONE

"THIS," said DS Nathan Strunk as he turned into the driveway of Gillian Hewish's house, "is a nice house."

Tina's Aunt Gillian – technically her mum's cousin – lived in a house off the Charmouth Road. There was a short track, a gate, and then a circular block-paved driveway with a carved stone birdbath at its centre.

Tina had been here once, back when Gillian and her mum were still friends. She'd forgotten how large the place was. It was like someone had transplanted a Spanish mansion to the Dorset coast.

A side gate opened and there was Gillian. She wasn't formally dressed, but there was something about her blouse and trousers that rose above casual. She held a massive toffee-coloured blob of fur and it took Tina a second or two to identify it as a cat. She struggled to wave at them without dropping it.

"What the heck's that?" muttered the DS.

"It's a Maine Coon," said Tina, pushing herself out of the car. "A monster cat." She waved. "Morning, Gillian."

CHAPTER THIRTY-ONE

"You found us OK," called Gillian. "Come round."

Gillian turned without waiting and the two detectives followed her through a side garden to a much larger rear garden. There was no back fence. Beyond the large patio and lawn the ground simply fell away to cliffs and the stony fossil beach at the east end of the town. The garden had uninterrupted views across the bay and, in the far distance, the island of Portland Bill.

A glass-topped dining table sat on the patio with a jug and glasses set out. Gillian dropped the huge cat onto one of the chairs. It flicked evil eyes at the humans and curled up.

"Sit, sit," said Gillian. "Help yourself to cucumber water. I've got a meeting at one but I'm yours till then."

Tina took a seat gratefully.

"They have you working in your condition?" said Gillian.

"She insisted," said Nathan.

"This your first child?" Gillian asked her.

"Second, Aunt Gillian," Tina replied.

Gillian smiled. "My, aren't you fecund? But we do need children, don't we? Someone to do the jobs when we're all too old."

Tina's Aunt Gillian had never had children nor, to the best of Tina's knowledge, a partner, at least not for long.

"We appreciate you giving us your time," said the DS. "I understand you have quite the property empire to oversee."

"Empire, is it?" Gillian sipped at a glass of water.

"Oh, I did a little research," he said. "You've got that building development off Haye Lane, and did I read that you're turning the old Regent Cinema on Broad Lane into an apartment and retail complex?"

The Regent Cinema had burned down in a fire some years ago, although the Art Deco façade was still intact. Tina saw the need to make use of the space but wasn't sure that knocking it down and putting a block of apartments there instead was the answer.

"We're creating housing where it's most needed," said Gillian. "People need homes." She gave each of them in turn a smile. "You'll have to tell me what this is all about. My assistant passed on your message, but I'm not sure I quite understand."

"It would have been nice to speak to you directly when we phoned," said the DS.

She shrugged. "I am a busy person. So much to do, I have to get other people to do some things for me."

Tina looked at her aunt over the top of her glass. *Sounds wonderful.*

"We're investigating the murder of Marco Callington, whose body was found the other day," said the DS.

"Yes. I read something. Found in a wheelie bin or something. Terribly undignified."

"It was a callous and violent murder," Tina said.

"Definitely murder, eh? But I'm not sure what this has to do with me."

Nathan consulted his notebook. Tina was sure this was for show; he had a good memory.

"We're interested in the Breaststrokes café bar, down at the seafront," he said.

"I see," said Gillian. "Or rather, I don't quite see. Not fully. But, yes, I've recently purchased it."

"Papers signed?"

She nodded. "Think the solicitors have some bits to finish off, but that's what solicitors are for, isn't it? Yes. Grand reopening soon, to which you're definitely invited."

CHAPTER THIRTY-ONE

"Are you aware that, up until his death, Mr Callington also had an offer on the place?"

Gillian pulled a face. Tina couldn't be sure if it was genuine surprise or not.

"I knew someone else had put in an offer. Fell through, didn't it? I didn't know it was this Callington chap." She frowned, wrinkles appearing in her tanned forehead. "I thought he was just some little shopkeeper."

"He owned a shop on Bridge Street, yes. And he was due to buy Breaststrokes."

Gillian seemed to be suppressing a smile. "Do I need my solicitor present for this chat?"

"Do you think you need a solicitor present?"

"It sounds like – apologies if this comes across as a little melodramatic – but it sounds like you are painting a narrative in which little old me, the mad old cat lady on the hill, murdered my rival Marco Callington, to make sure my offer on the café bar was the successful one."

"We're just building up a general picture," he said.

"Because if I was hellbent on getting that property – which I am, by the way – then surely it would have been simpler and cheaper to add an extra twenty thousand to my offer."

"I'm sure you're right, Ms Hewish."

She held out her hands. "Do these look like the hands of a person who could bash a man's head in with a rock?"

"A rock?" said the DS.

"Isn't that what it was? I'm sure that's what I heard."

He looked at Tina and then back at Gillian. "I'm not sure the police have released any information to that effect."

"Then I must have heard it from somewhere else," she said, her tone unperturbed.

The DS flicked through his pad. "But, just for the sake of our enquiries, can you tell me where you were between one and seven on the morning of the twelfth?"

Now Gillian did smile. "In bed, I should think. Asleep."

"Can anyone vouch for that?"

"Only Colonel Tom."

"Colonel Tom? Ah." Nathan wagged a finger at the Maine Coon cat, two seats along. The cat blinked and looked away.

"There's a security camera out front," said Tina. "Perhaps we could take a look to corroborate that no one left during that time."

"Sly," said Gillian.

"Sorry?" said Tina.

"Sly like a fox. You get that from your mum."

"I'll assume that was a compliment."

Her aunt gave a small shrug. "I'm always happy to help the police. They do sterling work in the community. But I think if you want to look at my camera, then that would be a matter to take up with my solicitor."

The DS leaned forward. "It wouldn't take long."

She gave him a level look. "It's the principle of the matter. There's expecting me to be helpful to the police, and then there's overstepping boundaries. I find that if you let people do things time and time again, they start to think it's their right. Applies to the police as much as it does to the rest of us. An Englishwoman's home is her castle, after all."

"So, we can't look?"

"No, Detective. If you want to set even a single foot inside my house, I suggest you go through the proper channels."

Tina kept her face composed. She was all but certain the

CHAPTER THIRTY-ONE

CCTV footage would reveal nothing at all. Gillian was no mad old cat lady, but a businesswoman with a reputation for ruthlessness and acumen. A busy woman.

If she wanted something doing – especially something like a little night-time murder – then she would pay someone else to do it.

CHAPTER THIRTY-TWO

AFTER LUNCH, Annie drove over to Naomi's house. Normally she'd have walked, but some things were too big to carry, especially up the steep hill.

She parked on the driveway. Snapdragons were growing in the borders of Naomi and Dougie's garden. She found one, leaned in, and squeezed the puffy little cheeks of its flower head. Its mouth opened and closed like a flower-shaped puppet.

"Well hello, Mr Snapdragon, I had forgotten that you could talk," she said in a high voice.

"You're going do-lally in your old age, lady," grunted the snapdragon.

"Well, that's just plain rude," she told it.

She knocked on the door.

"Hi, Mum," said Tina, opening it. "Were we expecting you? Naomi's not back from work yet."

"No. But wait till you see what I scored off the local buy-and-sell group. I couldn't resist." She bustled over to the car and opened the boot. Tina followed her, groaning.

Louis was at the door, clambering down the step to follow Tina and shouting to get Annie's attention.

She turned to him. "Hello Louis! Nanny's got a surprise. Now don't be like that, Tina, this is going to blow your socks off."

She wrestled the plastic slide out of the boot and slammed it shut. "Ta-da!"

Louis ran up to it and started to climb the tiny ladder.

"Hold your horses, Louis," said Annie. "This'll be better on the grass. Let's take it round the back, eh?"

"Mum!" Tina hissed. "This is something you should have mentioned before you just turned up with it. What if Naomi doesn't want this in the middle of her lawn?"

"What? It's perfect. With all the kids here it'll help them get outside in the fresh air. Besides, I had to grab it or someone else would have beaten me to it."

Annie picked it up and waddled with it round to the back garden. She set it on the lawn and waggled the top to make sure it was stable. "Perfect! You can have a go now, Louis." She helped Louis find his way onto the plastic steps and climb up to the top, which was only at waist height.

"Whee!" Louis went down the slide on his bottom, chuckling.

Tina stood nearby cradling her bump. "Nice one, Louis," she said.

"See, he loves it!" said Annie.

"Of course he does. That's not the point, Mum."

"Poppy will love it, too."

"I think Poppy's probably too big for it."

"Nonsense. She'll have a lovely time helping Louis on it. When the new baby's born, they can enjoy it, too, once they're up on their feet."

Tina sighed. "You stopping for a cup of tea? I'll put the kettle on."

"No you don't, that's what mums are for. You go and put your feet up."

While Annie was making tea, the front door opened and closed. Naomi, back with Poppy. Annie busied herself with the tea while listening to Naomi and Tina talk in the hallway.

"Mum's here then?" Naomi said to Tina.

"In the kitchen making a drink. She's bought a slide for the kids."

Silence. Her daughters did this; using facial expressions to communicate. She could almost hear the sound of rolling eyes.

Poppy came running through. "Nanny! Is there really a slide?"

"There is, my sweet! Want to go and see?"

"Yeah!"

Annie ushered Poppy out through the back door and showed her the slide. Poppy stepped up and slid down, even though it wasn't much of a ride for a six-year-old.

Tina and Naomi had followed them out, carrying their mugs. Louis ran over to the slide and Poppy helped him up the steps.

Annie beamed and turned to her daughters. "And that's what it's all about, eh? Gives them a chance to play together."

Tina and Naomi gave her a look.

"You know, there are kids in my class who want to have all the crayons," said Naomi. "It doesn't even matter if they're using those colours in their picture, they just want them all. I don't think it's because they want to deprive the other kids, it's more like some sort of crazy excitement gets the better of them."

Annie pouted. "Are you comparing me to a child?"

"I am. We teach the kids to be calmer and more even-handed. It's part of growing up."

Annie eyed her. "Well, maybe we squeeze too much joy out of our children in the name of growing up. I, for one, hope I never let go of my more childish impulses."

Tina and Naomi exchanged a look.

Poppy was experimenting with the slide, walking up the tiny slope and twirling on the top before jumping off the side with the steps.

"Look at Poppy!" said Annie. "She knows how to have fun with whatever's to hand."

"She's creative like that," Naomi replied. "Which is why she doesn't need new things every five minutes. None of them do."

"I can indulge them a little bit, though. I'm pretty sure it's in the job description for grandparents."

"The key phrase there is 'a little bit'," said Tina. "Please, Mum. You're getting carried away."

Annie wanted to find a smart retort, but she was conscious that Tina didn't have the slightest idea of just how carried away she was getting with certain other things.

She pressed her lips together and gave a bashful smile instead, then turned back to Poppy and Louis.

"Who wants to go again?"

CHAPTER THIRTY-THREE

THE NEXT DAY, Figgy decided it was time. Annie might have been overbearing, but she was right.

They needed access to the information Cameron had. And Figgy wanted to get to know him better.

She finished her swim and walked up to the Kiosk, heart pounding.

"Hey," he said, smiling as he spotted her. "The usual?"

She licked her lips. "Please."

She watched as he scooped her vanilla honeycomb crunch, wondering if he remembered everyone's order. She was imagining things, wasn't she?

You've got a job to do. As she took the ice cream from him, she cleared her throat. He was asking her about her swim, but she could barely hear him.

"Cameron. Would you like to meet me for a coffee later?"

He fell silent. He'd been closing the cover over the ice cream display, and his hand stopped moving.

"Yes," he said. "Yes, that'd be good."

Figgy resisted the urge to let out a whoop. *A date.*

Well, coffee. But it could be a date.

He gave her his number and she pinged him on WhatsApp.

"I'll message you when I get off," he said.

She nodded and smiled, then turned back to the beach.

She'd done it.

But now, she had to decide what she'd wear. She walked back to the caravan, turning over her wardrobe in her mind.

Did she want to look as if she'd dressed up for him, or did she want to look like her usual, casual self? Cameron was used to seeing her as she emerged from the sea, so regular clothes and dry hair would be a step up.

In the end, she settled on a nice blouse instead of a T-shirt, with just a small amount of make-up.

He messaged her just before three, telling her he'd be done in twenty minutes. She stuffed a fist into her mouth and checked herself in the mirror.

She looked fine. Good, even. She could do this.

They'd agreed to meet in the bakery café on Broad Street. She didn't want to seem too keen, so she browsed some shops on the way to slow herself down. She spotted Cameron coming up the hill and gave him a cheery wave. He wore a surfer T-shirt and jeans, casual but clean.

"Figgy." He glanced at his smart watch and nodded.

She grinned. They went inside the café and found a table.

"Do you come in here a lot?" he asked.

Figgy looked round at the décor and suddenly felt nervous. It was a café. Just a café. But now, sitting down at a table, opposite one another, it felt like they were in some posh restaurant.

"God, no," she said. "I barely go anywhere."

He laughed. "I know. This town isn't geared up for the likes of us, is it? Fancy fish restaurants and places with tourist prices. I'm not saying I want a McDonald's or a Nando's in town but..."

"You wouldn't mind if there was a McDonald's or a Nando's in town."

"Maybe. There's a place that does bubble tea and milkshakes on Silver Street."

"But this is OK?" she asked, worried.

"Oh, yes. Yeah. I'm just chatting." He twisted the menu in his hands.

Was he nervous, too? Was beautiful Cameron Winters actually nervous?

"So, what have you been up to?" he asked.

Figgy felt herself falter. She didn't want to tell him she'd spent the last few days reviewing CCTV footage and hiding in a car on a stakeout, looking for evidence that Cameron's mum had been involved in one or more murders.

She went for blandness instead. "Oh, you know, the usual. How about you?"

"Let me think." He frowned. "I'd say we've seen a higher than usual number of seagull incidents today. I reckon the score is seagulls fifteen, humans nil."

"Oh," she said, thinking of something she could tell him about. "I was given some stones, painted to look like seagull snacks. Helen's idea is that they'll train the seagulls not to bother."

"Helen?"

"This old lady who runs an art gallery in town. She's a... a free spirit. Like, she wears what she likes and doesn't give a damn, and I reckon that in a past life she was a bit of a character."

"I think I know who you mean. Does it work?"

"What?"

"The stones."

She shrugged. "It seems to."

He nodded. "I might paint some stones myself and put them round the Kiosk."

"Is painting something you like to do?"

"Maybe I'll give it a go. When you live somewhere like this it seems like you should, yeah? I'm a fan of making and doing things."

"My caravan has this picture window looking out over the beach. It's like a painting that changes all the time," said Figgy.

She berated herself. Did it sound too much as if she was inviting him round?

"Sounds amazing," he said. "Course, my mum would rather I 'did something' with my life."

"Like what?"

Cameron crinkled his nose. "I think she means something like get a job in a big company. Become an accountant or a stockbroker or a 'captain of industry'." He wiggled his fingers to make air-quotes.

A waitress appeared and they ordered mugs of tea and cakes. Figgy couldn't resist the chocolate and orange sponge, while Cameron went for a rocky road.

"That captain of industry thing. Is that what your dad is?" Figgy asked, remembering her secret mission.

"I guess so," Cameron replied. "He's a banker, anyway. He makes a ton of money, but I could never do what he does. It's so dry and soulless."

"And is he? I mean, dry and soulless?"

"Oh no. I mean, old people. They're all the same, but he has his moments. When I was younger, he used to take me to London. We'd see the sights and he'd talk about things so knowledgeably. If we went to one of the museums, it was like he worked there or something. He has this way of seeming like he knows everything."

"Not any more, then? The London trips?"

"No. He's been away for ages. Can't even remember the last time I saw him, to be honest."

"Oh. Like it's been weeks?"

"More than a month. Months. Mum and Dad have separate lives, I guess. I think that's normal. What about your parents?"

She jabbed a fork into her cake. "Never knew my dad, and my mum died from cancer a while back."

"Crap. Sorry."

She felt her stomach dip but forced a smile. "Oh, long, long time ago, really. That's why I came to live with my nan in the caravan. She's dead now though, so it's just me."

"That's tough."

Figgy shrugged. "I'm getting there. Two scoops of vanilla honeycomb crunch is helping."

Cameron laughed. "Well, if that's the kind of help that works for you, I'm happy to provide it."

"You're a craftsman," she said, affecting a silly bow, "and I salute your skills."

"I don't actually make the ice cream."

"Service with a smile. That's a skill."

"I want to know how that stacks up against the vanilla honeycomb crunch," said Cameron, pointing at her cake with his pastry fork.

Figgy took a forkful of the cake, which was made from the darkest chocolate with zesty pieces of orange. She closed her eyes, making a show of considering it. "I might need to alter my routine so I can accommodate both things."

He laughed. "Is it stupid to say I'm a bit jealous?"

"You can try the cake," she said, sliding it over.

"I meant having a place of your own, your own space. No, that's stupid. Your nan. I'm sorry."

She gave it some thought.

"I do have my own bubble, my own space. A cave. That's kind of cool."

"I think it is," he said.

"My therapist says I need to get out of the cave a bit more. No. That's a lie. I know I need to get out of the cave a bit more."

"There's a McDonald's over in Dorchester," he said.

"You're not liking your cake?"

He closed his eyes and shook his head at himself. "Cake's great. How can you ruin rocky road? I'm just saying, there's a world out there. You drive?"

"Nope. I need to learn."

He nodded. "I can drive. Not got my own car. I could borrow my mum's but..."

There was a sudden, pained look on his face.

"What?" she asked.

"Would I sound like a child if I said it feels like I need to stay in Lyme all the time to look after my mum?"

"Does she *need* looking after?"

His mouth twisted. "Protecting. She needs protecting. She's like forty-something years old and yet she gives off this vibe like she doesn't know how to do anything for herself. If she didn't get her supermarket shopping delivered, I think she'd die of starvation."

"I'm sure she's more resourceful than that," said Figgy, then stopped. "We want to care for them. You think I wouldn't do anything to protect my grandma? To get her back? It's cute that you care for your mum."

He laughed. "Cute?"

"Nice. Nice," she corrected. "Bloody hell. Eat!"

He dutifully cleaved away a chunk of rocky road and stuffed it in his mouth. He washed it down with a swig of tea.

"What I think," he said, "is that we need a breakout."

"Breakout?"

"McDonald's in Dorchester, maybe. Or something... you ever done coasteering?"

"That's the climbing, swimming and jumping off cliffs thing."

"Yeah. Like hiking and swimming rolled into one. They do that round Lulworth Cove."

"Maybe, or..."

"Wild camping on Exmoor," he said.

"Wow. Taking it up a notch."

He laughed.

"I'll take wild camping over jumping off cliffs," she said.

"It's dark out there on Exmoor. Don't they have werewolves or something?"

She snorted with laughter. "Where are you getting your information from?"

"Reddit," he said.

She laughed. "We start with McDonald's at Dorchester and take it from there."

She held up her mug and he chinked his against it in a toast.

CHAPTER THIRTY-FOUR

LYME REGIS's eighteenth-century road layout wasn't suited to twenty-first century traffic. The heart of the town was the sweep of road coming down from the Sidmouth Road and out along the Charmouth Road, curving just as it reached the Cobb Gate car park. Traffic, both human and vehicle, flowed through this space every day, bottlenecking at the height of summer.

The spot was often crowded and congested, which was far from perfect, but it was also one of the best places to have a business. The Cruickshank Gallery, Jurassic Fossils and A Traditional Childhood sat in a row in the middle of that most desirable spot, and when Annie went into the art shop that afternoon, she found Helen, her sculptor girlfriend Harper, and Solomon Matheson from the children's shop gathered together at a table in the middle of the gallery.

"Interrupting a business conference, am I?" she said.

Harper looked up. Someone had laid a tea towel over her chair so her grease-smudged overalls didn't mark the white paint. "Not quite."

On the table was a big roll of paper with a sketched plan of the three shops, the yards out the back, and the edge of the car park beyond which Marco Callington's body had been found.

Annie frowned. "Helping the police with their inquiries, are we?"

It was hard enough shepherding Helen and Figgy while they tried to find the answer to Marco's death. She wasn't keen on bringing Harper and Solomon into the fold, especially since they weren't aware of the body in the car.

"No," said Helen. "We're... well, we're thinking about the future."

"Deciding how they might carve up Marco's shop when it's back on the market," said Harper, leaning back.

"You're divvying up his shop?" Annie asked.

"Deciding which of us might make the best use of the space," said Solomon, gruffly.

"The man's not even been dead for a week," she said. "The police still have the shop taped up."

Solomon looked up at her. "Things move fast in business, Annie. He lived alone, has no local family to inherit. It might seem callous, but it's the way things work."

"It does seem callous," muttered Harper.

Helen looked at her. "Says the woman whose eyes lit up when I suggested we could expand her workshop into the fossil shop's rear yard. There's only a fence between them."

Harper grunted and peered at the map.

"More room for your junk and waste to spread," said Helen.

"Actually, I've tidied it all," Harper replied. "Shows what you know."

Annie looked closer at the map. Helen was right. It

wasn't just the Cruickshank Gallery and the fossil shop that were neighbours. Their small back yards were, too. The removal of the six-foot-high fence between them would double Harper's space for metal construction.

"Might I make a suggestion?" she said.

Solomon raised an eyebrow. "Yes?"

"You might want to keep this kind of discussion under wraps until the police have actually made an arrest. Unless you want their suspicious eyes drawn your way."

The gallery door opened, ringing the little bell. Helen folded the plan in half to hide it.

It wasn't the police, but Jason Mordaunt of the *Lyme Echo*. His satchel strap caught on the door as he came in and he stumbled, almost colliding with a stand of art print postcards.

"Oh, here he comes," spat Solomon. "The town muck-raker."

Jason attempted to laugh off the comment. "Mr Matheson, I hope you're not still harping on about the fair and honest review I wrote of your shop."

"Over-priced, you called me."

"'A higher price tag than one might find in a high street chain,' I believe I wrote," said Jason. "You have a perfectly charming shop, and you know it."

"That's not the impression I recall from your stitch-up review."

"The reading experience can be so subjective." He nodded at the others. "Ladies."

"Jason," said Annie with a firm nod.

"I don't suppose you've come here to buy some art?" Helen asked.

Jason tried not to look horrified at the idea. "I'm a man of simple tastes and meagre means." He gestured to the large piece *Viscera* on the wall. "Bit gruesome, that."

"Gruesome."

"Looks like blood and guts."

Helen tapped a foot. "The art experience is so subjective, isn't it? Its own little ink-blot test."

"Oh, really?" He shook himself and turned away from it. "Well, I'm here on business, journalistic business."

"Come to gather our opinions on Lyme Regis's seagull menace?" asked Annie.

"Very popular article, that," he said. "It's drawn a lot of comment and wider interest. But no, I'm here on less frivolous matters."

"Let me guess," said Solomon. "The murder."

Jason's mouth twitched. "Not really our scene. While a man's death is obviously – and sadly – very newsworthy, it doesn't seem to have much of a local angle."

"He died here," said Helen. "How much more local do you want?"

"Yes," Jason admitted, "but was he really one of us? Dodgy out-of-town type if ever there was one. Little more than a grockle, really. If you ask me, the police will find his death was a result of his activities beyond this town."

"You have evidence?" said Annie.

"Not as such, but Lyme Regis folk are hardly in the habit of bashing people over the head and stuffing them in wheelie bins. No, no. Not *Lyme Echo* material at all."

"So...?" said Helen.

"I thought I might do a series of in-depth articles on the leading creatives in the town. Artists."

"Ah, you want Clifford Muldoon's phone number, do you?" Helen said. The popular painter's works hung around

CHAPTER THIRTY-FOUR

the gallery and were among the pieces that got turned into cheaper prints and posters.

"Actually, I wondered if I could interview Harper McCoppin, here." He gestured at Harper.

"Me?" said Harper.

"I hear you work wonders in that workshop of yours. I think the reading public will be fascinated by your artwork and your process."

Annie had never thought of Harper as shy, but watching her reaction, it occurred to her that the sculptor normally let Helen do the talking for the pair of them.

"Er, I... I'm not sure," Harper said. "I'd have to think about it."

Jason picked up one of Harper's teaspoon dragonflies from the display by the counter. "I'm sure you don't often get the chance to talk to people about the nuts and bolts – I don't know if there are actual nuts and bolts – but the nitty-gritty of making your work."

"I don't."

"Then a photo tour of your workshop. Meet the metal mistress Harper McCoppin in her workshop."

"Oh, I don't want photos of me," said Harper.

"We can discuss that."

"And you're not calling her the metal mistress either," said Helen. "Total codswallop."

Jason held out his hands. "I'll give you full pre-approval on the article. Anything you don't want in there," he made a cutting motion, "out it comes."

Harper cocked her head. "I'd have to think about it," she said.

"We can do it now, if you like," he said, reaching for his satchel.

"She said she'd think about it," said Helen.

Jason nodded, pursing his lips.

"Tell you what," said Solomon. "You should write an article about the dog poop."

"Pardon?"

"People walking their dogs and not cleaning up after them. I could even point out the main culprits to you."

"Um, really?"

"If you think seagulls are a menace – pah! – you should write an exposé on the poop offenders."

"Maybe…"

Solomon stood. "Could take a walk down the promenade now. Terrible people. I'd hang the lot of them if I had my way."

"Hang them?" said Jason as he was led from the shop by Solomon.

As the door closed, Helen smiled. "He might be a crusty old so-and-so, but Solomon has his uses."

"I need to get on," said Harper, heading for her workshop. She didn't look best pleased by Jason's suggestion.

When she was gone, Annie tapped her finger on the folded map on the table.

"Really? Carving up his old business while we're still implicated in his death?" she whispered.

"You worry too much, Annie," Helen said.

Annie grunted. She reckoned she worried exactly the right amount.

CHAPTER THIRTY-FIVE

Annie took her phone to the beach when she went swimming. Sometimes she fastened it inside a freezer bag so she could take it in the water and get some action shots, but she knew of people whose phones had been destroyed by leaky bags, so she tended to leave it with her things on the wall. She knew you could get fancy kit and waterproof bags, even fluorescent ones that doubled as safety aids, for precisely this sort of thing. But Annie wasn't one for fancy kit.

Today provided spectacular early morning views of the sky across the bay, so she towelled herself down and dug out her phone to photograph the others as they emerged sparkling from the water.

Then she noticed the message in the WhatsApp group.

"Did you just take our picture?" asked Helen as she plonked down beside Annie on the wall. "Absolutely outrageous. Show us."

Annie waggled her phone. "I will in a minute, but we've had a message from Rosamund."

"Does she mention why she's not here?" asked Figgy. "It's not like her to miss a lovely morning like this."

"She doesn't." Annie sniffed. "It's a funny message. 'I'd really appreciate the three of you popping round to see me if you could. There's something I just don't understand, and I could do with your collective wisdom'."

Helen looked at her. "Say that again?"

"It's on your phone, too."

"My phone's tucked away somewhere. Repeat it, Annie."

Annie sighed. "'I'd really appreciate the three of you popping round to see me if you could. There's something I just don't understand, and I could do with your collective wisdom'." She looked up. "What do we make of that?"

"Goodness," said Figgy. "It can't be good, can it?"

Helen straightened her shoulders, looking across the beach. "No. It's probably not good."

Annie stared at them both. "D'you think she's trying to lure us round there to kill us because we know too much?"

The three of them pulled mildly sceptical faces at each other.

"We don't actually know anything," Figgy pointed out.

"We know she had a corpse in her car," Annie reminded her.

"Well then it's settled," said Helen. "We all go together, for safety. But first things first. I want to see that picture you just took."

The three of them got into their dry clothes and walked slowly up the beach.

"We can either all go home and regroup later," said Helen, "or we can grab my car and go right now."

Figgy and Annie shrugged at each other.

"Might as well go now," said Annie. The air was warm

today and she'd been able to dry off and change into her clothes.

They walked up to the gallery and climbed into Helen's Fiat. Annie messaged Rosamund to say they were on their way.

"Ground rules, then," said Figgy. "We're gonna need some."

"What sort of thing do you mean?" Helen asked.

"The basic ones, like how people in horror films always do that thing where they split up and it doesn't end well for them. We should definitely not split up. That's rule number one."

"I mean, Rosamund lives in a big house," said Annie, "but it's not exactly a haunted mansion."

"It's just a rule," Figgy said. "Now, what do we think about eating or drinking while we're there?"

Helen frowned. "Are you thinking she might make tea and poison us all? Good God, I suppose it's not beyond the realms of possibility."

"How about this?" said Annie. "We offer to make tea so she can rest her foot. I think we can make that work."

Figgy nodded. "Yeah, good."

As Helen pulled into Rosamund's driveway, Rosamund appeared at her door. Annie thought she looked anxious. She ushered them inside.

"Morning, love!" said Annie. "We came straight from the beach."

"I really appreciate it," said Rosamund. "Sorry? You didn't even go to the Kiosk?"

"A friend in need trumps morning caffeine. That's what I always say."

"I must make you a drink."

Figgy shot Annie a warning look.

"I'll do the tea," said Annie. "You take the weight off your foot. I can find what I need."

Rosamund put up no resistance, thank goodness. Annie went into the kitchen and emptied the kettle, then filled it with fresh water.

The teabags showed no sign of being anything other than normal, but she dug out the ones from the bottom of the box, just in case. She hesitated at the fridge as she fetched the milk.

Poisoning the milk ahead of time... that wouldn't be hard.

She reached into the back of the fridge and pulled out a fresh carton. She was messing up Rosamund's food rotation, but to hell with it.

She found an unopened packet of biscuits, too, and rather than putting them on a plate, she left them sealed to reassure the others.

She didn't really think Rosamund had any intention of poisoning anyone, but her mind couldn't help playing along with the drama.

"Here we go," she said as she carried a tray into the lounge. Figgy and Helen perched on the settee, while Rosamund sat awkwardly on a separate chair.

"The three of you being here makes me feel so much better," said Rosamund. "I've been getting agitated about something I found, and I really need to share it."

"Go ahead, Rosamund," said Annie.

Helen leaned forward, her skirt swishing against the coffee table. "We're all ears."

Annie tried to relax, but it was really warm in here again. She flapped a hand in front of her face to get some air.

Rosamund looked down at her hands. "I found some

CHAPTER THIRTY-FIVE

blood in my car. A... I guess you could say it would be a pool of it. Or it would have been before it dried. In the back."

"Blood?" said Figgy.

"It's really quite horrible. I was so worried about what it might mean." Rosamund looked up and searched their faces.

Helen and Figgy were mirroring Annie's expression. Shock, followed by mild confusion and then an attempt at a neutral look. Annie was going for mildly concerned interest, but if Helen and Figgy were anything to go by, it probably looked like she'd sipped tea made with sour milk.

"What do we think it means?" echoed Annie, buying time. "Hmm."

"There was a murder in the town recently," Rosamund said, turning her hands over in her lap.

"Yes..." said Annie, wondering if this might be the build-up to a confession.

"It made me wonder if my car was somehow connected," Rosamund continued.

Rosamund should be on the stage, Annie thought. Had she really invited them up to her house to probe what they knew with this elaborate ruse?

"Connected?" prompted Figgy.

But it was clear Helen had had enough.

"Oh, come on," she snapped. "This is ridiculous."

Rosamund blinked.

"Is your car connected?" said Helen. "I think you know the answer to that, don't you, Rosamund?"

Rosamund's brow creased with confusion. "Sorry? What do you mean?"

"Come off it, darling," said Helen. "The dead body was in your car at the beach. We know. You killed Marco Callington and shoved him in there."

CHAPTER THIRTY-SIX

Rosamund stood frozen, her face pale. A marble statue.

"Wait a minute," she whispered. "The body? In my car?"

"You can drop the act," Helen snapped.

Rosamund's gaze went to Annie. "You said as much. You said it. The other day. Was Marco's body in the car when you went to get it the other day?"

Annie and Figgy nodded in unison.

"You knew it was there," Annie said. "Please don't act surprised."

"No! There was no body in my car when I parked. I'm not a monster."

Annie gave her a smile. "No one's calling you a monster, love."

Helen twitched.

"No," Rosamund insisted. "Someone must have put him in there while we were swimming."

"No, they didn't," Figgy said.

Rosamund turned her gaze on Figgy. "You sound very sure about that."

CHAPTER THIRTY-SIX

Figgy nodded. "Your car was visible on the public webcam. Nobody went near it the whole time."

Rosamund's mouth fell open. "You've gone to all the trouble of looking through the webcam footage to see who went near my car, but you didn't even think to tell me about the body?"

"We tried," said Annie.

"Tried?" Rosamund spat. "Worse still, you've got it into your heads that I might have meant this man harm? Me?" She fluttered a hand towards herself, presumably intending to convey an impression of innocence and frailty.

Helen made a noise of scorn, mimicking the action. "Oh Rosamund, that's a good one. If only you hadn't had that stand-up row with Marco the other day. Hurled a glass of wine over him, too."

"What, him? That was the dead person?" Rosamund sagged. "Oh no. I didn't know who he really was. Just a really annoying chancer who wouldn't let a woman sit on her own in peace."

Annie huffed. Rosamund was a tough nut to crack. Every time they thought they had her on the ropes, she came back with just the reaction an innocent person would have.

"Look, you must know you've been acting weird," she said. "All this stuff with your house being red hot all the time. The CCTV cameras being 'broken'." She did air quotes.

"What? That?" Rosamund bowed her head.

A long moment passed, during which Annie, Figgy and Helen all shot each other puzzled looks.

Eventually Rosamund raised her head. Her eyes were moist. "David's left me."

Annie remained sceptical. "Your husband's left you, or your husband's 'left' you?"

Helen rolled her eyes at Annie's air quotes.

Rosamund's face screwed up. "What's wrong with you people? Do you have no empathy at all? I suppose you're going to tell me you think I killed David, too, now?"

There was a long awkward silence. Rosamund exhaled loudly.

"Was that a confession?" Helen whispered.

Rosamund scowled at her. "No. He's just gone. I keep telling people that he's away on business, but he's gone."

"And is that gone or 'gone'?" said Annie.

"Stop it! He's not dead, OK? Shall I tell you how I know?"

"Um. Yes?" Annie said.

Rosamund stood up and walked over to the wall. "I think I'll turn down the thermostat in here. It's warm, isn't it?"

She hit the buttons on the device.

"There we are. It's at eighteen degrees now, no need for any heating." She smiled at them all, then went to sit back down. "You can read the numbers from where you're sitting. If you don't mind keeping an eye on the display."

All four of them sat in silence. The only sound was the sipping of tea.

"There." Rosamund raised her cup. "Twenty-four degrees again. He likes to make it warm for me."

"Tech abuse," said Figgy.

"What?" said Helen.

"It's a thing. A form of abuse. Controlling the Wi-Fi, controlling smart devices." She pushed out her bottom lip in thought. "Is he doing this himself, or has he just left some presets that're overriding what you're doing?" she asked, getting up to take a look at the thermostat.

"I don't know," said Rosamund miserably. "I genuinely

have no idea. It's just that he used to deal with all of this stuff."

"Have you got an app?" asked Figgy.

Rosamund shook her head.

"Show me everything."

"Everything like what?"

"Just everything. Paperwork, router, boiler, control units. We can figure this out."

They seemed to have slid from accusations of murder to household maintenance. But Annie was genuinely intrigued.

"Can you figure it out, Figgy?" she asked.

"Don't know till we try, do we?" Figgy was already searching for something on her phone.

"Right," said Annie, with a cough. "Actually, I wonder if the three of us might speak privately for a moment, Rosamund?"

Rosamund looked resigned. "You want to discuss whether you believe me or not? Go ahead. Back patio's probably easiest."

Helen and Figgy followed Annie into the back garden.

"Well, this is awkward," said Helen. "We just accused Ros of all that stuff, and she's showing all the signs of being as pure as driven snow."

"I feel bad for her," said Figgy. "Technology is amazing, but not when it's out of your control like in this house. I want to help her."

"Are we all agreed that we think she's telling the truth?" asked Annie.

There were nods all round, the slowest from Helen.

"Then I guess we need to get back in there," said Annie.

They all trooped back in.

"Rosamund, we've been terrible friends," Annie said.

"We want to do better. Young Figgy here will try and help with your house and its mind of its own. We'll catch you up with all the sleuthing we've managed so far."

"Sleuthing? Is that something we do now?" Rosamund asked.

The group all shrugged.

"Yeah," said Figgy. "It's kind of fun."

"Let's see if we can build some bridges, eh?" said Annie. "And on that subject, you need to show us the blood in the back of your car."

"Is that because it's an important clue?" asked Rosamund. "Or because you have ideas on how I might get the stains out?"

Annie chuckled. "We're multi-talented. Both."

An hour later, Annie, Helen and Figgy drove away from Rosamund's house, each of them in silent thought.

"Do you think you can help with her heating?" asked Helen.

"I've got some research to do at home," replied Figgy, "but I'll give it my best shot."

"I can't believe she's been living like that," Annie said. "Poor woman."

Helen was about to pull off the main road to drive to the back of the gallery when she slowed and pointed to a group of young people on the pavement. They wore matching T-shirts and hats.

"*I heart Kevin?*" Annie said, reading the T-shirts. She gasped. "Oh I say, they're talking about your seagull, Figgy! There's a picture of him on there, look!"

Figgy gave a nod of resignation. "There's been loads of these. You need to see the hats in action to get the full effect."

Helen was still waiting for a gap in the traffic to turn off the main road. "Do we need to go round to your caravan? Shall I drive us down there?"

"Yeah, why not?" Figgy said.

Helen turned off her indicator, drove straight on and carried on round to Monmouth Beach car park.

"I can see more of them!" said Annie as they walked towards the beach.

"Come inside and you'll get the full picture," said Figgy. She unlocked the door to her caravan and the three of them approached the big picture window.

Helen climbed onto one bench seat, lying on her stomach, feet up in the air, chin in her hands so she could gaze out of the window. Figgy and Annie sat on the other side.

There were about twenty people out on the beach, all wearing those T-shirts.

Annie could see the purpose of the hats. They were bucket hats, with a tiny plastic basket mounted on top. The people outside were filming each other as they put edible treats into the basket and walked across the beach.

"I can't watch," she said, but of course they all did.

Seagulls swooped and clawed at the hats. Sometimes they came away with just the bread or cake, sometimes they took the entire hat, claws caught in the basket. Shredded hats littered the beach, and more than one person had blood running down their face.

"Well, my painted stones don't stand a chance against this sort of behaviour," said Helen. "Have these people got nothing better to do?"

"It's gone a bit viral," said Figgy. "*Hashtag FeedKevin* seems to be the centre of the activity."

"They can't all be Kevin," said Annie. There were dozens of gulls out there.

"No, Kevin's that one there," said Figgy, pointing. "You can tell by his eyes. These people don't seem to care which bird is which, though. You need a good eye to be able to tell them apart."

Annie definitely didn't have a good eye, because the birds all looked like identical screaming, swooping maniacs to her.

"I bet your neighbours love all this," she said.

Figgy pulled a face. "Not a lot I can do about it."

"I could bring some more stones," said Helen. "Bigger ones, maybe."

Figgy looked confused. "You said yourself those painted stones don't stand a chance against people with cakes on their heads."

"Oh, I don't mean we should paint them," said Helen, rolling onto her back and pushing herself up into a sitting position. "We should throw them at those idiots out there. We'd soon see them off."

CHAPTER THIRTY-SEVEN

"Tina, one of your copper friends is here," called Naomi.

Tina pushed herself forward in the armchair and brushed digestive biscuit crumbs off her front. They were perfect comfort eating. Crumbly, oaty, sweet, softened by a vigorous dunk in a cuppa. She'd recently added gherkins to her snacking regime. Gherkins and digestive biscuits was a less obvious and more embarrassing pairing, so she reached forward to put the lid on the gherkins. She'd managed to hide them away down the side of the armchair by the time Naomi entered, followed by DS Nathan Strunk.

"Cup of tea?" Naomi asked him.

"Oh, I never say no." He looked at Tina. "I hope you don't mind me dropping in."

"Not at all, as long as you don't mind joining us for a bit of *Bluey*."

She gestured at the TV screen. Louis was on the carpet, playing with his wooden train set, in front of the cartoon adventures of *Bluey*. He wasn't exactly watching it, but Tina knew he'd react immediately if she even thought about turning it off.

"*Bluey*, huh?" said the DS. "Whatever happened to *Teletubbies*?"

"Showing your age there, Sarge."

He sat down on the sofa. "I thought I'd come give you an update."

"Thank you." She stroked her abdomen. "Me and Acting Constable Bump here are always keen to hear what's going on."

"Well," he began, "we're still looking into the connection between Callington and Gillian Hewish. They both had an interest in the Breaststrokes bar but, on top of that, Marco Callington was seen in there the other week, with a woman, with whom he was having a heated debate."

"Heated debate?"

"A slanging match, according to Solomon Matheson. The owner of the—"

"I know him. Was it Gillian?"

He shook his head. "Don't know. But Dougie and Wendy are over there now getting the CCTV. That might give us some more clues."

"If it is Gillian, what then? Are we working on a hypothesis that Gillian either murdered him or had him killed over some business dispute?"

The DS pulled a face. "We're struggling for motives with this one. Marco Callington was not a well-liked man. His shop was a sore point among locals. His neighbours, both in the shops and the houses around, either didn't know him or had no kind words to say about him. And as for evidence, we don't have a murder weapon or any actual certainty as to where he died. There are spots of blood in the car park and near the gate to the back of his property."

Naomi came in with a cup of tea for the DS.

"Do have a biscuit," she said, pointing. "Tina's got some gherkins hidden away somewhere if you'd like one of them."

"I might pass on the gherkins," he replied, reaching for the digestives. "There is one more thing of interest," he said to Tina. "The delivery van."

"The delivery van? What, as in the road rage incident?"

"Maybe. Seems Marco was getting his stock deliveries brought to him in a van. There's little in the way of decent CCTV down that end of town, but we've looked at footage from shops up the hill and there's also a camera near the church going round the corner. Twice in the last week, there's been a white van, no markings, come down the high street and then up past the church. The delay between the two indicates it stopped somewhere on the way. Maybe it was parked up outside Jurassic Fossils to deliver stock."

"Got a registration number?"

He shook his head. "The cameras up the hill look straight across the road. No angle on the registration plates at all. The van's unmarked, but if you look closely there appears to be a little rubber duck on the aerial."

"Rubber duck?"

The DS shrugged. "Rubber duck. Like those people who put coloured balls on their aerials to help them find the car in a car park. Whoever it is, if they were delivering to Marco then they might well be the last person to see him alive."

"Apart from the killer."

"Apart from the killer," he agreed.

"So," Tina said, "the evidence at the scene doesn't point us in any useful directions. We've got no one with a solid motive for killing him but dozens of people with a general dislike for him. He's got his fingers in a couple of financial pies, but apart from a suspicious cash withdrawal, there's no specific sign of wrongdoing. And the best lead we've got at the moment is that he was seen having a shouting match with a woman in the bar he'd hoped to buy."

"That's the long and the short of it." He watched her.

"You expecting me to offer some stellar insights?" she asked.

He sighed. "I was hoping."

She took a deep breath, but not as deep as the deep breaths she remembered. The baby was occupying real estate that had previously been used by her lungs.

"The dead man was in a wheelie bin," she said.

"Yes."

"After having had his head bashed in."

"Yes."

She pursed her lips. "This doesn't strike me as a cool and calculated murder. If there's a scale, it's at the bungling and amateurish end of the spectrum."

"I agree," said the DS.

"And yet no one saw a bloody thing."

"Infuriating, isn't it?"

She winced as the baby kicked; the adrenaline was having an effect. "Maybe we are looking at a random attack," she said. "An argument with someone in that car park. An argument over nothing. A badly parked car. Litter. An argument very early that morning. Two strangers meet, argue, bosh, wallop, body chucked in a bin."

The DS grunted. "How rare are stranger murders?"

"Very rare," she admitted. "But maybe we need to do

some wider canvassing in the local area, find out everyone's movements overnight."

"That'll take a lot of resource."

"But we're sure it's murder now. What does DI Patterson have to say?"

"She's been called over to a suspicious house fire in Bournemouth. Three dead. This one's slipping down the priority list."

"You've asked HQ for help?"

He nodded. "And been given the usual runaround." His expression changed. "I bumped into your Mike."

She smiled. "And how is my husband?"

"Tired. Working on a number of cold cases and trying to repair the damage to your house. He showed me photos of his progress."

"Oh, really?" Tina hadn't been sent any. "And how's it looking?"

"It's surprising," he said. "You know how some people are just really good at one thing and really bad at everything else?"

"Yes?"

The DS smiled. "Your husband is a really good detective."

CHAPTER THIRTY-EIGHT

Annie had invited Figgy, Helen and Rosamund to her house for tea, cakes and murder chat. She hadn't used the actual phrase 'murder chat' in her message, instead falling back on their agreed code: 'tidal times'.

Rosamund hadn't been to Annie's house before, and Annie was prepared for any snooty attitude. Her place was at the opposite end of the scale from Rosamund's sleek show home, but Rosamund was polite and gracious, helping with the tea things and complimenting Annie on the grandchildren's drawings that covered the fridge.

"Right gang, here's the tea." Annie cleared space on the table. "Cherry Bakewell slice, chocolate chip muffins, Victoria sponge, pecan twists, rocky road and blueberry flapjack. The three nearest you are vegan, Helen."

"You haven't baked all these?" Figgy asked.

"God, no. Bakery café."

"Mm, delicious," said Rosamund, tucking into a slice of Victoria sponge. "Do you have these murder chats regularly?"

"Well, yes and no." Annie shifted in her seat. "I mean, we're just displaying a healthy interest in a bit of local drama, aren't we?"

Rosamund paused, cake halfway to her mouth, and looked around at the others. They all seemed equally sceptical.

"No?" Annie sighed. "Fine. In that case we're a bunch of nosy, persistent women far more interested in violent crime than we ought to be."

"Better," said Helen. "Less passive. More interesting."

"I'm mainly doing it to get out of the caravan," said Figgy. "But I can't pretend it's not fun."

Rosamund raised her eyebrows and ate the cake.

"Tell Rosamund about your cousin Gillian," Figgy said to Annie. "She looks like a prime suspect to me."

Annie eyed her young friend, realising she was too nervous to bring up the subject of Rosamund's car. "Gillian, yeah. She's Hewish Homes."

"I think they built my house," Rosamund said.

Annie looked at her. "Makes sense. She's my cousin, but she lives on a different planet. Life on Planet Gillian is all about making more and more money and then using it to live like some kind of royalty in a gated compound up on the Charmouth Road. She was spoiled even as a kid."

"A gated compound? We don't have properties like that around here," said Rosamund, in the tone of someone who'd have bought it herself if she'd known.

"You don't know it's there because she makes sure it's hard to spot. I think she might have a sign up saying it's a boarding kennel or something. Anyway, it's just her, her staff of servants, and her monster cats."

"Monster cats?" Figgy asked.

Annie used her hands to sketch out a giant cat shape. "The big floofy ones. Look like cushions until they uncurl and start killing things."

"Maine Coons?" suggested Rosamund.

"Yes, those. They've got their own studio apartment catio thing built on the side of the house. Bigger living space than young Figgy here."

"None taken," said Figgy, rolling her eyes.

Annie put her hand to her mouth. "Was that rude of me? Sorry."

"She has cats, then," said Helen. "Forgive me for nudging things along, but I get the impression that there's more going on there. The differences between you and her, I mean."

"The differences between us." Annie sighed.

"Give us three words that would describe her," suggested Rosamund.

"Huh." Annie thought for a moment. "Greedy. Ruthless. I think my third word would be 'smart'. I guarantee she'll be running rings round the police if they try to talk to her. Never gets her hands dirty, that one."

"Interesting," said Figgy. "I looked her up online and she seems squeaky clean."

"Exactly my point," said Annie.

"I think what you're saying," said Helen, "is that if she were to kill someone, a business rival, perhaps, then she'd definitely pay someone else to do it."

"I guess I probably am saying that," Annie replied. "It's funny, I can go weeks and months without thinking about Gillian. Our paths don't cross very often. When I do think about her, I picture her aged about eleven, when we both liked horses. It felt like we had things in common, for a bit. We had riding lessons together one summer holiday, and it felt almost like we were sisters. Then she got given her own horse. She never invited me round to ride. Not even once."

"She sounds frightful," said Helen. "Let's take her down."

Annie smiled at the others. "Listen. There's something else I'd like your advice on. This is a family thing."

"Go on," said Figgy. "I like hearing about family things. It's like being in one, but from a safe distance."

"You're not wrong for wanting a safe distance," Annie told her. "Honestly, they can be hard work sometimes. I've got in a bit of a pickle with Tina's new arrival. Both she and Naomi have been on my case for buying too much stuff, but it's something that gives me pleasure, you know?"

"What kind of a pickle?" asked Rosamund.

Annie put down her cup. "It'd be easier to show you."

She led them all upstairs to the spare bedroom. Now Tina was staying with Naomi, she'd had the luxury of being able to pile her purchases straight in there. Trouble was, she'd bought a little bit too much.

"Oh, dear me, Annie," said Helen. "You do have a bit of a problem, don't you?"

Annie looked at the room, seeing it through the eyes of her friends. Things were piled on the bed, on the floor, and on every horizontal surface. Each purchase had seemed like the essential piece of kit Tina's baby would really need, but now it was all together, it looked more like a mad jumble sale.

"I don't even know what some of these things are," said Rosamund. "It's a long time since I had a baby, but I don't remember needing quite so much equipment."

Annie stepped into the room and rocked the tiny bedside crib. "Some of it's only for when the baby's very small, like this is for newborns, so they can be close by when they need you in the night. I want things to go well for Tina and the new baby. It's such an important bonding time."

"Tina's already had a baby, though, hasn't she?" said Helen. "Surely she has most of the things she needs?"

"You sound just like her," said Annie, with a scowl.

"I wonder what my therapist would make of all this," Figgy said, running her hand over a rocking horse. "It's quite a lot."

"Your therapist can jolly well mind their own business," said Annie hotly.

Figgy reddened.

Rosamund turned to Annie. "You wanted our help, Annie. We're reacting to the scale of the problem, that's all. So tell us, what can we do?"

"Yes. Sorry for snapping, everybody. I need some ideas for getting these things to the new baby, under the radar."

Helen blinked. "You want to secretly give things to a baby without its parents knowing?"

"Well, obviously I can't arrange a secret rendezvous or anything like that," Annie said. "But I can't bear the idea of not handing these things over. Everything here was chosen with love."

There was a long silence. Were the others thinking hard, or just feeling embarrassed for her? Possibly both.

"Is Tina having a baby shower?" asked Figgy.

Helen frowned. "A baby shower? Do we have those in this country?"

"I mean, I've heard of them, but only really off the television," said Rosamund.

"Go on, Figgy," said Annie. "A baby shower is a possibility."

"I was just thinking," said Figgy, "that a baby shower is

where everyone brings the baby a gift, right? Well, what if you arranged one and these were the gifts that people brought?"

"Oh, you mean pretend they weren't all bought by me?" Annie said. "That's a genius idea, absolutely genius."

"It really is," said Helen. "You'd need to get lots of different sorts of wrapping paper, make it look as though the things have all come from different places."

"Then you pile them all up on the day," said Rosamund with a smile. "A little sleight of hand and it looks completely natural."

"Ladies, you are absolute lifesavers," said Annie. "Now, how do you all feel about coming to a baby shower?"

"I can't imagine anything worse," said Helen. She shook her head for a long moment. "Nope. I've thought about it, and I really can't."

"Helen!" said Rosamund. She turned to Annie and smiled. "What I think Helen is trying to say is that we will gladly support your ruse. A little bit of social time will be good for us. Clear the air."

"No, no, no!" Helen rolled her eyes. "How on earth are we supposed to clear the air when there will be people we're supposed to be nice to? We can only use the phrase 'tidal times' so many times in before people think we're utterly mad. No, I have a better idea. I will agree to come to this baby shower as long as we can have a proper evening of socialising beforehand. We let our hair down and trash talk anyone we suspect of murder. Which is a lot of people."

"I like that idea," said Figgy.

Rosamund nodded.

Annie clapped her hands in delight. "That's decided, then!"

CHAPTER THIRTY-NINE

Night fell over Lyme Regis. The sky was a glowing jumble of blues and reds, the setting sun throwing its final rays across the town. Only the most energetic seagulls were still flapping about and cawing at each other. Figgy closed the curtains, put a cup of hot chocolate beside her laptop and logged into her therapy session.

Figgy had weekly video call sessions with a therapist called Xandrea. She didn't know if Xandrea was the woman's real name or an online username. Either seemed equally probable.

She sat in the online waiting room, sipping her hot chocolate. There was a ping and Xandrea appeared.

"Hey, Figgy."

"Hey."

"How are you doing today?"

Figgy did a little self-audit. "Surprisingly good."

Xandrea nodded. "Surprisingly good? Let's unpack that and look at key behaviours. How's the Shipping Forecast?"

"Morning and night," Figgy admitted. "I still don't go to bed until I've listened to it."

"Have you tried my suggestion of just skipping it once?"

"I considered it. But I didn't actually *do* it. It just didn't feel right. But I did turn it down low. Like really low."

Xandrea nodded. "And we know why you listen to the Shipping Forecast."

"Because Grandma listened to it. And Grandma listened to it because of Granddad out at sea."

They had, over many sessions, discussed the deeper motives behind Figgy's pathological need to listen to the Shipping Forecast. Figgy's granddad had died, his trawler lost in a storm in the channel, many years before. Even though he was plainly lost, listening to the Shipping Forecast on Radio 4 two or three times a day had been a link to the sea for Grandma. That litany of names – Portland, Plymouth, Lundy – was like a prayer to the lost.

"It's a ritual," said Figgy.

"And rituals can be good things. A comfort. If they're not damaging. We've talked about the dangers of living in what amounts to a shrine."

Figgy frowned. "I like it here."

There was a flicker of light through the curtains next to her. She twitched them aside to see a light in Mrs Delacroix's caravan just across from hers. Grandma and her neighbour had died within a short time of each other. Figgy had seen a family member coming and going from the Delacroix caravan. She had no idea whether anyone was likely to move in soon.

"Anyway," said Figgy, "I have made some progress."

"Yes?" said Xandrea, eyes bright.

"I've kept up with the swimming club each morning."

"Very good. Are you enjoying it?"

Figgy pushed her lips together in thought. "The swimming? No. It's cold for one thing, and if I'm not careful, I start thinking about what might be in the water at the bottom of the sea."

"Like what?"

"Like great white sharks."

"We don't have great white sharks in England."

"I know, but I think about it. And crocodiles. But I've been going along to the club. Annie says it isn't a club, even though it obviously is. But I've kept it up. And I've started seeing some of the women a bit more, outside the swimming bit."

"Oh, that is good. Socialising at various times of the day?"

"Yes. There's Annie and Helen and Rosamund and... I mean, they're all quite old, so it's not like we're proper friends."

"Old? How old?"

"Like at least forty," said Figgy.

"Yes," said Xandrea. "That does sound old."

"But we've..." She hesitated. "Xandrea, we have client privilege thing, don't we?"

"Yes."

"Anything I tell you, you can't tell anyone."

"Unless you tell me something that means you or someone else is in danger."

"I'm not in danger," Figgy assured her. "And no one else is. Not anymore."

"Anymore?"

CHAPTER THIRTY-NINE

Figgy took a deep breath. "So, the other day – quite a few days ago now – we found a body in Rosamund's car."

"I'm sorry?" said Xandrea.

"Me and Annie found a body because Rosamund had trod on a razor clam and needed taking to hospital and Helen went with her, so me and Annie went to move her car. And when we got to the car, there was a man sat in it. His name was Marco Callington. He ran a local fossil shop."

"And he was dead?"

"Mmm-hmmm. Dead. Whacked over the head. There was wet blood on him like he'd just died." She sniffed. "Like he'd really just died. There and then. Anyway, we didn't know what to do."

"Did you call the police?"

"We wanted to check with Rosamund first, you know, get her side of the story. So we took him to the hospital."

"I thought you said he was dead."

"He was. Rosamund was at the hospital. But she wasn't saying anything because, it turns out, she had no idea he was there. So then me and Annie took him back to his shop. Helen was with us by that point."

"And why did you do that?"

"I'm not saying we were looking for a place to dump him, but, yeah, I suppose we were looking for a place to dump him."

"OK, this all sounds quite alarming, Figgy."

"You're meant to be non-judgy, Xandrea. It's all fine, honest. Anyway, while we were there, somehow Marco's body got itself from the car to a nearby bin, and that's where the police found it."

"So you did tell the police?"

"We're kind of lying low at the moment. We know we didn't do it. And although Rosamund looked guilty, the whole body in her car thing seems to be a coincidence. She's going through a lot at the moment. Her husband's left her but he's still making her life hell. You know about technological abuse?"

"I do."

"Well, there's a bit of that going on. He's run off with another woman, or something. Anyway, the four of us are doing our bit to work out what's going on. Marco's shop has a prime position on the high street and the shop owners to either side, Helen and Solomon, might be eyeing it up, so there's motive there."

"Is this the same Helen as before? I thought you said she didn't do it."

Figgy wiggled her jaw. "I don't think she did it, but she'd have a reason. Then there's Solomon on the other side. He's really angry deep down. I saw him shout at a dog owner the other day. He had..." She curled her fist. "...real fire."

"So, you're questioning suspects?" said Xandrea.

"Not exactly. Also, I think our main suspect is Annie's evil cousin, Gillian, because she wanted to buy a bar that Marco, the dead guy, was also going to buy."

Xandrea took a while to respond. "So, one of your 'friends', this Rosamund, had the body in her car. Another – Helen, was it? – wants to get her hands on the dead man's shop? And a third one has a cousin who you think actually did it?"

"Um, I mean, when you put it like that, it doesn't sound so good."

Onscreen, Xandrea spread her hands. Xandrea wore a lot

CHAPTER THIRTY-NINE

of rings on her fingers. It looked impractical, but Figgy was quite jealous.

"Figgy, this is not a safe situation for you to be in," she said.

"I mean, legally it's a bit *whoa*, isn't it? But I'm safe. I mean, unless the police want to charge me with concealing a death or being an accomplice to murder, which is possible."

"And are you sure these women aren't grooming you?"

"Huh." That gave her pause. "You think they might have drawn me into some sort of wicked plot?"

"It sounds quite fantastical. In fact, I have to ask. Has this actually happened? This isn't some fiction or roleplay or anime thing?"

Figgy wasn't sure how this could be some sort of anime thing. She enjoyed Japanese animation, and in her experience, it tended not to feature middle-aged English women running around trying to solve mysteries.

"No, it's not. It's real, Xandrea. And I should point out all the good it's doing me." She held up her hand to tick things off. "I've had friends over. Both Annie and Helen have been here, which is something that wouldn't have happened six months ago. I've been to a bar with them. And I've asked a boy out."

Xandrea blinked. "You asked someone out?"

"Uh-huh."

"Like someone your age?"

"Cameron. He's nineteen. So, a bit younger than me." She decided not to mention that as well as being a nineteen-year-old boy, Cameron was also the son of former suspect, Rosamund.

"Oh. Oh, that is big news. And you went out? Like on a date?"

"Daytime. Café. Chitchat. Normal stuff."

Xandrea was momentarily speechless. "That is progress," she said. "Big steps."

"Thank you," said Figgy.

"Although I think we might need to discuss this murder thing a bit more."

Figgy nodded. "I thought you might say that."

CHAPTER FORTY

THE NEXT AFTERNOON, Annie called in at the gallery to find Helen before meeting Figgy and Rosamund for their evening out.

"Listen, Helen. I'm really glad you suggested this. Rosamund's been wound so tight, I hoped we might loosen her up a bit."

"We're on the same wavelength, my dear! Now, just to check, do you want her wine-loose, or should I try to acquire us some special smokes?"

"Goodness no! Let's just go for wine. The moment I attempt something a bit dodgy, we're bound to run into Tina or Dougie or one of their colleagues. That's the trouble with having police in the family."

Helen let out a cackling laugh. "Yeah, let's all pretend that the police are squeaky clean. But we'll go with wine."

Once Helen had locked up and said goodbye to Harper, the two of them walked up the hill to the Nag's Head. Figgy and Rosamund were already there, Rosamund waggling a bottle of white wine at them from a corner table. "Want a glass?"

Annie grinned and nudged Helen.

"I would love a glass," said Helen, throwing herself into a chair. "I've been stock taking and it's exhausting work."

Rosamund poured wine into glasses and gave Helen a curious look. "I didn't know you had that much stock."

"More than you'd think," said Helen. "And while I'm an excellent businesswoman, I detest the tedious business of counting things."

"I can help next time," said Figgy. "I like counting things."

"Well blow me down," Helen replied. "I will definitely take you up on that offer, Figgy. Who knew there were such people in the world?"

"My cousin Gillian," said Annie. "I picture her like Scrooge McDuck counting all her money. She loves it."

The four of them sniggered at the image.

"This is so nice," said Rosamund. "I haven't known what to do with myself for weeks."

"Since David left, do you mean?" Annie asked.

Rosamund nodded.

"Question," said Helen. "Did he tell you he was leaving? Like, did he do the whole flouncing out with a fanfare thing?"

Rosamund slumped back in her chair. The bar was getting busier now, and people were standing near them. She lowered her voice.

"I wish he had," she said. "I might have been on a more solid footing if I knew for sure what was going on. Real life's not like that though, is it? It's messy."

CHAPTER FORTY

"Real life is messy," agreed Annie. "I think we can all raise a glass to that."

There were murmurs of agreement as they all took fresh slurps of wine.

"Messy how?" asked Helen.

Rosamund wrinkled her nose. "I don't know any of this for sure, but I'd had suspicions for a while that he was seeing someone else. Those business trips getting longer and more frequent. Then the last time, he took way more stuff with him than he normally would, but I didn't even realise until days after he'd gone. I was putting some of his laundry away and his wardrobe was all but empty. That was four months ago, and I haven't seen him since."

Figgy and Helen looked aghast. Annie put a comforting hand on Rosamund's arm.

"I'm sorry that happened, Rosamund," Figgy said.

Rosamund's face crumpled slightly, and a tear slid down her cheek. "Thanks, Figgy. It means a lot to have the three of you to talk to."

"He's not been in touch at all?" asked Helen. "I imagine you've tried to contact him."

Rosamund shook her head. "He's ghosting me. He obviously knows everything about me from all the technology in the house, but he doesn't want me to know anything about *him*."

"We'll fix that," said Figgy, her face set. She licked her lips. "But I'm curious. What does Cameron make of it? He told me his dad's on a business trip."

Rosamund gritted her teeth. "I've embellished the thing to make it less painful for him. Extended project abroad, that sort of thing. With the heating in the house I just said that I was feeling the cold."

Annie found it hard to believe Cameron hadn't realised something was up, but perhaps he and his mum were each secretly trying to protect each other.

"I'm delighted that you've let us in, Rosamund," said Helen. "No more of this nonsensical stiff upper lip thing, if you please."

"Oh, I get it, I do," said Annie. "We all want to give the appearance we're doing alright, don't we?"

"I tried, I really did," said Rosamund. "When I was young, we had a little plaque in our kitchen that said 'Be a swan. Calm and unruffled on the surface, paddling like the devil beneath.' It's been my life's motto. Control is important. It's why I take myself for occasional meals out. It gives the impression of being in control of my life."

"But then you met Marco," said Annie.

Rosamund nodded. "I definitely lost my cool. I think I poured out some of the frustrations I'd bottled up over the past few weeks. He was being extremely irritating. He behaved as if I owed him attention, you know? Came swanning up to me, stinking of the minty vape he'd just been smoking outside. Moved like he was the bloody king of the jungle."

There were nods all round.

"And when I told him I wasn't interested," she continued, "he did that whole 'Hey, I'm just having a friendly chat. Don't you like being friendly?' thing." She shuddered.

"Y'know," said Figgy, "sooner or later the police'll do what we did and find you through the CCTV."

The group fell silent as they pictured the net closing in on Rosamund.

"But I'm innocent," she said miserably. "It's still a mystery to me how he came to be in my car."

"It looks much better since we deep cleaned the carpet," Helen told her. "You can't even see the stain."

"I'm pretty sure they can find traces of blood if they look properly," said Figgy. Annie gave her a look.

Rosamund shrugged. "I think I'll need to sell the car anyway. David's changed the password on our joint account, so I shall be penniless fairly soon if I don't do something. I could probably do with getting a job."

"Is he even allowed to do that?" Annie asked. "We should look into it. And while I'd normally say hurray for you, you should get a job, you do know we need you for murder chats, don't you? We can't have you going off into the world and being useful to other people."

"I'll have that piece sold for you soon," Helen added. "I'm pushing it with a few buyers I know."

"What piece?" asked Annie.

"*Viscera*," said Helen. She'd had a few drinks and the word whistled through her teeth as she over-enunciated.

Annie thought of the red and purple picture on the gallery wall and then remembered the empty space on Rosamund's living room wall.

"Selling off the valuables," said Annie.

"It was never really my thing, that painting," said Rosamund, turning to Helen. "Sorry, but it wasn't."

Helen shrugged. "Doesn't bother me, I didn't paint it. It's a bit... corporate for my tastes. But it's only been in the shop since... well, since the morning of the, ahem, Marco incident. It's got time to sell yet."

CHAPTER FORTY-ONE

THE GLASSES of wine kept coming. When Figgy checked her phone, it was nearly eleven.

"Oh, I have to go." She stood up. The alcohol rushed to her legs, and she stumbled.

Helen tittered, but Rosamund and Annie reached out to grab her before she fell. The pub was full now, and Figgy had crashed into a group of men standing near them. She felt her cheeks redden.

"Whoa there, your royal Figgyness," said Annie.

"Sorry." She realised she was drunk. "I've got to go."

"We've all got to go," said Helen. "But there's no rush, is there?"

"Young people can't handle their drink," said Annie. "They haven't had as much practice as us more mature ladies."

"You putting me in that bracket, are you?" said Rosamund, arching an eyebrow. "Just when I was starting to like you."

"I have to get home," said Figgy. "For the Shiffing Porecast."

"What?" said Helen.

Annie smiled. "She means the Shipping Forecast."

Figgy nodded, the room blurring before her.

"Still doesn't make any sense," Helen said.

"It's my thing, OK?" Figgy broke free of the arms holding her up.

"You alright walking?" asked Annie.

Rosamund stood up. "I'll go with her."

"It's not in your direction," Figgy said.

"It is. Sort of. Besides, I need to clear my head."

Helen threw her hands in the air. "And that's it! Party's over!"

"Oh, we can order a nightcap, love," said Annie. "The last of the party animals, us two."

Rosamund was at Figgy's elbow as they walked to the door. Behind them, Annie asked, "So when exactly did Rosamund bring that painting to your shop?"

Figgy didn't hear the answer above the noise of the pub. She and Rosamund stepped outside and onto the narrow pavement of Silver Street.

Rosamund held onto her arm and pointed up the dark street. "You live in those caravans on Monmouth Beach, don't you?"

"Yes."

"Good. Then it's this way." Rosamund steered her up the road a way, and then they crossed to go over the hill that was Pound Street.

There were streetlights in Lyme Regis, but they were well spaced and only just bright enough to pick out the shape of the road, to add texture to the town at night. Pound Street was dark, most of the windows unlit.

The sea air, carried on a soft breeze, was cool and refreshing. It woke Figgy up, but only enough for her to recognise she'd drunk far too much and would regret it tomorrow.

"So," said Rosamund, with a bright forcefulness. "You and my Cameron have been getting pally, haven't you?"

Figgy blinked. "Um. Yes?"

"He says you've been out for tea and cake."

Do we have to have this conversation now? "We have."

"I don't know if that's code for something else."

Figgy frowned. "Code?"

"Like Netflix and chill."

Figgy looked at Rosamund to see if she was joking, but the dimness made her face unreadable.

"What? No? We had tea and cake. Literally, tea and cake."

Rosamund nodded stiffly and was quiet for a while.

"You know, Cameron is going through a lot at the moment. He's finished school, and although he's not gone yet he really ought to be going to university."

"Is that what he wants to do?" asked Figgy, realising it sounded like a challenge.

"And he's going to find out about his father soon enough," Rosamund continued. "A lot of changes. A lot of upset."

"I see."

At the end of Pound Street, they crossed the road to walk through the Holmbush car park and down the footpath to the front. It was a steep path through lush public gardens, a pleasant walk in the daytime. At night, it was dark and isolated, and as far as Figgy was concerned, more than a bit scary.

CHAPTER FORTY-ONE

Rosamund held Figgy's arm tightly in the darkness. "What I'm trying to say, Figgy," she said, "is that Cameron needs protecting."

A laugh escaped Figgy's mouth. She clapped her hand over it.

"You think it's funny?"

"He said the same thing about you."

"Did he?" Rosamund made a strangely satisfied noise. "I want him to be his own person, but it's nice that a mother and a son can look out for one another."

Figgy shrugged. "I guess."

She stumbled on the steps zigzagging down towards the seafront, but Rosamund had hold of her.

"I like you, Figgy," said Rosamund.

"Er, thank you. I like you, too."

"No. I mean it. I admire you. You are a young woman forced to face some of life's challenges far too early."

"I just try to get on with life."

"Mmm, yes. You've had to fight to keep going."

"Er. Not sure I'd put it like that."

Rosamund's other hand patted Figgy. The woman practically had her in an embrace. "I myself settled down too early, and, it seems, with the wrong man."

"Uh-huh." Figgy had no idea where this conversation was going.

"In fact, I was not much older than you when I met David, and I was pregnant with Cameron a few years later."

"Right."

"I have regrets."

"I'm sorry." It seemed like the right thing to say.

"Why are you sorry?"

"Because you regret what you did."

"I don't regret it," said Rosamund sharply. "I got Cameron out of it. My special man."

"Oh. OK."

The lights of the promenade were visible below them. There was the muffled sound of electronic dance music, possibly from Breaststrokes café bar.

"The point is," said Rosamund, and Figgy realised the woman was as drunk as she was. "The point is, we shouldn't be too quick to settle down with someone else and get tangled up in their drama."

The grip on Figgy tightened.

"Do you understand what I mean?" Rosamund asked.

Figgy wasn't sure what she was supposed to say. She nodded, relieved not to have any follow-up questions to answer.

They walked silently until they reached the seafront. There were lights coming from a couple of buildings on the prom, and the sparkle of reflected light on the sea between the beach and Cobb wall.

Figgy tried to untangle herself from Rosamund, and almost panicked when Rosamund seemed briefly to resist.

"I'm this way," she said, pointing towards the track leading further along the front to the caravans.

"I know," said Rosamund.

"Are you OK to get home?"

Rosamund stood there, swaying. "Perfectly fine. Strong, independent woman, me. I will Gloria Gaynor this thing."

"Oh. OK."

Figgy backed away. Rosamund held out her arm and wagged a long finger at her.

"But we understand each other, right?" she said.

CHAPTER FORTY-ONE

"Cameron's got prospects. He's got a bright future waiting for him if he can just get through this... this hiccup."

Figgy was going to nod and walk away. It was the sensible thing to do. The easy thing. But then she stopped and faced Rosamund.

"Are you saying you don't want me to spend time with Cameron?"

Rosamund frowned. "Figgy. Figgy. I like you, Figgy. I really do."

"Uh-huh."

Rosamund stared at her for a long moment and then nodded. "We understand each other."

She turned away and walked off down the promenade.

CHAPTER FORTY-TWO

Figgy woke to a screech, a pounding headache and a message on her phone.

The screech came from Kevin, who accompanied his complaints with a furious scraping of his beak against her picture window. The headache was entirely expected and probably less than she deserved considering the number of glasses of wine bought for her the night before. The message, as she saw once she'd managed to roll herself out of bed and peel open her bleary eyes, was from Cameron.

Did my mum say something last night?

Figgy blinked several times to clear her eyes and read it again. She sent a reply.

Something? Like what?

There was no reply for a while, time enough for her to get up, go to the bathroom, throw some water on her face and gulp down the splashes that made it into her mouth, by which time he'd responded.

Maybe nothing. She seemed kind of weird and kept saying you were a really nice person.

Figgy chuckled and shuffled through to the living room, where Kevin was throwing a tantrum on the window ledge. The painted stones had confounded him for a few days, but now hunger and annoyance were kicking in. These were the squawks of a gull who wanted restitution.

Figgy considered Cameron's message. She could be honest.

Yeah. Your mum did say something, Cameron. She said you were her special little angel and that it was her job to look after you and she didn't want the big bad woman with messed up problems of her own getting in the way of your perfect little life.

She wasn't about to send that message.

Instead she wrote, *We were just chatting. Nothing big.*

The three dots bounced for a long time. Then they stopped. Then started again.

His reply was one word: *K.*

"K?" she said in exasperation. "K?!"

What the hell was *K* supposed to mean? Was it a casual, no-worries, 'OK, don't worry about it'? Was it a passive aggressive, short and to the point 'OK, I'm onto you, missy'? What kind of OK was *K*?

Had he fallen out with her? Was he annoyed with her? And if so, why the hell was he annoyed with her? It was his mum who'd accused her of ruining her son's life. And with what? A piece of cake and a cup of tea.

Her head was still pounding, the cymbals of Kevin's screeching bashing along to the drums in her brain. The noise and the pounding and the unfairness of everything made her blood boil and Kevin – poor, stupid, greedy Kevin – was going to get both barrels of her fury.

Still in the T-shirt and pants she'd slept in, she went to the door, flung it wide, and shouted, "Just bog off, will you!"

Rosamund Winters, standing at the edge of the little garden that surrounded Figgy's caravan, took a step back and dropped the hand that had no doubt been raised to knock at the door.

"I'm... I'm sorry."

"Oh, God," said Figgy. "I didn't mean to... I was shouting at Kevin."

Kevin jumped from the window ledge and flew straight at Figgy. Drawing on energy she hadn't expected, Figgy launched a fist at him. It didn't connect – thank goodness – but the sheer rage in the movement was enough to startle him and send him reeling into the air and away.

Across the way, a man stood in the doorway of old Mrs Delacroix's caravan. He was thin, with blue hair and a scruffy beard. He stared at Figgy.

She waved at him. "Morning!" she called. "Just shouting at the seagull."

He nodded dumbly and closed the door.

Figgy looked at Rosamund. "Really, I was shouting at the seagull."

Rosamund nodded. "I... I think I owe you an apology."

"Do you?"

"I think I said some things last night. I think I was a bit... I was a bit of a bitch, wasn't I?"

"Hey, let's not use words like that."

"I was a bit..." She waved her hands. "I was a bit *me*, I think. Probably told you to get your snatching claws out of my darling baby boy."

"Er..." Those hadn't been the exact words, but the sentiment was about right. "Not as such."

CHAPTER FORTY-TWO

Rosamund looked down at the scruffy ground at her feet. Figgy could hear Kevin somewhere above, still screeching.

"I can be overprotective," Rosamund said.

"That's understandable, Mrs Winters."

Rosamund looked up. "Oh, it's Mrs Winters now, is it? Not Rosamund?"

Figgy winced. "Sorry. I don't know. Are you being Cameron's mum, or Rosamund who I go swimming with?"

"I would really rather I was Rosamund."

"I'd like you to be Rosamund, too."

Rosamund nodded and shifted from foot to foot. Figgy could see the tiredness and frailty in her face.

"Hangover?" Figgy asked.

"Yeah." Rosamund looked back at her, shielding her eyes. "We kind of went for it last night, didn't we?"

"Um, I think we did."

"Can I... can I buy you a coffee or something?" Rosamund asked.

Phew. "I'd like that. I might have to get dressed first."

"I can wait."

Figgy stepped back. "Come inside."

"Oh, I don't want to intrude."

Figgy held the door wide. "You won't. Make yourself comfortable." She looked at the sky and tried to pick out Kevin among the wheeling birds. "Feel free to shout at Kevin if he comes back."

CHAPTER FORTY-THREE

Helen kept looking towards the rear of the shop.

Annie had popped in that morning to discuss 'murder stuff' with Helen and had accepted a cup of tea. But Helen was clearly distracted.

"What is it?" Annie asked.

"That journalist is here."

Annie frowned. "Jason whatshisname?"

Helen nodded, chewing on a pencil. "Doing his feature piece on Harper's art."

"You look worried."

Helen stuffed the pencil into her hair and readjusted a stand of art event brochures on the counter. "I'm not worried. It's just that... Harper isn't exactly a people person."

"She seems perfectly sociable to me."

"She can turn it on if she needs to, but interacting with strangers isn't her forte. Anything outside her comfort zone makes her anxious."

"Really?"

CHAPTER FORTY-THREE

"She hasn't said anything, but the last few days she's made some very fretful dragonflies."

Annie raised an eyebrow. "I, for one, would like to see these fretful dragonflies."

Helen shook her head then went to the display cabinet and took down three small, welded dragonflies, constructed from odds and ends of cutlery and scrap. She arranged them on the counter.

"Normal, normal, fretful," she said, pointing to each in turn.

The dragonflies were beautiful. Annie might have called them cute, although that would probably have annoyed Helen and Harper. But she didn't think any of them looked anxious or fretful.

"I'm sure she's doing fine," she said. "And any publicity is good publicity."

Helen didn't look reassured. "I'm just going to check on her. Supportively." She made for the back door.

"Spy on them, you mean," Annie said.

Helen cast her a look. "Supportively."

Annie went with her, through the narrow back corridor and out into the yard. Jason Mordaunt was taking photos and poking around the large artworks that filled much of the yard.

"And tell me about this piece," he said.

Harper turned to the two-metre-tall metal bird sculpture he'd indicated. "This is called Phoenix," she told him. "It's made from the remnants of machinery from an abandoned quarry over on Portland. That's a chunk of Portland stone at its base."

"Ah. Ah, yes." Jason didn't seem all that interested. He

poked around the material gathered by the fences enclosing the yard, taking photos without looking.

"Getting everything you need?" Helen asked.

Jason flinched, then turned. "Oh, yes. Very fruitful. I love this work. Recycling Dorset's industrial past to say something new and meaningful."

"I didn't have you down as an art lover."

"I try." He smiled.

Helen fixed her girlfriend with a look. "You let me know when you're done here, or when you've had enough."

She ushered Annie back through the shop.

"I like that big phoenix sculpture, too," Annie said.

"Oh, good. Want to pay us six thousand pounds for it?"

Six thousand pounds? "No, you're alright, thanks. I haven't got anywhere to put it."

Annie glanced out the front of the shop. Her daughter Tina was leaning against the wall in front of the Cobb Gate car park, with Dougie standing beside her.

"Oh, dear," she said.

"Oh dear?"

"I'm trying to lay low for a bit. Tina hasn't taken too well to my, er, generous gift buying for the new baby."

"You've bought even more?"

Annie considered the items that had been in her spare room when she'd shown her friends, and the subsequent additions to that room. "Not *too* many more. But some. Anyway, I did convince her to have a baby shower on Sunday, and you lot are going to be the smokescreen for my gift-giving."

"But you're still hiding from her?"

"I think she might be onto me. And apparently, my girls

sometimes find old Annie Abbott a bit too much. I'm allegedly a little bit irritating."

Helen nodded. Annie cocked her head.

"Oh, God," said Helen. "You wanted me to disagree with you, didn't you?"

"A little back-up would be nice."

Helen shook herself and brushed a strand of hair away from her face. "I can do it. Let's do a retake. Give me the line again."

"No, it's fine," Annie huffed. "Clearly I *am* irritating."

"You... you have your ways."

"What *ways*?"

"You are, if I may indulge in a horrible cliché for a moment, the stereotypical mother hen. You fuss. You fuss around all of us, noisily, too. And you chivvy."

"Chivvy?"

"Chivvy. I think it's your main skill. You chivvy and encourage and badger. Quite a bit of badgering, too. You get people to go along with your plans."

Annie frowned. "I know you're trying to make it sound like a good thing, but that's not coming across."

"Oh, it is a good thing. Most of the time. Figgy was right, you know."

"Figgy? How?"

"We *are* the Lyme Regis Women's Swimming Club. Once upon a time, there was just a bunch of solitary early morning sea-swimmers, and we might nod to each other. That's how it was for years. But then you come along, and suddenly it's a routine and a ritual. Coffees together at the Kiosk. Corralling us all to do the Lyme Lunge on New Year's Day. That's you, that is. The enthuser. The club-maker.

You're like that man – oh, what's his name? – the one with the flute?"

"James Galway?"

Helen shook her head. "The Pied Piper of Hamelin! You toot your flute and expect the rest of us to come running."

Annie tried to remember the story. "I never thought of myself as a flute tooter."

"It's a metaphorical flute."

"Metaphorical or not, I didn't think it was a thing I did."

"Ah, but that's the thing about the persistent flute tooter. The flute tooter toots their flute so often they don't even know they're doing it."

Annie wasn't sure about that. "And I'm doing it all the time?"

Helen smiled. "Probably tooting it right now and neither of us realise."

She nodded, considering. "It's a subtle flute I'm tooting, then."

Another nod. "But it *would* be understandable if your girls have got a little tired of your flute tooting."

Annie sighed. "Because I'm an interfering and overbearing helicopter parent."

"Uh-uh. A flute tooter. I prefer my analogy."

There was the sound of footsteps as Jason Mordaunt came through from the rear, clutching his satchel to his side.

"All done?" asked Helen.

"Fascinating stuff," he replied. "Now, I must dash. Next important story to get."

"No rest for the wicked," said Helen, watching him go.

The journalist slipped out the front and almost collided with Tina on the pavement.

"Ah, Mr Mordaunt," Annie heard her daughter say. "Just the man I was looking for."

"Me?" he replied, his voice wobbling.

Tina steered him away. As she did, she looked through the shop window and gave a little wave to Annie and Helen.

Annie gave a stiff wave back.

CHAPTER FORTY-FOUR

"You mind walking with me?" Tina asked Jason.

Jason Mordaunt nodded.

"Don't worry," she said. "We're not walking far. Probably only as far as that bench."

Jason looked at her bump. "You're a police detective?"

"Detective Constable Tina Abbott."

"Can I see some ID?"

She fished out her ID. "Happy?"

"Yes."

She sat on the bench by the Cobb Gate car park. "You're welcome to sit with me. Got to rest my ankles." She lifted her feet to regard them. "I *used* to have actual ankles. I'm sure of it."

Jason eyed her, not sitting. "You had questions."

"Mmm. Me and my colleague, PC Anderson here." She gestured to Dougie, who had followed them. "We're interested in your relationship with the late Mr Callington. Marco."

CHAPTER FORTY-FOUR

"There was no relationship."

She squinted at him, wishing he'd sit down. The town was busy, locals and tourists passing and Dougie nodding hellos.

"Yes," she said, "but you wrote articles about his shop and put them in the *Lyme Echo*."

"One article."

"I know. I read it."

Jason looked gratified. "What did you think?"

She wrinkled her nose. "Some would say it was an outright attack on a local shopkeeper's business." She tilted her head. "Or, one might view it as a firm, fair and insightful exposé of less-than-ethical business practices."

"I didn't write anything that wasn't true," he said.

"Didn't say you didn't," replied Tina. "If you could summarise, what would you say were Mr Callington's major... failings as a businessperson?"

"I thought you read the article."

"I did. Please humour me."

Jason sighed and clutched his satchel tighter.

"His shop wasn't a fair reflection of the history, geology or culture of the town. Compare it with – oh, I don't know – the Lyme Regis Fossil Shop, which has local fossils, some beautiful displays and clear labels. Jurassic Fossils was just a low-brow dinosaur tat shop. An overpriced one at that. Not only was Marco Callington importing fossils and selling them off as local finds, but he was also selling fake fossils."

"Fake fossils?" asked Dougie.

Jason glanced at him. "Models of fossils. Moulded resin models. 3D printed. And that's fine, I suppose, as long as people know what they're buying."

"And he wasn't making that clear?" Tina asked.

"Very poor labelling."

Very poor labelling hardly sounded like a crime.

"Did Mr Callington read the article?" she asked.

"Probably."

She gave the journalist a long look.

Jason sighed. "He did. We... spoke about it afterwards."

"I guess he wasn't happy."

"No."

"And?"

He blinked. "And? I'm a journalist. I'm used to people not liking the truth."

She gave him a thin smile.

"Perhaps," suggested Dougie, "you might like to describe the details of that conversation."

"I dunno. It would have been in his shop. One afternoon. I don't know when. A good couple of weeks ago. He told me he thought the article was unfair. No. A 'stitch-up', he called it. Said he could sue. People say things like that sometimes."

"To you?" Dougie asked.

"Pardon?"

"People often say things like that to you, do they?"

"Are you implying I'm a... a disagreeable person, Constable?"

Dougie pulled a face but said nothing.

"And how did that conversation end?" asked Tina.

"We agreed to disagree. He was busy with new stock. I had things to do."

"And you didn't talk about the newspaper article after that?"

"No."

CHAPTER FORTY-FOUR

"Or before?"

He shook his head. "That one conversation."

Tina nodded. "And do you know the delivery van that comes to his shop?"

He frowned. "Can't say I've seen one."

"Very good, Mr Mordaunt. That's very helpful."

The journalist nodded. "Can I go?"

"Of course."

He went through to the Cobb Gate and approached a large Land Rover, old but in good condition, parked just the other side of the wall.

"Not ideal for Lyme's narrow streets," Tina called to him.

Jason smiled at her. "My job takes me all over the county. Up hill and down dale in all weathers."

Tina didn't bother pointing out that Dorset didn't exactly have dales. "By the way, are you quite sure that was the only time you and Marco spoke after the article came out?"

"Yes," said Jason, brow furrowing.

"No calls, no messages?"

"No. Don't think so."

"Think?"

"No, Detective. We didn't meet or talk or anything."

"Until that conversation. So you sought him out."

His frown deepened. "Pardon?"

"You met in his shop. You went in. You sought him out. You instigated the conversation."

Jason shrugged. "I guess."

She shrugged back at him. "Why?"

"Follow-up. I wanted to know what he thought. Just standard journalistic practice."

"Fair enough."

He hovered a moment. When she didn't ask anything more, he got in his vehicle and drove off.

Tina shared a glance with her brother-in-law. "What d'you make of that, Dougie?"

"Dunno. Journalism. It's an odd business."

CHAPTER FORTY-FIVE

Long after Tina and Jason had gone, Annie stood in Helen's gallery and stared out over the road, watching the comings and goings of the locals, the holidaymakers, and the cars trying to get past the people dodging across the road in front of them.

"You know what?" she said to Helen as she gazed over towards the Cobb Gate car park. "We should get the others over here. I've been thinking."

"Steady! Do you mean right now?"

"Yes. Right now."

Helen tapped a message into the group chat.

Annie looked down at her phone to read it. "Cheeky mare! I do not need a lie down in a darkened room to recover from thinking, thank you very much."

In less than twenty minutes, Figgy and Rosamund arrived together, chatting with a bonhomie that Annie hadn't seen between the two of them before. Had Figgy been ingratiating herself with her future mother-in-law?

Helen handed them mugs of tea and looked at Annie,

hands on her hips. "Come on then, Aristotle. Let's hear the results of your great ponderings."

Annie closed her eyes to try and locate the feeling she'd had a short while before. "I thought I was on the verge of getting to an important point."

The other three looked at her, saying nothing. Helen made a rolling gesture with her hands: *get on with it*.

Annie took a breath. "Rosamund, your car was in three places on that morning when Marco was in it."

"Was it?"

Annie nodded, growing in confidence. "It was at your house first thing. Then it was here, wasn't it?"

"Um, yes. It was. I dropped the painting off before swimming."

"Right, you talked to Helen and then you moved it over the road to the Cobb Gate car park. Is that correct? Did you stop anywhere else?"

Rosamund shook her head. "No, those are the only places."

"Talk us through the bit when you came here to the gallery," said Annie. "What did you see and do?"

"I mean, what is there to say?"

"As much detail as you can remember."

Rosamund closed her eyes. "I put the painting in the boot, and I set off from home. It was early but I was already overheated from being in the house, so I was grateful for the aircon in the car. I drove round and then I got to the turnoff for Helen's. It's not obvious where to go when you come off Monmouth Street."

"So you came round the back?" asked Figgy, pointing to the rear of the shop.

Rosamund nodded. "I parked. I got the painting out of the boot."

"*Viscera*," said Helen, indicating the painting.

"Yes," agreed Rosamund. "I came inside, and we chatted about you selling it for me." She glanced around at the group. "I probably lied and said I was tired of it or something but now you all know I'm struggling financially."

"We get it," Figgy said.

"What happened next?" Annie asked.

Rosamund shrugged. "I briefly thought about leaving the car here while we swam, but it seemed cheeky, so I got back in and moved it over to the Cobb Gate car park and met up with you all at the beach."

Figgy had her lips in a small 'O'. "Your car has central locking, yeah?"

"Of course," said Rosamund.

Annie couldn't imagined Rosamund ever having owned a car old enough to lack central locking.

"So, when you were carrying the painting into the gallery, did you lock the car?" Figgy continued.

"I don't know."

Figgy gave her a serious look. "Think."

Rosamund closed her eyes again and held out her hands, grasping an imaginary painting. "I was definitely worried about damaging the painting, so I didn't want to put it down on the ground. I carried it in through the door and followed Helen inside."

Figgy was nodding. "Boot still open?"

Rosamund still had her hands out. "Yes, but only for a few minutes."

Annie clenched a fist. She'd been right. "You see?"

"No," said Helen, frowning. "Please fill in the blanks."

Annie looked at Rosamund. "Did you drive here today, Rosamund?"

A nod. "I'm parked at the Cobb Gate. I was meeting Figgy, and I'd planned to drive over to the Waitrose in Bridport for a few essentials."

Annie smiled, wondering what Rosamund considered essentials.

"Right," she said. "Go fetch it. Bring it round the back and I'll show you how Marco Callington ended up in your car."

Rosamund frowned. "Aren't the police still doing crime scene things?"

"Packed up yesterday afternoon," said Helen.

Five minutes later, Annie, Figgy and Helen were in the back yard. Helen held an unused canvas of a similar size to the *Viscera* painting. No one else was around; the neighbouring alleyways and paths were empty. *And a good job, too.*

Rosamund drew up.

"Park like you were before," Annie told her.

Rosamund hesitated, then turned her massive Audi round in the parking area. The back of the SUV had a large boot door. Figgy opened it and Helen inserted the painting. There was a deep boot space before the seats, but they still needed to fold down part of the rear seat to fit it in.

"That's how it was before," Rosamund said.

Annie clapped her hands together. "You're going to do everything the same as you did that morning. Helen, you, too. Go back inside and come to the door when you realise she's there."

Helen headed back towards the shop.

Annie could feel it coming together. "I'll be Marco" she said, "and—"

CHAPTER FORTY-FIVE

"What?" said Helen.

Annie looked at her. "I'm going to be Marco," she repeated.

"Was he here?" asked Rosamund.

"If my theory is correct then he was. Figgy, can you observe and video scene number one."

Figgy had her phone out. "Wait, scene number one?"

Annie winked. "There's more after this."

"Tell me when to start," said Rosamund, getting into the driver's seat.

"Action!" shouted Annie, feeling the thrill of directing a movie.

Rosamund got into the car, then got out again. She went and rapped on the door at the back of the gallery.

"Morning Helen!" she shouted.

"Bring it in, my dear!" shouted Helen.

Figgy was rolling her eyes, but she had her phone held up, capturing the scene.

Rosamund went to the boot of her car and opened it. She put her keys into her pocket and grabbed the large canvas. She backed carefully away and then walked inside the shop, leaving the boot wide open.

"Here's me staggering into the back of the boot," Annie said to Figgy.

"Marco is staggering, right," said Figgy. "Why?"

"Because I've been hit on the head." Annie clutched her hand to her imaginary head wound. "Oof, I've collapsed in the back. See how I've crawled forward a bit onto the back seat so I can have a lie down? My head wound is bleeding into that rear footwell now."

Rosamund's voice carried clearly from the shop. "I'm

back to close the boot now, but I don't actually step outside, I'm just using the plipper."

The boot closed behind Annie. Remote-controlled. *Posh*.

"And cut!" she shouted.

She waited for someone to open the boot, and she climbed out. "And as they say in show business – ta-dah!"

Helen looked confused. "Wait. What?"

Annie grinned. "Marco got in the car here. Right here. It's the only explanation."

"Someone stuffed him in the car?" asked Rosamund.

Figgy shook her head. "No. He got in. It makes sense. It crossed my mind when I first saw his body in the car. He was still warm. The wound was still wet. I'm sorry to be icky, but it was. He was alive when he got in the car."

Rosamund pulled an expression of disgust. "What on earth did he do that for?"

"And you're saying he was killed here?" interrupted Helen.

"Attacked here," Annie said. She gestured at the space around them and the back of Marco's fossil shop. "Someone attacked him, but he didn't die right away. He was mortally wounded. That's the phrase. He was hurt, and yes, he was going to die, but he was moving around. He came out here and got in the boot."

"Maybe it's like cats," said Figgy.

The others looked at her.

"I read that when they get hit by cars and things, they crawl off somewhere to hide. And then they die."

"That's really sad," said Rosamund.

"And not necessarily the kind of instinct fossil shop owners might share," Annie added.

"He was hurt," agreed Rosamund, "and he stumbled out

CHAPTER FORTY-FIVE

here and he saw a car, open. He needed help. He needed to get to a hospital. He came to the car for help and crawled inside."

"Maybe he was hiding from the person who hurt him," said Figgy.

Annie nodded. "A decent theory."

Rosamund shook her head. "I drove him down to the Cobb Gate car park and didn't even realise he was back there? He didn't say anything?"

"Easy enough to miss," said Annie, "especially in a car the size of the Starship Enterprise. He might have been drifting in and out of consciousness."

Rosamund had paled. "Maybe he was already dead."

"No," said Figgy. "Because we found him in the front seat. He moved."

"This, I reckon, is what Marco did while we were in the water, swimming," said Annie. "He used whatever energy he had to crawl forwards and sit in the passenger seat, but then he just died."

"Stone the crows," Helen whispered.

"And other expressions to that effect," Annie agreed.

CHAPTER FORTY-SIX

"So someone whacked him on the head near here?" Rosamund scanned the yard as if she might be able to see the murderer.

Figgy pressed buttons on her phone. "I've shared the video on the group chat. Did you say there was another scene, Annie?"

"There most certainly is!" Annie replied. "Something happened when we came back here. Let's walk through the return trip, shall we? Now, Figgy, how long would you say we were inside the shop when we were looking for a way to move Marco's body?"

"Ten minutes, maybe?"

"So let's shoot another scene. You can film again, Figgy, and keep time. I'm Marco's body, in the front seat of the car, and then an unknown somebody comes along and puts me in the wheelie bin. That's you, Rosamund and Helen."

Rosamund and Helen both looked equally reluctant, but Figgy had been swept away with the filmmaking bug.

CHAPTER FORTY-SIX

"Cameras are rolling!" she shouted.

"And action!" called Annie. She shut the door and tried to act like a corpse, but a corpse that was keeping one eye open so she could see what the others were doing.

Rosamund and Helen shrugged at each other and walked towards the car. Helen opened the door and the two of them muttered back and forth about the best way to move the body.

"A shoulder each. Can we manage that?" Rosamund asked.

They managed to drag her out of the seat. Annie found it tricky to stay floppy when she wasn't convinced that they had her properly supported. Once they were on the flat, they grabbed her more securely and carried her awkwardly over to the bins.

"Which one?" hissed Rosamund.

"The recycling one should be less disgusting," replied Helen, flipping open a lid.

Annie caught a smell and tried hard not to identify it. *Curry. Definitely curry.*

"We're doing this, then?" Rosamund asked.

"Oh yes. It's what dead Annie would have wanted."

Dead Annie took a deep breath and held it, confident that her ladies would manage this.

"On three!" said Helen.

Annie was lifted and levered head-first into the bin. Marco wouldn't have felt its lip pressing painfully on his stomach, but Annie gritted her teeth rather than call out.

She felt her weight shift and shot downwards. She was relieved not to have smashed her head in, but there was something gross and unidentified seeping onto her scalp.

"Did you get that, Figgy?" asked Helen. "Is this the end of the scene, Annie?"

Annie tried to make an affirmative grunting sound without opening her mouth.

"I think that was 'yes'," said Rosamund.

There was a long, long pause. Annie wondered what was happening.

"Figgy," said Helen eventually. "Do you have any bright ideas about how we get her out of there?"

"Oh. Yeah. Tricky," said Figgy. "Maybe the best thing would be to tip the whole bin on its side, and she can wriggle out?"

"That could work. Come and give us a hand, will you? We want to do it as gently as we can."

Annie waited for what seemed like an eternity while the three of them organised themselves.

"Right, on my count!" said Helen. "One, two, three."

Annie was relieved to be tilted gently, but not so relieved to find herself lying face down in whatever it was that had leaked out from the recycling.

"Annie, you can come out backwards now," Rosamund said.

Annie squirmed out, scuffing her knees on the gritty shale of the ground. She knelt down to get her bearings before standing up.

"Oh dear." Helen looked horrified. "I'd better get something."

Annie wiped the stuff from her face. "What is it? What have I got on me?"

Figgy grimaced. "By the smell and colour, I'd guess biryani."

CHAPTER FORTY-SIX

"We'll get you all cleaned up, Annie," Rosamund said. "That was a good job, you make a rather convincing corpse."

"You got the video, Figgy?" Annie asked.

"Oh yes. It's a classic."

Helen reappeared with a tea towel and Annie finally stood, wiping the gunk off her face.

"Have you learned anything new now you've seen the world from a corpse's point of view?" Rosamund asked.

"Yes." Annie fixed Helen with a steely gaze. "Some people should really rinse their recycling a bit better. I need to get washed and changed."

"And I need to get off to Waitrose before all the good avocados have gone," said Rosamund.

"What have we learned?" said Figgy. "Does this help us understand who killed Marco?"

Helen and Rosamund turned to Annie, who nodded.

"It explains why Rosamund couldn't possibly have done it," she said.

"Thank you," Rosamund said. "Some of us knew that all along."

"I mean, assuming that the killer and the person who moved the body were the same person."

"That means none of us was the killer," said Figgy. "Annie, Helen and me were in the shop while the body was being put in the bin. And you were at the medical centre, Rosamund."

Helen nodded. "So, the killer was someone else, someone else who had reason to be here. And they dumped the body while we were in the shop."

"Or an accomplice did," suggested Annie. "Someone who could be alerted while we were in the shop."

Figgy drummed her fingertips against her chin. "Motive, means and opportunity."

"Hmmm?" asked Helen.

"That's what the police look for. Why they did it, how they did it and the opportunity to do it."

"Well, everyone hated him," Helen replied. "And clearly someone whacked him over the head."

"With what, we don't know," Figgy said.

"Opportunity, though," Annie added. "The police don't seem to know who did it, so that makes it anyone who could have been here, unseen, that morning."

Figgy gazed about the enclosed parking area and the grey windows looking onto the space.

"So, anyone in Lyme Regis, then?" she said.

"You know," said Helen, "I remember seeing this thing on telly once about John Napier. You know him?"

"Can't say I do," Annie said.

"Scottish chap. Invented the decimal point."

"Oh, him." Annie still didn't have a clue who Helen was on about.

"Anyway, when something was stolen from his house, he made all the servants go into a darkened room and touch his black cock."

"Helen!" exclaimed Rosamund, scandalised.

"A bird! A bird!" said Helen, grinning. "He owned a black cockerel, and he told all his servants that the bird could detect guilt."

"A magic chicken?" said Figgy with a grin.

"So he said. And they believed him. And they went into the room and stroked the cockerel."

"And what did the magic bird do?" Figgy asked.

"Nothing. It was just a bird. But what he *had* done was

CHAPTER FORTY-SIX

cover it with soot. The guilty servant was the only one without soot on their hands. Guilt and fear made the thief refuse to touch the bird. He tricked them."

Annie nodded thoughtfully. "And you think we should do something similar with all of the people of Lyme Regis?"

"I don't even know where we'd get hold of a black cockerel," said Figgy.

"Ridiculous," said Rosamund.

CHAPTER FORTY-SEVEN

Tina nudged DS Strunk as Rosamund Winters turned into her driveway.

"She's here."

The DS grunted. It was early afternoon, and they'd been waiting half an hour for the woman's return.

Tina levered herself out of the car and went to the back seat to get Louis out.

"You know, the police don't really do 'bring your children to work' days," the DS said.

"Mum's busy with her little friends, and Naomi isn't a child minder. She's got her own stuff to be getting on with." Tina unbuckled Louis and stood him on the pavement, then spotted the DS's expression.

"I see that look," she said. "It was you that got me involved in this case."

He shook his head. "You got yourself involved."

"And you value the support. The team's understaffed as it is."

CHAPTER FORTY-SEVEN

He frowned. "As long as you don't plan on giving birth on my watch."

Tina rubbed her bump. "Got another week or two." She gestured ahead. Rosamund Winters was making for her front door with two bags of supermarket shopping.

The DS called out to her. "Mrs. Winters! Excuse me!"

Rosamund turned, a shiver passing through her.

"DS Nathan Strunk." Nathan gestured to Tina. "This is DC Tina Abbott." A pause. "And her child. I wonder if we could ask you a few questions."

"What questions?" Rosamund asked.

"It's about the other night, in Breaststrokes café bar. We're investigating the murder of Marco Callington. You might have heard what happened."

Rosamund Winters froze. Tina stepped onto the driveway, holding Louis's hand.

"You were with Marco Callington in Breaststrokes on the evening of the ninth," prompted the DS.

The manager of the Breaststrokes café bar had been helpful. Or possibly just indifferent. Barbara 'call me Babs' Spiro had not been at all surprised when they'd called in with their questions, and she'd produced the relevant CCTV footage in minutes. Tina had recognised Rosamund as one of the women Annie regularly swam with. It hadn't been difficult to pull up an address.

"What's this about?" asked Rosamund.

Tina decided to spell it out.

"Marco Callington is dead," she said. "We're still trying to work out his movements in the hours and days before he died. You might have been one of the last people to see him alive. You and he were drinking together on the ninth."

Rosamund scoffed.

"No?" said Tina.

"Is your husband at home?" the DS asked.

Rosamund gave him an icy look. "Away on business."

"Since when?" asked Tina.

"For a while. I don't know when he'll return."

Tina noticed that the security cameras pointing at the driveway and the front door had been covered with sheets.

"What was your relationship with Mr Callington?" she asked.

"There was no *relationship*. None. I was drinking, alone. He came over and pestered me, as some men think they have a right to do. That's it. End of story."

"The story ended with you throwing a drink at him," said DS Strunk.

"So? You never get angry at people?"

The front door of the house opened. A tall young man with a mass of curly hair looked at the two detectives. Reaching into her memories of her mum's chitter-chatter, Tina thought this had to be Cameron Winters.

"Everything all right, Mum?" he asked.

"Everything is fine," Rosamund told him. "These police detectives are doing general enquiries about the dead man."

"What? Door-to-door?"

The DS shuffled his feet. "That's right. Door-to-door."

"I didn't see anything," the young man said.

"See anything?" prompted his mum.

He was nervous, but not on the scale of his mum. "I guess you wanna know if people have seen anything suspicious. I didn't see anything."

"That's good to know," said the DS.

Cameron nodded and moved away from the door. "I've got work, Mum."

"Course you have," said Rosamund, waving him off. When he was through the gate and away, Rosamund looked from Nathan to Tina. "You're Annie's daughter, aren't you?"

"Yes," Tina said.

"I believe Annie is insisting I come to some sort of baby shower thing on Sunday."

Tina nodded wearily. She wasn't looking forward to it, either.

"Do anything for your children, wouldn't you?" said Rosamund.

"That's the default position for parents," Tina agreed.

Rosamund pointed in the direction Cameron had gone. "He's got himself an interim job selling ice creams to tourists, but he'll make something of himself one day. He's a lovely boy."

"I'm sure he is."

"And he's very protective of me," she added. "He worries more than a teenage lad should."

Tina waited for her to continue. The DS was watching them.

"My husband, David, is not here, and the reasons for that are none of your bloody business. And if I wanted to, I could be drinking at all hours with anyone I liked."

"Didn't say you couldn't," said the DS.

Rosamund inhaled through her long, elegant nose and gave them a haughty look.

"I was just enjoying a drink by myself when a self-important lout who I now know to be Marco Callington came over and tried to chat me up. I gave him short shrift and left him with little doubt that I was not interested. *That* was the conversation."

"I see," said Tina.

"Is that enough for you?"

Louis slipped from Tina's hand and ran over to the SUV parked on the driveway. He slapped both hands on it, like he was playing a game of Tag.

"I suppose so," said Tina.

CHAPTER FORTY-EIGHT

Annie needed no excuse to visit Lyme Regis beach. It was the town leisure centre, dog-walking park, natural history wonderland and, on this fine Saturday morning, free entertainment for the grandkids.

Today she was with Poppy, who was collecting pebbles in a bucket. Annie occasionally picked up a pebble and held it out for her granddaughter's inspection, but Poppy was the bucket gatekeeper, and Poppy had standards. Most of them ended up back on the beach.

When the bucket was almost too full to carry, they walked down to the shoreline and threw the pebbles into the sea.

Poppy and Louis had both learned that Grandma wouldn't let them take all of the prettiest pebbles home. Perhaps it taught them something about the importance of preserving the beach. And of course, throwing pebbles into the sea and hearing them 'plop' into the water was a lot of fun.

When the bucket was empty, apart from one smooth and

holed stone that Annie put in her pocket, she and Poppy brushed the sand from their hands and marched back up the beach to the promenade.

"Ice cream, Grandma?" said Poppy.

"Do you, dear?" Annie said. "How often?"

Poppy groaned. "Can we have an ice cream, Grandma?"

Annie gave a theatrical tut. "What's the magic word?"

"Abracadabra."

Annie pursed her lips, pretending to be coming to a decision. "I would also have accepted 'hocus pocus' or 'piff paff poof'," she said. "I think Granny's purse can stretch to a couple of ice lollies."

As they bought the lollies, Annie watched workmen raising a banner beneath the sign for Breaststrokes café bar. A grand re-opening was promised for the following Friday.

On the promenade beside it, the journalist Jason Mordaunt was taking photos of the building.

"This way, lovey." Annie wandered over. "Is 'Café Bar Under New Management' going to be this week's front-page news?"

Jason turned. He had a black eye. Or more accurately, a red eye, with angry swelling all around his left eye socket.

She pulled back, reflexively putting a hand in front of Poppy. "Oh, my goodness."

"Huh? Oh, this? Got whacked in the face with a brolly. I'm going to be charitable and say it was an accident."

"And was it?"

Jason pressed his lips together. "I was doing some vox pops with the locals about the dog fouling problem. One of the shopkeepers along the road has a real bee in his bonnet about it."

"I remember."

"I approached a lady whose Lhasa Apso had just done its business, and she whirled round and..."

"Ouch."

"Ouch," muttered Poppy, ice cream circling her lips.

"Quite," said Jason. "Journalism has always been a business fraught with danger."

"In Lyme Regis?" Annie asked.

The man gave a smile. "I took a post at the *Lyme Echo* when I realised that journalism in the big city was going to lead me to an early grave."

"That dangerous?"

"The commute, the fast-food lunches, the cutthroat editorial meetings. My blood pressure was through the roof. But, yes, also the danger. I did some work on the abuse of migrant workers in the nail beauty industry."

"Seems a bit niche."

"It's big business. Abuse, fraud and money laundering on a massive scale. I have a nose for crooked business practices."

"Ah, that's why you're into writing consumer articles about local shops."

"Hardly the same thing," he said, "but, yes, I did tread on the toes of some nasty people back in the day. Had to go equipped to defend myself."

"A gun?" Annie asked in a horrified whisper.

Jason tittered. "I'm talking about Bristol here, not Mogadishu. Pepper spray, rape alarm. Some weight training and I did a few self-defence classes. A man has to be prepared. Thank goodness, Lyme is a bit calmer, this current injury notwithstanding." He nodded. "Of course, the money's not quite up to big city salaries, but you make do."

"You do," she agreed. "Cheap and cheerful's the way to go."

She turned to direct her granddaughter towards home, and was already pulling out a tissue to wipe the ice cream away when Jason said, "If I could bother you for a moment, though..."

"Yes?" she said.

He had his big digital camera in his hands. "Like I say, I've been doing some background on the dog foul menace..." He skipped through some pictures and stopped on one. It only took Annie a moment to recognise herself with the neighbour's dog, Dex, on East Cliff Beach at the other end of town, down among the rocks and the fossils.

"Nice photo that," she said. "The sun and the shadows..."

"And then this," said Jason, flicking to another image. It was a close up of a dog poo on a concrete path. He flicked from that to the dog picture and back again.

"But that's not us," said Annie. "We didn't do that."

"The camera never lies," he said.

Annie heaved an agitated breath. "That's a picture of a dog, and then a picture of a poo. *Not* evidence. I'm a conscientious poop collector. Got a little roll of bags on me right here. Bag 'em and bin 'em."

Jason said nothing but gave her a knowing look. Annie felt her anger rising.

"You're making it up!" she snapped. "And I can see why people 'accidentally' clobber you with their brollies!"

"Is that a threat?"

She looked the man up and down.

"Come on, Poppy." She swept her granddaughter away.

CHAPTER FORTY-NINE

It was Saturday afternoon, but that didn't mean rest, not when Figgy had work to catch up on. Having a new social life with the Lyme Regis swimmers and a sideline in amateur murder investigation was all well and good, but it did cut into her working time. And flexible working hours didn't mean no working hours. It all needed doing sometime.

She'd been focused on her laptop for a few hours but had registered plenty of movement on the beach from the corner of her eye. She put the kettle on and went over to the window to take a look.

The now familiar sight of the Kevin T-shirts explained the crowds, even larger than the regular influx of tourists. Thankfully, there weren't as many of the hats today. Maybe people had heard about the danger of attack. A risky way to get a cool selfie.

As the kettle came to the boil, Figgy realised that while the number of people was high, the number of seagulls had definitely gone down. She shifted along the bench seat to get a closer look. The seagulls wouldn't have been put off by a crowd, opportunists that they were. Something else must have affected them.

Then Figgy saw one of the T-shirted women step towards the caravan and place something small on the ground. She craned forward to see what it was. The woman did a small bow and backed away.

It was a stone. And it wasn't the only one.

Figgy needed to see this properly.

She stepped outside and stood in front of her bay window, somewhere she didn't go often. As always, she was surprised by the briskness of the wind.

She looked down and saw dozens of painted stones on the ground, maybe more than a hundred. She struggled to pick out Helen's originals, because there were so many. Each was painted to look like a dainty snack; it was like looking across the counter of a well-stocked bakery.

"Wow." She took some photos of the stones and looked up to see that the woman who'd just placed one there was watching her.

"You painted this, um, Battenberg?"

"I did," said the woman. "Isn't it cute? Everyone wants to pay tribute to Kevin, don't they?"

"So it seems," Figgy said.

She decided not to explain that the stones had been an effort to teach Kevin boundaries, instead waving goodbye and retreating to her door. Someone was approaching Mrs Delacroix's caravan. It was the man with the blue hair she'd seen the other day, carrying a box from a van parked up the track.

"Hi," she called over. "You moving in?"

He turned. "I am. It was my nan's place."

"Oh? Mrs Delacroix was your nan?"

CHAPTER FORTY-NINE

The man nodded and put down the box. He stepped over to shake Figgy's hand. "Braydon."

"I'm Figgy. My nan knew your nan." It sounded a bit lame, but it was all she had.

"Mrs Edmunds?"

She felt a little pang at the memory of her grandmother. "That was her."

"Nan mentioned her. Good to make your acquaintance. You've got a right circus going on over there." Braydon nodded towards the beach. "Saw you in the paper."

Figgy gave a small shrug. "It's been weird. It'll be nice when it calms down a bit and it's just the gulls and me."

Braydon gave a nod of understanding. "Yeah. We all just want to be left alone, eh?"

He withdrew into his caravan and shut the door.

Figgy went back into her own place, trying to decide whether Braydon was the ideal neighbour who wanted to keep himself to himself, or just a tiny bit rude.

CHAPTER FIFTY

"How's your foot, Rosamund?" Annie asked as the four of them walked back to the wall after their Sunday swim. It was a bright morning, but a chill wind had them walking quickly, eager to get dry and dressed.

The twins, Sally and Peg, were still out there, and the young athletic Australian, Juniper, seemed to be aiming for some sort of record, but for most of them it had been a brief dip.

"It's barely sore at all now," Rosamund said. "I think I'm declaring myself fit."

"Wish I could say the same." Figgy grimaced. "I thought you told me this would get easier."

"Oh, stuff and nonsense, Figgy," said Helen. "Your speed and distance have improved no end. Not that we're counting. This is a relaxing swim, after all. No rules."

"It's true, Figgy," added Annie. "But don't be tempted to compare yourself with others. That way madness lies."

"You're right." Figgy nodded. "It feels like it's doing me good."

CHAPTER FIFTY

"It's doing us all good," Annie said. "The benefits of open water swimming are legendary." She wrinkled her nose. "Well, they're not just legendary. Science has things to say on the matter, too."

"It counteracts all the vices one might be inclined to indulge in," added Helen with a wink.

Figgy pulled a face. "I don't really have any vices."

"Then get some! What might I recommend, hmmm?" Helen looked thoughtful as Rosamund nudged her.

"Did I ever tell you that you look like a smoker?" asked Annie.

Helen frowned. "Look like a smoker?"

Annie nodded. "You do this thing with your hands." She flicked her fingers about, trying to make elegant shapes. "It's like you've got a cigarette holder in your hand."

"Like Cruella de Ville," added Figgy.

Annie clicked her fingers. "Like Cruella de Ville, exactly."

Rosamund smiled at Helen. "You'd make a good Cruella."

Helen gave her a sharp look. "You'd better back that statement up."

"I don't mean in a puppy-murdering sort of way."

"Glad to hear it."

"But in your free and easy, high-class sort of way."

Helen pursed her lips. "Debonair?" she suggested.

Annie wasn't so sure. "Decadent," she countered.

"Louche," said Rosamund, savouring the word.

"Oh, I can definitely do all three of those," said Helen, pleased. "And for your information, I did smoke in a former life. But that was a long time ago, and I was a completely different woman then."

Rosamund put up a guilty hand. "Smoked as a teenager."

Annie put her hand up, too. "Ditto. Everyone did it at least once, didn't they?"

"Well, I haven't," said Figgy.

Annie waved her away. "The younger generation are all so clean-living."

"And it's all vaping now, anyway, isn't it?" added Helen.

They were all more or less dried off now, wriggling into their warm clothes. Annie noticed a deep frown on Figgy's face.

"What is it, Figgy love?" she asked.

The frown remained while Figgy spoke. "Rosamund, you said that Marco smelled of vape in the bar that night."

"I did. Mint something. He was wreathed in clouds of it as he came in."

"But he had cigarettes in his pocket when we searched his body."

"You searched his body?" Rosamund asked.

"We were being thorough," Annie told her. "What were those funny cigarettes called, Figgy?"

"Furongwang," Figgy replied.

Rosamund scoffed. "There's no cigarette called that."

Annie took out her phone and scrolled back through the pictures. "Yes. Furongwang. Furongwang." Annie repeated the word, tasting it in her mouth.

"Show me," said Rosamund.

Annie passed the phone over. "Odd that he would have both cigarettes and vape, don't you think?"

"I can imagine that a person might want to have both vapes and cigarettes," said Helen. "Different social situations and so on. But I really don't see Marco as someone who would be sensitive to such things. If he felt like lighting up a fag, he'd just do it, you know?"

"These look classy," said Rosamund, looking at Annie's phone. "Old-fashioned. Not sure why."

"It's all that talk of cigarette holders and Cruella de Ville," said Helen, peering over to look. "Ah. You know why."

"Why?"

"No health label."

Annie took her phone back. Helen was right. Why hadn't she spotted it before?

All cigarettes now had those big health warning labels. Bold letters, pictures of diseased organs or coughing people. It wouldn't be long before the whole pack was one big warning label.

"Didn't know you could get cigarettes without the government warning," she said.

"You can't," said Figgy. "You really can't. Those are illegal."

"Dodgy fags," said Helen. "Imported without paying duty."

"You mean smuggled?" asked Rosamund.

"Ooh," said Annie, feeling a tingle of excitement. "So our Marco Callington is not only a nasty so-and-so and a shoddy businessman, but he also buys dodgy fags."

"Maybe he's connected to the mob," suggested Figgy.

"Whoa," said Helen. "He buys knock-off fags from someone who probably picked them up on a package holiday to Turkey or something. Doesn't mean he's in with the mafia."

"But it means he knows dodgy people," Annie said. "We *are* looking for a murderer."

Rosamund cleared her throat. "The *police* are looking for

a murderer. We're getting a little carried away with ourselves."

"Don't spoil the fun," Annie told her. "We can do a bit of snooping. See if we can find anyone selling dodgy cigarettes. We just need someone dodgy to ask."

"We're going to ask dodgy people about dodgy cigarettes," said Helen. "I'm dying to hear how we might do this."

Annie shrugged. "I think there's probably a hierarchy of dodginess. You start off with someone a teeny bit dodgy, they'll know slightly more dodgy people, and then you work your way up."

She sketched out a pyramid of dodginess with her hands.

"But do we want to do that?" asked Figgy. "It sounds dangerous."

"We only want to go far enough up to find those cigarettes," said Annie. "Now, who might we know that can start us off?"

"Babs?" Helen suggested.

Annie looked round. Breaststrokes café bar was opening up for the day. "Babs Spiro!" she agreed. "Let's do it!"

She grabbed her bags.

Figgy grabbed hers, too. "What are we doing? We're going to start knocking on doors and asking difficult questions?"

"Apparently," said Rosamund.

CHAPTER FIFTY-ONE

"So let me get this straight." Babs frowned. "You lot want to know where you might find someone who's flogging dodgy cigarettes?"

They nodded.

The manager of Breaststrokes looked like the sort of woman who should be somewhere on Annie's imaginary hierarchy of dodginess, but right now she seemed more likely to call the cops on them instead.

She shook her head and slapped a hand on the counter. "You all know how to wipe tables?"

Annie frowned. "I, er. What?"

"I'll give you some cloths. Go and wipe all the tables, inside and outside. We'll talk when you're done."

Annie wasn't sure who was the more outraged, Helen or Rosamund. Figgy just took a cloth and got on with it. Rosamund sniffed her cloth and pulled a face. Helen flounced. She'd often said that a clean house was a sign of a wasted life.

"I think this is proper gangster," said Figgy, throwing herself into the task.

A few minutes later they presented their cloths to Babs.

"Now will you talk to us?" demanded Helen.

Rosamund sniffed her hands.

Babs took the cloths and dropped them into a bucket of grey water behind the counter. Rosamund grunted.

"Right, will you tell us now?" said Helen.

"Where do we get hold of dodgy cigarettes?" asked Annie.

"No idea." Babs smiled. "But I know a man who might. There's a guy, Tez, who services the toilets. I can't guarantee what he knows, but he's the person I'd ask if I wanted to know. He'll be here in ten minutes. You can have a cuppa while you wait."

Tez pulled up in a small van at the exact time Babs had said he would.

He carried heavy rolls of paper for the huge dispensers that Annie thought were the most annoying way of delivering toilet paper ever invented.

Babs waved him over. "These ladies are after some information. The sort of thing you might know."

Tez grinned. "How can I help you guys?"

Annie thought he looked like he spent his afternoons surfing. Maybe he did. He had the deep tan and the blonde highlights.

Annie nodded at the rolls he'd plonked on the table. "Those toilet rolls. The ones that only let you tear off one piece of paper at a time. Don't people complain about them?"

"All the time. Businesses love 'em though, because there's less mess and waste. Was that your question?"

"Oh. No, I was just wondering. Sorry. The actual thing

we want to know about is where we might find some unusual cigarettes."

Tez pulled back. "Weed?"

"No, not weed."

"Unless you offer competitive rates," added Helen. She looked at the others. "I think my guy is taking advantage of me."

Figgy looked scandalised.

"Not weed," said Rosamund. "What my friend is trying to say is that we're interested in who might be selling foreign cigarettes. Duty free, as it were."

"If I had any information about that, it wouldn't come for free," said Tez.

"Oh, for goodness' sake, are we cleaning the toilets now?" Rosamund snapped.

"I was thinking more like cash to be honest," said Tez. "Tenner."

There was a brief pause while they all fished through their emergency cash hideaways. Nobody wanted to leave loads of cash on the wall while they were swimming, but between them they managed to rustle up ten pounds.

"Thanks all," said Tez, pocketing the cash. "Anyway, I don't know who's selling them but I can keep my ear to the ground."

Rosamund cocked her head. "You don't know? We just paid you ten pounds for information you don't have?"

"I said I'd listen out and..." He leaned in. "You're not the only ones asking about these."

"Sorry?" Annie asked. "We're not the only ones asking about weird cigarettes in Lyme Regis?"

"That's what I said."

"Who else is asking?"

He shook his head. "Couldn't tell you. I don't take names in this game, you know how it is."

"The toilet paper game?" Figgy asked.

Helen rolled her eyes and nudged Figgy. "Thank you, Tez. You've been most helpful."

Tez wandered off, hefting his toilet roll. The four of them leaned in to talk.

"Someone else is interested in the Furongwang cigarettes?" Annie crowed. "I'd say that's pretty interesting, wouldn't you?"

They all nodded, then sat back to finish their drinks.

"Now, don't forget Tina's baby shower is this afternoon," said Annie. "I need as many people as possible so I can sneak those gifts under the radar. You'll all be there, won't you?"

CHAPTER FIFTY-TWO

ANNIE SPENT the rest of the morning preparing snacks and wrapping Tina's baby shower presents in as many different types of paper as she could find. She hid some bags full of gifts near the front door, shoved some into the cupboard under the stairs, and piled a few into the kitchen cupboards. She just had to drip-feed them into the living room without Tina noticing.

There were banners to put up and balloons to inflate. By the time the guests began to arrive, she was exhausted, but there was nothing more energising than a get-together.

Tina arrived with Naomi and Dougie, Poppy and Louis in tow.

"Hello, my lovelies!" Annie swooped in for cuddles. "Will Mike be able to join us, d'you think?"

"He's on his way. You know what the traffic can be like."

"Go through to the living room. Snacks on the side and balloons to play with. How high can you bop a balloon, Poppy?"

Poppy giggled. "Up to the ceiling!"

"You'd better practice and show me."

As the family went through, the doorbell rang again: Figgy, Rosamund, and Helen.

Annie glanced over her shoulder to make sure Tina was out of sight.

"Right, quickly!" She removed a raincoat from the rack by the door to reveal several carrier bags hanging from the hooks, bulging with gifts. "Take these. Two bags each."

"Crikey, Annie," said Helen. "We barely know Tina. Don't you think this looks excessive?"

"She asked me questions about Marco Callington. Won't this look like bribery?" Rosamund asked.

"All you need to do is go in there and shove these onto the gift table during the general hurly-burly. If you want to hang back till some other guests arrive, that's fine."

"No," said Helen. "I cannot wait another moment until I wrap my lips around a prosecco. You did mention prosecco?"

"Um. I'll find you some."

Helen led the others into the living room, exchanging greetings with Annie's family members.

Annie bustled through to the kitchen, indulging in some nanna-dancing as she passed Poppy and Louis.

"Hey, Dougie! Mind opening this for me?" She waved a bottle of prosecco.

Dougie followed her into the kitchen and opened the bottle.

She handed him a carrier bag. "Oh, Dougie, if you're going back in there, could you pop this on the gift table? Someone's left it in here."

Dougie looked briefly confused but did as he was asked.

Things were going well. Annie was about halfway through the bags of gifts, and Tina didn't suspect a thing.

CHAPTER FIFTY-TWO

The doorbell went again, Annie's cousin Gillian. She had been invited, but Annie hadn't actually expected her to show.

"Gillian! How nice to see you." They exchanged air kisses and she led Gillian through, picking up an extra bag of presents on the way and pushing them onto the table as if Gillian had brought them.

"Gillian's here, everybody!" she said, mainly for the benefit of Figgy, Helen, and Rosamund.

There were more arrivals after that, people from the police station that Annie only half recognised, and some others who might have been from a local playgroup. She surveyed the room, beaming.

Rosamund was talking with Gillian. *Good*. Rosamund wouldn't be cowed by Gillian's wealth and status. But was she investigating the murder or checking up on the value of her house?

Annie took the opportunity to drop a couple of extra bags onto the gift table. She'd put some of the larger items underneath, tied with a bow. They'd have to come from her, there was no getting away from that.

Figgy and Helen stood next to Tina, who sat in the carver chair from the dining table. Figgy gave Annie a discreet but urgent beckoning signal.

"Hello all!" Annie approached with a smile. "My actual family and my swimming family, all in the same room."

Helen turned to Annie, her face a picture of innocence. By Helen's standards, at least.

"Tina is involved in the investigation of Marco Callington's death," she said. "Fascinating job she has. She was explaining that they're looking for a van. It sounds distinctive enough that it ought to turn up sooner or later."

Rosamund and Gillian had turned at the sound of Helen's voice. The circle of people shuffled politely so they could join in.

Annie cleared her throat. "So, should we all be looking out for this van?"

"We're not asking the public to get involved," Tina said. "Last thing we want is to put someone in danger."

"Oh yes, of course." Annie and the other members of the Lyme Regis Women's Swimming Club avoided each other's gaze.

Tina smiled. "It's not a secret. The van we're looking for is a Transit style and at the centre front of the roof, just above the windshield, there's a rubber duck securing the radio aerial."

Annie frowned. "Is 'rubber duck' the name for a type of aerial? Like in the olden days, when people said things like 'breaker one nine rubber duck'? People did used to say things like that, didn't they?"

Tina gave her an *Oh, Mum* look. "No, Mum. It's an actual yellow rubber duck." She mimed the action of playing with a rubber duck in the bath. "Someone's used it to hold the aerial on, or maybe for decoration."

Annie nodded. "Well, that should be easy enough to spot."

CHAPTER FIFTY-THREE

Annie shuttled between the kitchen and the living room, making drinks and bringing through the remaining bags of gifts. She exhaled with relief.

She'd made teas and coffees for most. She handed the rest of the Prosecco bottle to Helen.

"Nanny?" asked Poppy, tugging at her arm.

Annie bent down to her granddaughter's level. "Yes, sweetheart?"

"Where do you keep bringing those bags from?"

Annie froze. How loud had Poppy been?

She pulled on a smile. "Oh, I've been helping other people with their bags, sweetheart. Most of the gifts on there are from the kind people who've come along to celebrate the new baby."

"You've brought a lot in from the kitchen."

"Kitchen," added Louis.

Naomi lifted Louis onto her lap. "Mum?"

Annie kept her gaze on Poppy. "You're very observant, Poppy. I hope you know how clever you are, young lady."

Tina cleared her throat. "Mum, it sounds like there's something underhand going on. Anything you'd like to share?"

Annie decided to brazen it out. "No." She met Tina's gaze.

Tina clenched her jaw. "I don't have the energy for this. Naomi, help me out, will you?"

Naomi stood up and went to the gift table. Annie's shoulders slumped.

Naomi lifted a bag. "Who brought this?"

Annie waved her hands. "Fine, fine! We don't have to do this. I'll admit I added a few extra gifts. You've got me bang to rights."

Naomi raised her eyebrows at Tina.

"I'll take it from here, Naomi, thanks," said Tina. "Let's take a different tack. If there's anyone in this room who has brought a gift for the baby, can you go get it and bring it to me here. I'll open it."

Annie's heart swelled as her swimming buddies went to the table and each lifted up two carrier bags. Naomi and a couple of others also picked up much smaller bags.

"Thank you, Helen," said Tina, as Helen dropped the bags at her feet. "Now, I don't want to appear suspicious or paranoid, but would you mind telling me what's in there? I'm testing a hypothesis."

Helen was a world-class bluffer. "Oh, Tina my dear," she said airily. "I will confess to you now that I went round to Solomon's shop and just asked him to wrap me up some age-appropriate gifts. You'll need to forgive me for being so very lazy. I wanted to show willing, but I genuinely have no clue about babies."

Annie could see that Rosamund and Figgy had their

hands inside their carrier bags, squeezing and prodding at whatever was wrapped up inside.

Tina smiled at Helen. She asked Rosamund the same question.

"Gosh," said Rosamund. "It's been a couple of weeks so my memory might not be entirely correct, but we have a board book, a little outfit and a toy."

Tina narrowed her eyes. "What kind of a toy?"

"A squishy one."

"In the shape of…?"

Annie had to step in. Her friends were being tormented for their loyalty. "Enough! It was all me. They're just being kind. Trying to cover for me."

Tina's face was stony. "I see." She looked up at Naomi and her nursery friends, standing in line and looking awkward. "I'll open the gifts from these people who actually bought them themselves, without playing games or trying to trick me. The others I'll leave here."

Annie felt herself crumple. "Oh, but there are some lovely things there, love! I just wanted to buy some stuff for the baby."

Tina sighed. "Mum, this is not 'some stuff'. I don't even know how to describe half of it, much less fit it all in my house. It's too much and you know it. I've run out of ways to be polite about this, so now I'm just going to say it. You need to back off. I'll be keeping my distance until you calm down. A lot."

Annie felt her eyes pricking. She felt humiliated. But worst of all was the prospect of seeing less of her family.

"Let's have a chat, eh?" she said. A room full of people had their eyes on her.

"I think I'm done with chat," said Tina. She levered

herself out of the chair just as the doorbell went. "I'm really hoping this is Mike and he can give me a lift."

"No worries if it isn't. You can come with us," said Naomi, as she ushered Dougie towards the door.

This was a disaster. "Are you leaving your *own* baby shower?" Annie asked.

Tina looked at her. Her face had softened a little; was there regret there? But then she pushed her shoulders back. "I believe I am."

Tina reached the door just behind Naomi and Dougie. Poppy looked back at Annie, but Tina ushered her forward.

"Hi everybody!" said Mike, smiling at them from the doorstep. "Did my best to get here on time but the traffic was... What's going on?" He looked from Tina to Naomi and Dougie and then to Annie.

"We're going back to Naomi's," said Tina. "I'll tell you what's happened on the way." She marched outside, taking Mike and Poppy with her.

Two minutes later they'd all gone, and Annie was forced to go back inside.

She glanced around the room. The swimming group were clustered together. The nursery group were gathering their bags and preparing to leave.

Annie's cousin Gillian stood up and stretched. "What a lively lot you all are. I should come round more often, it's like watching a soap opera."

"So very kind of you to come," Helen said, pulling herself up haughtily. "It looks as though you're about to leave. If you brought a gift for Tina's baby, would you like me to make sure it gets to her?"

Gillian looked briefly affronted by Helen's dig but then gave a small laugh. "No, I didn't bring a gift. Maybe I have

CHAPTER FIFTY-THREE

the gift of second sight, eh? The person who didn't bring a gift is looking like the smartest person in the room right now, aren't they?"

After Annie had shut the front door behind the nursery group and her cousin, her three swimming companions folded her into a group hug.

"That was tough, Annie," said Figgy.

"We're here for you," added Rosamund.

"Your cousin's a monster," said Helen. "But your daughters will come round."

"I don't know," said Annie. "I just don't know. I really think I've messed things up with them."

CHAPTER FIFTY-FOUR

Tina dropped into the comfiest wheeled office chair in the Lyme Regis police station and let out a sigh. She rubbed her chest. Heartburn. She'd never had heartburn before her first pregnancy. Now, anything seemed to set it off.

PC Wendy Sharman looked across at her. "It's Sunday. It's almost like you don't have a home to go to."

"Hey, Wendy. I'm... I'm finding everything annoying today."

"I'm sure you have your reasons."

"Especially my mum."

"Shame you can't arrest mums for being annoying."

"Yeah, a big shame." Tina reached out and flicked at some papers. "The DS here?"

"DS Strunk is out making enquiries."

"I see."

"Which is code for gone out for some fish and chips and a sulk at the sea front."

"He not happy either?"

"Frustrated. No closer to finding the killer."

CHAPTER FIFTY-FOUR

Tina picked up the piles on the desk. It looked like DS Strunk had been going through Marco's financial records. They had statements from what they believed were all of Marco's bank accounts. The shop accounts were dull. The only thing that leapt out at Tina was a number of cash deposits.

"People use bank cards round here, don't they?" she said.

Wendy pursed her lips and nodded. "Lyme Regis *has* recently moved into the twenty-first century."

"Is there any reason why Marco's fossil shop would be doing so many cash transactions?"

Wendy shrugged.

"Kids spending their pocket money on dinosaur toys?" Tina suggested.

"Reckon kids these days have their own cards or just use their parents'."

Tina nodded.

There was a lot of money coming in and out of the fossil shop account, and yet the shop itself had seemed anything but busy. Old stock on the shelves. Toys and books fading and yellowing in the sun.

"Are fossils big business?" she asked.

Another shrug from Wendy. "Maybe online. I reckon a lot of shops – you know, book shops, antique shops and so on – do most of their business online. The shop's more like a showroom."

She could be right, yet Marco was making money somehow and earning a chunk of that in cash. If he'd squirreled enough aside to put an offer in on Breaststrokes, then he must have been doing well. Tina thought of the fossil they'd found on the shop counter and the piece of paper it had been resting on.

She sorted through the papers on the desk until she found the folder of CSI photographs. She flicked through until she came to the image.

"'How much is this worth to you?'" she read out.

The fossil was a fake. A resin cast or something. It was worth nothing except as an ornament, but someone had written that note.

"Wendy?"

"Yes, Tina?"

"Have we still got all the evidence stored here?"

"Anything forensics haven't taken, or which they've already returned."

Tina held up the picture. "This fossil and the paper it's stood on. Have we got those?"

Wendy came over and peered more closely. "I can check."

"D'you mind?"

Wendy headed out of the door and to whatever cupboard they'd commandeered for evidence. Tina looked at the picture, stretched her aching back and tried to find a more comfortable position.

Her unborn child objected to the movement, twisting inside her and making her feel tight. She'd not had any Braxton Hicks or false contractions with Louis, but she knew that every pregnancy was different.

"You're not ready to come yet, are you, lovey?" she muttered.

She was only a week away from her due date. She liked to think she'd have some sort of pre-warning, beyond her waters breaking, but there was no knowing. Could it...?

The baby's movements subsided. Either it had found a more comfortable position, or it had given up trying.

CHAPTER FIFTY-FOUR

"Here," said Wendy, as she came back in. She placed two clear plastic evidence bags on Tina's desk.

The items were as she remembered. A big fake ammonite fossil in a lump of fake rock, and the piece of paper it had sat on.

How much is this worth to you?

It wasn't a sheet of printer paper or something torn from a notepad. It was thin, sheer and crinkly. She turned it over and looked at the printing on the reverse. There was a gold band and the beginning of some large words in a golden script.

Tina frowned, realising what it was. It was the paper used to wrap a block of ten or twenty cigarette packets. Not something she saw often, especially not these days. In the normal course of events, as soon as cigarettes hit the shops, the block would be unwrapped and the paper thrown away. But they had a crisp, smooth quality, and always made her think of Christmas wrapping paper.

She couldn't make out the brand from this ragged section, but that didn't change things.

She called DS Strunk.

"Hello," he said, his voice obscured. *Fish and chips.*

"I've had an idea, Sarge," she said.

"Yeah?"

"The 'How much is it worth to you' piece of paper."

"Huh?"

"The piece of paper on the counter in the shop..."

"Oh, yeah. Yeah. That." There was the sound of gusting wind and the faint call of gulls.

"It's from a cigarette wrapper. Not an individual one, but a big pack."

"Marco ran a fossil shop, not a cigarette shop."

"Yeah," she said. "So where did it come from?"

She remembered the Chinese import label they'd found in the untidy rear room. "Marco Callington imported goods," she said.

"Fake fossils and that," he agreed.

"Right. But what if fake fossils weren't the only dodgy thing he was importing?"

"OK..."

"What if the shop was basically a front and he was importing fake cigarettes, or smuggling them in? That would explain how he could make ends meet with – let's face it – a shop full of tat. Sure, he sold fossils, but maybe he was also importing black market cigarettes."

"Oh, I like this," said the DS, his voice more energised. "So the 'what's this worth to you' message..."

"Wasn't about the fossil. It was about the paper itself. It was a message."

"Someone knew that Marco had a dodgy import business and was threatening him?"

"Blackmail," said Tina.

The DS laughed.

"What?" she said.

"He withdrew five thousand in cash three days before he died."

"A pay-off for the blackmailer?"

"Oh. This sounds credible, and it gives us a motive. I'm going to the shop again, see if there's further evidence."

"I'll meet you there."

She ended the call and tried to propel herself out of the chair. Her body didn't really want to move anywhere. She grunted as she pushed herself upright.

"Sorry, bump," she said.

CHAPTER FIFTY-FIVE

ANNIE HAD SPENT all afternoon moping.

She'd moped as she tidied away the snacks and did the washing up. She'd moped as she put all the baby gifts back upstairs, wondering what on earth she was going to do with them. Then she'd made herself a cup of tea and sat by the window to concentrate on her moping.

A message from Helen appeared on the WhatsApp group around teatime.

Found some leftover booze from a launch we had last month. Any chance the three of you can come and help me tidy this lot away?

The message was accompanied by a picture showing Helen holding up several bottles of wine and pulling a funny face.

Annie smiled, cheered that her friends would do that for her.

I can be there within the hour. It's a dirty job but somebody's got to do it!

It felt good to close the door behind her and walk into town. To step away from the moping for a while.

When she got to the Cruickshank Gallery, Figgy and Rosamund were already there.

"You lot are lifesavers!" said Helen theatrically. "Honestly, I would have attempted to drink this all by myself and it would not have ended well."

"You can stop pretending now," said Annie. "The idea of leftover wine! Thank you for dragging me out of the house. I'm grateful."

"Let's get the real glasses out, shall we?" said Helen. "I'll pop upstairs and grab some. They're a bit nicer than the cheapo event ones. We have to assume that people will break things at events."

"People," said Figgy with a shudder. "By the way, I'm meeting Cameron later, but I told him I was coming here first."

"Good for you," said Annie. She looked at Rosamund, who gave her a kind smile.

Helen turned as she reached the stairs. "While I fetch the glasses, would the three of you be kind enough to pop out and see Harper? Not sure if she wants wine or a cup of tea. My money's on tea while she's working, but you never know. She might ask you to help her move the big sculpture she's working on. Needs a few pairs of hands."

"Yes, of course. Happy to help," said Annie.

Annie, Figgy and Rosamund went outside and looked across the yard area.

"It's so strange to think that Marco died here," said Rosamund. "We still don't really know what happened."

They all nodded and made their way to Harper's workshop. Annie knocked on the door.

CHAPTER FIFTY-FIVE

Harper opened up. There was an oily soot mark across her broad freckled face.

"Helen wants to know if you'd like a cup of tea or some wine," Annie said.

Harper produced her giant mug in response. "I reckon tea for now. Might join you in a wine once I get this thing stable."

She gestured towards a large piece of metalwork. Bits of it were rusty and other parts were a blueish colour from whatever Harper had done to them. Annie tried to work out what she was looking at.

"Is that a really massive dragonfly?" she asked.

"It is!" replied Harper.

"I can see garden tools in there," said Figgy, pointing.

"Yep," agreed Harper. "I got a load of old tools in an auction. Forks are good for feet. The wings are made from an old lawnmower."

"It's rather stunning," Annie said.

She could see the cutting cylinder from a lawnmower, which Harper's skill had turned into a dragonfly wing with only the faintest memory of a lawnmower.

"It must be tricky to hold everything in place while you're making something like this," said Rosamund.

"I have various clamps and anchor points that I use," Harper told her, pointing to the ceiling where a beam hung down, a few chains attached to it, "but I have to get creative sometimes. Helen was pestering me to clean up the yard so I'm using some stones from outside as supports."

Annie looked at the ends of the wings. They were tilted to join the body at a pleasing angle, and each one sat on top of a stone.

"Helen said you might want some help moving this?" she asked.

"If you're up for it. I'm ready to join the body onto the legs now, so I need a lift."

Harper handed them each a pair of gloves and positioned them around the sculpture. Then she asked them to lift carefully as she directed them.

"And down," she said. The body and wings were now perfectly positioned on the legs. "Thanks all."

"No problem," said Annie.

One of the stones in the pile in the corner caught Annie's eye. It wasn't really a stone, not in a conventional sense. It was a fossil, an ammonite as broad as her hand, embedded in a chunk of marble-like stone. She picked it up. It was heavy, like a bag of sugar.

"What's this, Harper?"

"What's what?" said Harper, without looking up. She was too busy adjusting her half-formed sculpture.

Figgy sidled over to Annie and looked down at the object. Annie gently lowered the fossil rock into her friend's outstretched hands, so she could feel its heft. As she did, it rolled over, revealing a dark reddish-brown stain on the reverse.

Figgy stared at Annie, eyes wide.

Annie gave Rosamund the same wide-eyed look and jerked her head towards the door.

"Back with your mug of tea in a minute!" she told Harper, her mouth dry.

Harper grunted, fixated on her work.

Outside, with the workshop door shut behind them, they looked at the rock still held in Figgy's hands.

"That's a blood stain," said Figgy. "Yeah?"

Rosamund goggled at the rock. "Where did that come from?"

"In there!" Annie hissed. "Just sat on the floor!"

"Let me see. Let me see." Rosamund pushed forward and scratched at the ruddy marks on the stone.

"Don't tamper with it!" said Figgy.

"Your fingerprints are all over it," Rosamund shot back. "Oh, God. That *is* blood. That's blood. This is..."

Annie nodded. "The murder weapon."

CHAPTER FIFTY-SIX

Annie saw Figgy's brow creasing as she tried to comprehend the fact of the murder weapon being right in front of them.

"Hang on. So, the murder weapon is here?"

"The fatal blow was struck here," said Rosamund.

"Wait." Figgy turned around on the spot. "*Here* here? Like..."

"Helen *did* want the shop next door," Annie pointed out.

Rosamund considered the space. "He was struck here. No. He can't have been. I came to see Helen earlier that morning."

Annie nodded. "He's attacked in his own back yard and then, when you come to visit Helen, he crawls out to your car—"

"Like a wounded cat," said Figgy.

"Like a person seeking help," said Annie. Her heart was pounding in her ears.

Figgy nodded. "And then we bring him back here in the car because we don't know what to do."

CHAPTER FIFTY-SIX

"But Helen was with us..."

Rosamund pointed silently to the workshop. "Harper's strong enough. She could..." She mimed hefting a body onto her shoulder.

"Oh my God," whispered Figgy.

They stared at each other in silence, the only sound Harper moving around inside the workshop.

Annie licked her lips. "There's only one thing for it," she said. "We need to confront her, and we need to do it right now." She rapped on the door to the gallery, even though it was open.

As she waited, she tried to tell her heart to just flippin' well slow down. It ignored her.

"What's the matter?" Helen asked, appearing in the doorway, wine glass in hand. She glanced down at the rock in Annie's hand. "Good grief, is that...? That's not the murder weapon, is it?"

"I don't know, Helen. Why don't you tell us?" Annie stared at her.

"Hmm? What?"

"Is it possible that you hid this in Harper's workshop so that the police wouldn't find it?"

Helen laughed. "Really? You're going to throw the accusation at me now?"

"We've found the murder weapon in your shed."

"Oh, stop being tiresome, Annie. You surely can't think that I killed that silly man?"

"You did want his shop," put in Figgy.

"And you were right here at the scene of the crime," added Rosamund.

Helen put her hands on her hips. "Think it through,

Annie. I was also with you when the killer moved the body, wasn't I? Come on, you don't seriously believe I did this?"

"Maybe you had help," said Figgy, pointing at the workshop.

Helen glared at her. "Don't you dare draw my Harper into this!"

"I hate to say this, Helen," Annie said, "but I know how good you are at lying when you're put on the spot. I saw it today when you pretended you'd bought those presents."

"Lying about presents is not the same as lying about murdering someone! And you're an ungrateful mare, considering I was attempting to get you off the hook for your frankly quite unhinged behaviour. I'm not surprised your daughters left like that."

"You're meant to be on my side!"

"You've just accused me of murder!"

"Oh, don't worry!" snapped Rosamund. "I've been accused of murder by you lot. It's about time it was someone else's turn."

"I'm not the one who had the stiff in their car!" said Helen.

"What's this about a stiff?" asked Harper, emerging from the workshop.

Annie was trying to formulate some sort of answer when there was a creak from the adjoining fence and a head appeared over the top. She couldn't remember his full name, but she recognised him as one of the police detectives – Nathan something.

"Did I hear someone mention accusations of murder?" he asked.

Annie was suddenly aware of the deadly rock she held in her hand. She shoved it behind her back.

CHAPTER FIFTY-SIX

"Is that my mum over there?" called Tina's voice from the other side of the fence.

"No," said Annie.

"I'm coming round."

There was a scraping and a click and a few seconds later, the back gate to Helen's yard opened. Tina stood there, her expression grim.

"What's that?" she asked, pointing at the fossil.

"It... it..." Annie didn't want to say it was the murder weapon. She didn't want any of this.

Tina took a step towards her. The yard suddenly felt very small. "I think someone had better bloody tell me what's been going on here."

Annie glanced at Figgy, Rosamund and Helen. They all had their eyes on her, as if she'd somehow get them out of this. "Well, I guess you could say that we've been trying to help you solve the case."

Tina's face was even stonier than when she'd walked out of the baby shower. Annie felt herself shrink.

"Can you summarise what it is you've been doing to help?" Tina asked.

Annie licked her lips. "I'd rather not say."

Tina's nostrils flared. She couldn't have looked more like an enraged bull if she'd pawed the ground.

She turned to her colleague. Annie felt herself breathe again.

"Sarge, I think we need to get this lot down to the station. In handcuffs if necessary."

CHAPTER FIFTY-SEVEN

Tina studied Rosamund Winters while the DS made the introductions for the benefit of the recording. She wasn't supposed to be there, maternity leave and all that, but there were no other members of CID around, and the DS had said he'd rather there were two of them present. She'd promised not to speak.

Rosamund held herself with a calm, formal poise. She was like a woman of substance sitting for a painter, chin held high, hands crossed on her lap. But Tina only had to look a little closer to see fear fizzing beneath that calm exterior.

"We spoke to you the other day," DS Strunk said to her. "You said you didn't know Marco Callington and had no real dealings with him. Would you like to give us a more honest version of events?"

Rosamund's jaw shifted but she didn't speak.

"Let's start with the fact that Marco Callington's body was in your car," he prompted. "Forensics officers are analysing it now. We may have to make a thorough investigation of your home."

CHAPTER FIFTY-SEVEN

"You don't need to," said Rosamund.

"Is your husband in if we pop round now?"

"No."

"Maybe we should contact him at work—"

"He's left me."

They waited for her to continue.

"Weeks ago now. He's run off with a... with a woman. A business associate. If you must know, he'd been having an affair with her for I don't know how long. And then, without discussing it with me, he left. He went on one of his business trips, and he hasn't come back. Didn't even give us a chance to discuss it like adults."

Tina nodded.

"He stopped paying the bills, stopped paying into the housekeeping. He did all the bills. It's his login for all the accounts. He's left me alone but it's only him who can log into the smart hub and the security cameras. The smart hub speaker in the kitchen kept playing his Spotify playlist, at random intervals. Do you like rap metal?"

"Not sure I know what rap metal is," said the DS.

"I had to unplug the thing," said Rosamund. "He's gone but his presence is still there in the house."

She paused, her hands very still on the table between them. Tina heard the faint shriek of a gull outside.

"I didn't lie to you," Rosamund said softly. "I only knew Marco Callington from that one evening at the bar. Everything I told you was true. Had I gone there alone for a drink? Yes. It was a sort of bet with myself. If *he* could go off and enjoy a new life then maybe I could, too. Maybe some bit of me would have liked the idea of meeting another man there, to prove that I could still do it."

She sniffed. Tina listened, unsure if this was relevant.

"Twenty years, David and I had been together. Twenty years with just one man and he'd made a mockery of it, just like that. I did want to prove to him that he wasn't the only one who could move on. But I wasn't looking for anyone, not really. I certainly wasn't looking for Marco Callington."

The DS leaned forward. "We heard you talking with the others. Marco's corpse had been in your car."

"I was more surprised by that than anyone. I had no idea. He was *not* in my car that morning. I didn't see him when I went down to the front for a swim and then…" She pointed to her leg under the table. "I hurt myself. I was given a lift to the medical centre. And I gave my car keys to Annie so she could move it." She scoffed, and Tina could see anger there, alongside the fear. "What kind of murderer would give someone the keys to her car knowing full well there was a dead man sitting in the front seat?"

"But he must have got there somehow," said the DS. "And no one else had access to your car that morning, except you."

"Ah, well, we have a theory about that. A possible theory. Annie and Figgy would be able to tell you more about that."

"You tell us."

"If I must."

CHAPTER FIFTY-EIGHT

THERE WAS a part of Figgy that was utterly terrified by the enormity of the trouble she was in.

She wasn't a lawbreaker. Maybe she'd downloaded some gaming software that she'd not exactly paid full price for, but that was as far as it went. Her parents, and then her gran, had instilled in her an absolute respect for law and order and for authority figures. She'd been a timid and compliant teenager and had never contemplated doing anything that might draw the attention of the police.

This situation, right now, sitting across from two police detectives in an actual police interview room, like on TV, was her worst nightmare.

But despite herself, she couldn't help feeling excited.

She was in an actual police interview room! Like on TV!

She was already wondering if she'd get to appear in court and stand in the dock. How would she hold up under questioning? What would she say?

And prison! There was a mad part of her that wanted to know what that would be like. Horrible and scary obviously, full of dangerous thugs. And yet Figgy found herself fantasising about how she'd fit into prison life.

She tried to control these thoughts as she looked from the younger pregnant detective to the older male detective.

"My therapist told me I should get out and meet new people," she heard herself say.

The male detective, DS Strunk, he'd said, scratched his chin. "You were telling us about how you think Marco Callington got into Ms Winters' car."

"Oh, yes," she said. "So, we think it all happened at the shop or round the back of the shops, right? That was where Rosamund stopped before she went swimming. She was selling some art back to Helen who runs the gallery. Rosamund's husband has left her, and she needed the money, so she carried this big painting into the back of the art shop. She didn't have any hands free to shut the boot, so she left it open, and we think Marco, already injured and bleeding, crawled into the back of her car."

She took a breath. Was she garbling? The female detective wasn't speaking. DC Abbott, she'd said. She was huge. And she was Annie's daughter, Figgy reminded herself. She blushed at the thought of the baby shower.

Focus.

"It's got a massive boot," she continued. "Marco was hurt. Maybe he was looking for help." She shrugged. "He might have been delirious. I'm guessing getting whacked on the head might do that."

"You say whacked on the head," said DS Strunk. "How do you know he was hit on the head?"

Wasn't that obvious? "We saw the injury when we went to move the car. There was a lot of blood. And I guess, when we found him, he might have just died, right before. The blood was still, er, sticky. So, he climbed in the car, Rosamund came back and closed the door, drove down to the beach and... yeah, that would be it."

"The post-mortem shows that there was some inflammation around his eyes," said Strunk. "A chemical reaction. Did you notice that when you saw him? Did you do anything to make that happen?"

Figgy shook her head. "I don't think I got a proper look at his face."

"But you initially said he was in the front of the car when you found him."

Figgy nodded. "We think – that's all of us – we think he'd been lying in the back, maybe unconscious. We think that with the last of his strength, he crawled through to the front. But I didn't want to look at him. I'm a bit squeamish."

DS Strunk consulted his notes. "Helen Cruickshank tells us you did not then put him in the wheelie bin."

"That's correct. We went to take him home and then – just like that – he vanished from the car."

"Are you saying he just got out and put himself in the wheelie bin?"

Figgy stroked her chin. "I thought about that. We were definitely certain he was dead when we found him. And I've been thinking over that since, and I'm worried we got it wrong, and he was alive all along."

"And?"

She shook her head. He hadn't been alive. "He was dead. Definitely dead."

"But he was somehow magically transported from the car to the wheelie bin."

"Glitch in the Matrix?" suggested Figgy and immediately wished she hadn't.

The male detective gave her a penetrating stare. "Are you being flippant, Miss Edmunds?"

"Yes. I mean, no. I mean it's kind of likely we're living in a computer simulation and all that. But I'm not being flippant. Or mad. The moving body thing is a real mystery, isn't it?"

CHAPTER FIFTY-NINE

ANNIE WAS next in the interview room.

She sat at the table opposite DS Strunk, Tina beside him. Tina wasn't making eye contact. She sat back in her chair, arms crossed, fury all over her face.

The DS leaned forward. "So, Mrs Abbott."

"Oh, Annie," she said. "Call me Annie." She glanced at Tina. "Everyone does, don't they love?"

Tina looked down. Annie felt her shoulders droop.

"Annie," said the DS. "Tell me everything you know."

"About... about Marco?"

Tina sighed.

"Yes," said the DS. "About Marco."

Annie knew she should say as little as possible to try to recover the situation. But the truth was she was proud of how much their little group had managed to find out. The police would need to be told everything sooner or later. She sighed and counted off the main points on her fingers.

"We found Marco's body in Rosamund's car after swimming. We've got ideas about how he came to be there; we did a reconstruction and reviewed the CCTV footage. But after we realised it wasn't Rosamund's husband, we took him back to, erm, to put him in his own shop. That was when he was moved. Not by us. By someone else."

Annie took a breath, running over the events in her mind. She had to admit, when she heard it out loud, it didn't make much sense.

"We thought Rosamund had killed him for a while," she continued. "We staked out her house and Figgy dated her son to ask him questions, but we think she's innocent, even though we found out that she argued with Marco in a bar." She took a breath and glanced at Tina.

No change in her girl's furious expression.

"We found out Marco was trying to buy Breaststrokes bar," Annie continued, "competing with cousin Gillian, so *she's* definitely a person of interest in your investigation." She looked at the DS. "Shouldn't you be writing this down?"

He said nothing.

"Finish your story, mum," said Tina in a tight, icy voice. DS Strunk shot her a look.

Annie narrowed her eyes. *So Tina's been told to keep quiet*. She wasn't supposed to be working, right now. She should be at home, with her feet up in front of the TV. She looked uncomfortable in that hard-backed chair.

"Um," she began. "We got to thinking about how Marco had cigarettes on him when he was a vape smoker, so we were on the trail of the brand. Furongwang." She made a writing gesture at the sergeant, but nobody was writing anything down. She sighed. "They're knock-off cigarettes. No health warning labels on them, you see. We didn't find out where they come from, but we did discover that someone else in town has been asking about those cigarettes, too."

CHAPTER FIFTY-NINE

"Who?" asked DS Strunk.

She shrugged. "We don't know."

He nodded slowly. "That matches with everything your friends have said."

"Well, it would," she replied, "because it's the truth."

He laced his fingers together on the table. "Here's the thing, Mrs Abbott. A man has died. Murdered. A violent death and a town in shock. The police do their best to investigate these things but, because of your... antics, vital clues have probably been lost. At the very best, you've created delays in our investigation. There is a strong chance that your actions from the very start have enabled the killer to escape justice."

Annie looked from him to Tina. Why had she allowed all this to happen? "Yes, I can... see that, detective. We didn't mean to—"

Tina thumped her hand on the table, stood up and stormed out of the room as fast as a heavily pregnant woman could storm. The door slammed behind her.

"Detective Constable Abbott has left the room," said DS Strunk, for the benefit of the recording.

"I should go after her," Annie said.

"Listen to me, Mrs Abbott. Are you aware there is a criminal offence of perverting the course of justice?"

"I think I've heard it on a telly programme."

He grunted. "I will consult with the DI and possibly even the detective superintendent, and we'll decide whether to ask the Crown Prosecution Service to consider bringing charges against you. That could mean a two-year prison sentence. Up to seven if the judge thinks you did it deliberately and it prevents us finding the actual killer."

Seven years. Annie gulped.

"You have done a reckless and foolish thing here, Mrs Abbott," he said. "Even more reckless given that your own daughter..." he laughed bitterly "...and both your sons-in-law are serving police officers. DC Abbott's credibility as an investigating officer will certainly be called into question if the murderer ever goes to trial."

That was the worst thing of all. "I am sorry."

"Sorry doesn't make a difference," he replied. "Now, you've not been arrested, so you and your friends are free to go. But, if the police do decide to charge you, you will be arrested and brought back here. Understood?"

"Very much so," she said, her voice thin.

He escorted Annie out to the reception where Figgy, Helen and Rosamund waited. They stood to greet her as she came out. She tried to smile.

Dougie was at the reception desk. She approached cautiously.

"Dougie, is Tina about?"

Dougie looked up. "Oh, Annie. I don't think that'd be a good idea, do you?"

"I just wanted to say—"

He raised an eyebrow. She stopped speaking.

"What Tina said to me," he told her, "was that you were a liability, a loose cannon and an embarrassment of a mother." He glanced down. "Her words. Not mine."

Annie felt the words strike her. She tried to find something to say but had nothing. Dougie continued.

"I love you, Annie. I do," he said. "We all do. But as a mum and a grandma you, well... This thing you do, this thing you think is being a kooky grandma—"

"I'm not kooky."

"Kooky, zany, wacky. This unpredictable but smothering

CHAPTER FIFTY-NINE

behaviour. Whatever it is. It's going to drive a wedge between you and your daughters. You need to stop and reflect."

She pulled a face. Annie wasn't used to her son-in-law being so direct.

"Naomi suggested that maybe you haven't got over the death of her dad," he continued. "I dunno. I think... I think perhaps you need to grow up a bit."

Annie felt her mouth fall open. Dougie, looking sheepish to his credit, gestured to the door with the pen in his hand.

"You're all free to go," he said, and returned to the paperwork in front of him.

CHAPTER SIXTY

Annie, Figgy, Helen and Rosamund walked across the car park. They'd all be taking different routes home from here, and it felt to Annie like part of her world was being stripped away.

She wanted to pull them all in for a hug, but in the current sombre mood it felt like the wrong thing. And she didn't have the energy.

"It's been a strange day," she said. *Understatement*.

"Yes." Rosamund tightened her cardigan around her. Annie wondered how Rosamund made a boring thing like a cardigan look as dramatic as a cloak. It was the way she tugged it and looked into the middle distance. Like Meryl Streep.

"Dreadful." Helen scowled. "What absolute idiots."

Was Helen talking about the police? Themselves? Annie?

Figgy said nothing, but looked like she might cry.

"I guess we're all heading home," Annie said. "I'll see you for swimming in the morning?"

CHAPTER SIXTY

Silence.

"Bye then." She croaked the words as they all set off.

She walked home. Her mind was a whirl of emotions, crowding out the practical things that normally made up her thoughts. She arrived at her door with no idea how she'd got there.

She unlocked the door and went inside. The house was still in disarray from the baby shower, and every room contained a reminder of her own stupidity. She picked up a balloon that had drifted into a corner and held it for a moment, cradling it like an infant. There would soon be a new grandchild, and she'd messed up her chances of spending quality Nana time with all of her grandchildren. She rocked the balloon. Annie Abbott didn't do tears.

She carried the balloon baby through the house, jigging it as she walked. It was uncomfortable and ugly to be confronted by all these emotions, but she needed to let them in.

She came to the room where she'd put all the gifts for the new baby, looking at them afresh. She no longer felt the same excitement as she had when she'd bought them, a tiny, future bonding moment with a new member of the family. Instead she saw the desperation of a woman who hadn't properly come to terms with living on her own.

She walked over to the pile, pulled out a plush unicorn toy and held it to her cheek, squeezing a small grain of comfort from its touch. She took it into her bedroom and lay down on the bed, still clutching it to her face. She lay for a long time with the unicorn plushie, and eventually, at some point, she realised that she was crying freely.

CHAPTER SIXTY-ONE

ANNIE WOKE with the morning light streaming through her window. She hadn't drawn the curtains. She'd fallen asleep from emotional exhaustion the night before.

She lifted her head and touched her face. The imprint of a plushie unicorn marked her cheek.

"Well, you were good company last night." She put the unicorn on her pillow. "You need a name. I shall call you Rodney. Thanks, friend. You helped me through a dark time, and I'm grateful."

She levered herself off the bed without looking at the clock. She'd been there a long time, but maybe that was what she'd needed.

"Do you know what today's going to be, Rodney?" she asked. "Today's going to be the day I find creative and useful things to do with all those baby gifts. I behaved badly, but I can make amends, can't I?"

Rodney the soft toy had no reply. *Perfect.* Annie had made up her mind.

CHAPTER SIXTY-ONE

She ate some breakfast, keeping an eye on the WhatsApp group. There was nothing from Helen, Rosamund or Figgy.

On a piece of paper, she listed ideas for some of the gifts. *Sell, Donate, Keep, Re-use.*

The categories seemed sensible, but she needed more detail. She could sell some of the bigger things, so she decided to tackle those first. She made listings in the local forums for the crib, rocking horse and the huge fancy buggy. She specified that the money was going to charity. That felt important.

"Hey, Rodney!" she called upstairs. "I think we're in business."

Annie searched for the details of the nursery Tina and Naomi had mentioned. Little Stars. She rang and asked if they'd like some donations. They seemed keen to come and take a look and not surprised by her call. Yesterday's meltdown had clearly been thoroughly circulated on the local gossip channels. Hardly surprising.

She arranged for them to visit later, when they could choose what they wanted to take. As she sat with another cup of tea, she dared to think she was getting on top of things.

She sent a message to her swimming buddies.

Thinking of you all. I'm trying to be a better person, starting today.

No response. Annie sighed. What if they all blanked her?

But then the dots started bouncing. Helen was messaging.

You big old drama queen, you! Don't be too much better or you'll lose everything that's fun about you.

Annie laughed.

Rosamund joined in.

It's certainly true that you make life more interesting, Annie. I missed swimming today.

Annie raised her eyebrows. For Rosamund, that was a big overture.

It took several minutes for Figgy to reply.

I'm getting better at navigating change and dealing with setbacks. It seems a life without those things is quite dull. I haven't found a way around all of them YET (my therapist tells me I must use the word yet when I say I can't do something). You're part of my life now, Annie. There's a lot about you that inspires me.

"Well." Annie walked around the house repeating the word to herself. There was genuine warmth in the messages, and she felt overwhelmed.

She inhaled deeply and looked at them again. If the women of the swimming club could find it in their hearts to forgive her, then surely she could find her way back into the affections of her two daughters?

The doorbell rang. Time to see what could be donated to the nursery. She put on her game face and went to answer the door.

A few hours later, Annie had made progress in clearing the baby gifts. She raised a cup of tea in a silent toast to her efforts and looked at what remained.

She went back to the WhatsApp group and shared a before and after photo of the pile with the swimming group.

Thought you might like to see how far I've got in moving on these presents. Only a few items left.

One thing I don't think I should sell is this vintage seesaw (yes, I know!). I think it might be decorated with lead paint. Helen, do you think Harper might be able to use it in one of her art pieces?

A few minutes later there were some smiley faces, and Helen replied.

I asked her and she says she can definitely use that. You've done a great job there, my dear. Are we all swimming in the morning?

Annie felt lighter. Almost light enough to float away. Her friends were there for her.

CHAPTER SIXTY-TWO

FIGGY DID her best to enjoy her morning swim.

She was glad the business with the police hadn't destroyed the Lyme Regis Women's Swimming Club. Morning swimming was an ongoing thing at the beach, but it was only by Friday that she felt confident Annie, Rosamund and Helen had settled back into their own patterns.

Annie and Helen were bobbing on the waves fifty meters out with a semi-regular swimmer called Tammy or Pammy. Rosamund, her foot healed now, was engaged in an informal swimming race to the buoys with the much younger Juniper. A few older women did little more than get in, get wet to their shoulders, and come out again. And that was fine. There was no judgment here.

Figgy went into the sea, swam the requisite fifteen minutes she enforced upon herself while trying not to think about sharks and crocodiles and monstrous octopuses, then stepped out to get dry. She looked enviously at the dry robes Annie and others had waiting for them. They were fifty, sixty quid minimum online.

Maybe she could save up for one. She needed a new job if she was going to start being extravagant.

She dried off and did the towel shuffle, swapping her cossie for clothes without embarrassing herself. The others were still out at sea, so she grabbed her bag and strolled along to the Kiosk. She'd get herself a drink or even an ice cream and then come back to meet them.

There was no queue. It might be warming up to be an ideal beach day, but it was still early, and it was a weekday.

Cameron grinned as he saw her. "The usual?"

"Actually, just a mocha," she said. "I might come back for an ice cream in a bit."

"Right you are." He pressed buttons on the complicated coffee machine. "I enjoyed the other day. You know, tea and cake."

"Me, too." She smiled. "We ought to plan that big breakout."

"Pardon?"

"Breakout," she said. "It was something you mentioned. You know, wild camping on Exmoor or—"

"McDonald's in Dorchester. Right." He smiled as he passed her mochaccino over.

She paid and walked off. She'd not gone a dozen yards before she heard footsteps behind her and turned. Cameron was there, having come out from behind the Kiosk.

"I have to ask," he said.

She frowned. "Have to ask?"

He wrung his hands together. Figgy had seen his mum do that. "You and me. Tea and cake."

"Yes?"

"Something my mum said." He pressed his lips together, uneasy. "You thought my mum had killed that man."

"I didn't."

"You and the..." He flung an arm out. "Batty swimming crew. You thought she'd done it, right?"

"The body was in the front of her car."

"And then you asked me out. Like, you've been buying ice cream from me for months and then you decided to ask me out and you were full of questions."

She felt her stomach sink.

"I didn't do it because of that. I've..." She hesitated; her cheeks hot. "I've wanted to ask you out for, like, ages. You're..." She smiled. "I like you."

"Right. I mean, thanks. I like you, too. So you didn't ask me out because you wanted to grill me about my mum, the potential murderer?"

"No, I..." She hesitated. *Damn.* Why did she hesitate? "OK, so Annie did suggest I have a word with you, but I honestly—"

"Oh, I see," he said, crestfallen.

"No, no, no. Not 'I see'. I really wanted to ask you out. And I'm really glad I did."

"But you did it because you were being Scooby Doo."

"Velma," she heard herself say.

"Hmmm." He frowned. "Lot to think about there."

He turned away.

"I like you!" she shouted after him.

"Oh, I like you, too," he replied, and went back to work.

Figgy trudged back along the promenade, the warm cup of coffee in her hand. She didn't want it now. She felt like she'd betrayed Cameron, betrayed their little relationship before it had really got off the ground. And the worst bit was that Cameron clearly thought the whole thing between them had been a lie.

CHAPTER SIXTY-TWO

But it wasn't. It wasn't a lie at all. Every word, every emotion she'd expressed towards him had been genuine. That was what felt so unfair.

As she neared the stone sea wall, where Annie and some of the others were now drying themselves off, there was the slapping of running footsteps behind her. She turned, half-hoping, dreaming, that it was Cameron rushing up to tell her that none of what had gone before had mattered, that he was into her the same way she was into him, and he was going to sweep her off her feet, into his arms, and...

It wasn't Cameron.

It was a tanned guy in a surfer T-shirt with blond highlights in his hair. Tez, the toilet roll guy from Breaststrokes.

"Ah, it's you," he said.

"It usually is," she replied, too disappointed to think of anything sensible to say.

"I did what I said I would," said Tez.

"Yes?"

He ran a hand through his long scruffy hair. "Kept my ear to the ground."

"And did you hear anything?"

"Yeah. Tell your mates there's a feller who sells cigarettes out the back of his van up by the building site on Haye Lane."

"At the building site? Right now?"

"That's his spot, can't say he'll be there right now though" said Tez. He backed off, giving two thumbs up. "Tell your mates. Job's done. Tez always delivers."

Figgy watched him go then hurried to Annie and the others, who were in various stages of dried or changed.

"The building site on Haye Lane," she said.

"What's that?" asked Helen.

"I just bumped into Tez."

"Do we know a Tez?"

"Toilet Tez from Breaststrokes. The one we gave ten quid to. He says the person dealing in dodgy cigarettes is based out of the building site on Haye Lane."

"Hey, we're not doing that anymore," said Rosamund. "Are we? We're officially off the murder case, right?"

"Like we handed in our badges and guns?" said Figgy.

"You know what I mean. We're in enough trouble as it is."

"I didn't say we should do anything about it. Tez told me. I'm telling you."

"Will the police arrest us again if they find us snooping?" Helen asked.

"Well, we're not officially investigating the murder," said Figgy. "We're investigating illegally smuggled cigarettes. Whole different thing, isn't it?"

Helen looked at Annie. "What do you reckon, Annie?"

Annie puffed out her chest and let out a slow hum. "I'd say we should stay clear..."

"There you go," said Rosamund.

"But—"

"There doesn't have to be a but!" said Rosamund.

Annie frowned. "But the Haye Lane building development. That's the one owned by my cousin, Gillian."

"Ooh," said Helen.

Figgy let that sink in. A dead man, feuding with Gillian Hewish over the Breaststrokes bar. And now the dodgy cigarettes found on his body were being sold from work.

"Maybe we should take a look," she said.

Annie chewed her bottom lip. She'd perked up. "Just a little look," she said. "Couldn't hurt."

CHAPTER SIXTY-THREE

THE NEW HOUSING estate was situated in the wide green area between Haye Lane, Roman Road and the River Lim. It was a decent distance from the sea front. Annie decided to go home, get her car and pick up the others on the way.

"First chance for you to try a stakeout," Helen said to Rosamund as they picked her up last.

"Just to be clear," said Rosamund, "I'm not involved in any further investigations into the murder. I do *not* want to be sent to prison for perverting the course of justice. Can you imagine me in prison?"

"I think you could be top dog," Figgy said.

"Really?"

"Yeah. Like queen bitch of some white supremacist prison gang."

"White sup..." Rosamund drew back, brow furrowed. "I don't have a racist bone in my body, Figgy! I swear."

"I didn't mean that!" said Figgy. "It was probably just the blonde hair."

"Oh. Oh, OK."

"I think you'd look good with prison tattoos," Helen assured Rosamund, patting her hand.

"Oh. It's tattoos now, too, is it?"

"I bet you've got tattoos, haven't you, Helen?" Annie said, trying to change the subject.

"I think we'd have seen," commented Rosamund.

Helen winked. "You don't know where I've got them."

Figgy laughed. "We should all get matching tattoos."

"Matching?" Helen said.

"The LRWSC. In a little logo."

"LR...? Ah, the swimming club."

"We're not a club," Annie grunted.

"Soon to become the Holloway Prison Women's Jogging Club," said Rosamund.

Haye Lane was narrow and winding, and had been widened in parts to allow construction vehicles to come down from Lyme Road. Annie indicated and turned into the new road that led to the housing estate. Roads in various stages of completion branched off, surrounded by plots of land and houses also in various stages of completion. Partway down was an expensive looking Portakabin office with a row of flagpoles outside, from which flew Hewish Homes flags. A show home stood alone, grass slowly coming through in the patchy lawn.

There was a loud honk and Annie glanced in her rearview mirror to see a yellow dumper truck. She pulled over onto an area of muddy ground and pulled on the handbrake.

"Now what?" said Rosamund.

"Now we..." Annie shrugged and turned off the ignition. "We wait and see if the man with the dodgy cigarettes shows up."

CHAPTER SIXTY-THREE

They sat and looked at the vehicles, the people in hard hats and luminous jackets going about their business.

After five minutes, Figgy said, "I spy with my little eye something—"

"Is it a man selling dodgy cigarettes?" Helen asked.

"No."

Helen shook her head, tutting. "We need to stay focused."

Figgy nodded. After a pause, she said, "It was a squirrel, actually."

Annie grinned at her. "Good one, Figgy."

"What I don't understand," said Rosamund, "is why an extraordinarily successful businesswoman like Gillian Hewish—"

"Destroyer of green spaces around Lyme," put in Helen.

"Yes."

"And the main reason why locals can't afford to live in their own town," added Annie.

"That, too. But I don't understand why a captain of industry like Gillian Hewish would be involved in something as petty as dodgy cigarettes. It sounds like a step down."

"Two point eight billion pounds," Figgy said.

"Pardon?"

Figgy waved her phone. "I looked it up. The amount of money lost to the government through illicitly imported cigarettes. That's money going straight into the pockets of criminals. Two point eight billion last year."

"Blimey," Rosamund said.

"A lot of it's used to finance weapons, drug smuggling and people trafficking."

The four of them gazed blankly as they tried to comprehend the numbers.

"Do you think your cousin Gillian is doing people trafficking and that?" Helen asked Annie.

Annie was stumped. It was a ridiculous idea, but everything she knew about Gillian... her cousin would do anything if it made business sense.

"All these construction vehicles coming in and out," said Rosamund. "Gillian will have suppliers on the other side of the channel. If she wanted to make money off illegal cigarettes, she's already got a supply network set up."

"But how does Marco Callington fit into that?" asked Figgy.

"He's just buying his own dodgy cigarettes from her, isn't he?" suggested Helen.

Rosamund didn't look convinced. "But he vapes rather than smokes."

"Maybe he was in competition with her," said Helen.

Annie liked that. "Oh, rivals for the café bar but also rivals in the cigarette business."

"A David to her Goliath," Helen said.

"A motive for her to kill him," added Figgy.

There was a sharp rap at Annie's window which made them all jump. How had they managed to be snuck up on by a man in a hi-vis jacket? It wasn't like he'd even tried to sneak.

Clutching her pounding chest, Annie lowered the window.

"Hello," he said, removing his hard hat. "Ms Hewish asks if you'd care to join her in the reception suite." He indicated the posh Portakabin. "She asked me to tell you there's complimentary coffee and biscuits."

CHAPTER SIXTY-FOUR

THERE WAS INDEED coffee and biscuits in the reception suite.

A seating area composed mostly of leather and steel tubing had been arranged around a fake fire on the wall. There was even a sheepskin rug on the floor.

Gillian Hewish reclined on a seat, sipping coffee from a tiny cup.

"Ah, the intrepid women of Lyme Regis," she said as they entered. "Come. Have a seat. Timpson here is making the drinks."

The man, who looked more like a site engineer than a barista, took off his hi-vis jacket and hard hat and moved over to the coffee machine.

Gillian smiled. She had good teeth, Annie noticed. White, but not too white. Straight but not weird straight like an American actor. Annie could imagine she enjoyed the services of the very best dentists.

She checked herself. *Stop looking for things to dislike about Gillian.* She didn't have to. The woman's business practices and attitudes to Lyme were more than enough to condemn her.

"I assume this is some sort of WI exploratory visit," Gillian said. "Touring round local businesses."

"We're not in the WI," Rosamund responded, as the four of them sat down on two sofas.

"Shame." Gillian waved a hand across at them. "You've got a real cross-section of society going on here." Her hand paused as it gestured at Figgy. "Tapping into the millennial Gen-Z market. That's important these days, I hear." She smiled at Figgy. "If you're looking for a new home, we've got some great one-bedroom help-to-buy properties with a forty-year mortgage."

"I already have a home," Figgy said, her lips thin.

"Good for you!"

Timpson put two coffees in tiny saucers on the table in front of them and went back to make two more.

"If you wanted to speak to me, you could have waited until this evening," said Gillian. "The grand re-opening of Breaststrokes café bar. Under new ownership. You are coming, yes?"

"We hadn't planned to," Helen said.

"Complimentary drinks. And I'd love to have a chat with your little friend, Harper, about getting a piece of dramatic art installed out front. I'm thinking a statue of a swimmer, made from old anchors or something. Whatever. I'm not an art person. It's the impact that matters."

"Girlfriend," said Helen.

"Sorry. Girlfriend. I'm not up to date on everyone's relationship status."

"We know about the cigarettes," said Figgy.

CHAPTER SIXTY-FOUR

Annie felt her mouth fall open. She'd been planning on leading up to that subject gradually.

Gillian's smile froze. "Cigarettes?"

Figgy held her gaze. "Two point eight billion pounds."

"OK. Are we just talking in random non-sequiturs now?"

"I'm talking about the illegal cigarettes you're importing into the country," Figgy said.

The look of confusion on Gillian's face seemed genuine.

"We have evidence," said Helen. "We have it on good authority, well, some authority, that illegal cigarettes are being moved through your business. Right here."

Gillian looked at Timpson. Timpson straightened up from delivering the second set of coffees.

"Are they referring to...?" he said.

"I think they are." Gillian composed her expression. "I'm really not sure what this is about, ladies, or if it's any of your business at all, but yes, I am aware that a dirty little oik was selling counterfeit cigarettes from the back of his van on the very spot where you yourselves recently parked."

"Sounds convenient," Figgy said.

"It was a nuisance," Gillian replied. "Pestering our workers. Harassing honest folk on their way to work."

Rosamund had an eyebrow arched so high Annie was worried it might merge with her hair. "So you reported him to the police?"

"We threatened to, and then the blue-haired lout realised he was skating close to danger and drove off."

"Never saw him again," agreed Timpson.

Annie watched her cousin, thinking. It did all sound very convenient. But that was the thing with the truth, it could be convenient or inconvenient. And, annoyingly, she reckoned Gillian was being honest.

Irritated, she reached forward for her coffee and felt her phone buzz. It was Tina. She answered, her mouth drying.

"Hi, Tina."

Was this Tina her daughter, or Tina the investigating officer, the detective who would take a dim view of her mum poking her nose into criminal affairs again?

"Mum?" Tina sounded breathless.

Annie felt the tension leave her, replaced by concern. "You all right, love?"

"Baby's coming," Tina panted.

"Oh. Oh, my."

"I need you to come over here."

Annie swallowed. "Of course. You at Naomi's?"

"Will be... Dougie's driving me there to collect the baby bag."

"OK. OK. I'm on my way."

She stood up and was already moving when she realised that the others were looking at her.

"The baby's coming! I've got to go!"

"We'll walk back," said Helen.

"Yes, I believe we're done here," said Gillian.

"Congratulations," added Timpson.

Annie ran out. It was a ten-minute drive to Naomi's, which she managed in six. She was careful to drive within the speed limit, but her usual generosity towards other road users had gone.

She emerged from her car to find a police car out front and Tina waiting at the door, a bag in her hand, doing breathing exercises.

"Do you need me to drive you?" Annie asked.

"No. Dougie and Naomi are doing that. I'm going to

need you to look after Louis and then collect Poppy from school, please, Mum."

Annie didn't hesitate. "Yes, of course." She checked the time. "I can pop and get Poppy in a short while."

Tina nodded, then her focus went inwards as she breathed into a contraction.

"Oh darling! You're doing so well. I know you've got this."

"Thanks, Mum," said Tina when she was through the worst of it. "They're coming quite fast now. We do need to be off soon."

"What about Mike?" asked Annie.

"Meeting us at the hospital in Dorchester. It's all..." She stopped as she struggled. "It's all in order."

Naomi and Dougie came out of the house. Dougie, still in his uniform, helped Tina to the police car. A crying Louis, confused and upset by the commotion, was scooped up into Annie's arms.

"Let's wave them off," she said to him, jiggling his hand in a farewell wave as Dougie circled round in the cul-de-sac and drove away.

Annie's two girls and another grandchild, as yet unborn, were in that car. She swallowed down her anxiety.

"Right, my little man," said Annie. "Let's take a walk around the garden. We should inspect the flowers, see if any new ones have emerged. We also need to see if there are any interesting insects to be found. After we've done that, it will be time to go and get Poppy from school. What do you think?"

CHAPTER SIXTY-FIVE

Figgy said farewell to Rosamund at the top of the Holmbush car park and walked down through the gardens to her caravan. The route was easier and less spooky in daylight.

The Jane Austen Gardens path met the promenade not far from Breaststrokes café bar. As Figgy walked past, she saw balloons and banners being hung for the evening's grand re-opening.

The fact that she was giving serious consideration to actually going along was testament to the changes she'd made over the past few weeks. She knew she wasn't going to go. That was certain. But if she cast her mind back only a month or so, she saw a Figgy Edmunds who only left her caravan to go to the shops and doctor's appointments.

At a couple of spots along the prom, someone had tied signs to the railings. The signs, laminated and stuck to cardboard, read *'Poop and run is a crime!'* Below the text were pasted-in Google images of a dog waste bin and a rather contrite-looking terrier.

CHAPTER SIXTY-FIVE

Figgy shook her head. This was clearly the work of Solomon Matheson, engaged in his one-man crusade against the pavement foulers of Lyme Regis.

She continued past the Cobb Arms pub, the last building on the prom, and crossed the road leading down to the harbour slipway and the jutting stone arm of the Cobb itself. Beyond was the lifeboat rescue building, a car park and then the rows of caravans.

The journalist, Jason, was crouched in the car park, walking in an uncomfortable-looking waddle as he tried to approach a seagull with his camera.

"Don't you already have enough pictures?" she called.

He saw her, almost toppled over, then stood. He leaned against the bonnet of his elderly Land Rover and smiled.

"I'm trying to get some action shots," he said. "Seagulls being just normal birds are dull. Angry squawking seagulls are the money shot."

She nodded.

"Did I hear you got arrested the other day?" he asked.

Figgy held her chin high. "Helping the police with their enquiries, we were."

"Bit of a Miss Marple, is what I hear. Is that where you've been just now?"

She grunted. "Following up a tip-off from Tez the toilet paper man."

"Ah." Jason nodded. "Give him my best. Knowledgeable bloke. You off to the Breaststrokes re-launch thing later?"

"I don't know."

"Might get a few newsworthy snaps there."

She shrugged and walked over to her caravan. She couldn't tell if the number of stones painted to look like tasty snacks outside had increased. There were so many of the darned things. If any seagull was daft enough to think this smorgasbord of fake confections was real, it would take them the best part of an hour to check all of them.

Figgy let herself in, dropped her bag onto the bench seating and thought about dinner.

The Radio 4 Shipping Forecast was broadcast three times a day. The longwave radio signal was still available, but Figgy's grandma had switched to an FM radio several years ago. Currently that meant Figgy could – and would – listen each day shortly after five a.m., just before six p.m., and the event that signalled it was time for bed, at a quarter to one in the morning.

She put together a simple dinner and turned the radio on to catch the end of the news programme. When the Shipping Forecast began, Figgy felt the familiar shiver of comfort run through her.

"Viking and North Utsire," began the announcer. "Variable becoming mainly northerly or northeasterly, three to four, possibly five later in Viking. Slight or moderate. Drizzle patches until later. Moderate or good, occasionally very poor."

Figgy ate fish fingers and chips as the announcement continued. The actual content didn't matter. The words were a formality.

But they were a prayer. As close to a religious incantation as anything Figgy knew. They were a hymn to the sea, to this island nation of fishermen and a comforting reminder that there were forces at work that paid no mind to the petty concerns of the people on land. The tide and the waves and wind didn't care for people. They'd sweep and roar for aeons to come. And somehow, that was a source of comfort.

As the forecast ended, Figgy stood and turned off the

radio. She picked up the last fragment of chip, ate it and took the plate to the sink to wash up.

Beyond the window, she spotted movement outside. For a moment, she thought it was Jason, out there stalking seagulls, but he was still up at the car park. The movement was her new neighbour, Mrs Delacroix's grandson, returning to his caravan. He was carrying another box in from his van parked up at the edge of the car park.

He smiled as he saw Figgy watching, his floppy blue hair bouncing with each footstep.

A thought struck her.

"Blue-haired lout," she whispered.

CHAPTER SIXTY-SIX

POPPY AND LOUIS were on their puddings, bananas and custard, and the three of them were being decadent, eating on the sofa and watching *Hey Duggee* on TV.

Annie's phone rang and she leapt upon it. She'd had a message from Mike when he'd met Tina at the hospital in Dorchester but, since then, there had been radio silence on the new baby front.

But the caller was Figgy. She resisted a groan of disappointment.

"Hi Figgy. Can't talk long. Got to keep the line clear."

"Oh, yes. How's the baby?"

"No idea. Waiting to hear. I was twenty hours giving birth to Tina, so it could be a while. Anyway, I can't talk long—"

"I've found him," Figgy said.

"Found who?"

"The man. The dodgy cigarette man. The one your cousin Gillian called a blue-haired lout."

"Oh?"

CHAPTER SIXTY-SIX

"It's Braydon Delacroix. My new neighbour. I didn't stop to think. He's just moved in, but he's got blue hair, and he's got a van. It could be him."

There were clicks and a change of sound on the line.

"Where are you?" said Annie.

"I'm just creeping out to have a look," Figgy whispered.

"What?"

"Taking a look at his van. Should I challenge him? I could just go up to him and see what he has to say."

Bad idea, Annie thought. Then she remembered something. "His van. Does it have a rubber duck on it?"

"What? No. It's just a regular white transit van."

"I mean on the aerial. Has someone stuck a little rubber duck on it?"

"Hang on." A pause. "Yes! There is! How did you know?"

"Weren't you in the room? That's the van the police are looking for. It's been parked up in front of Marco's shop. It's like their main lead or something."

"Oh," said Figgy. "Then Braydon has to be our man."

Annie clutched the phone. Beside her, little Louis was giggling at the TV. "Right. You need to back off, Figgy. You can't go creeping around at night and—"

"It's still light," Figgy argued.

"No. No. You can't go in without back-up."

There was a new noise on the line. A creak, and then a man's voice.

"What the hell are you doing?" it said.

Figgy started to say something and then there was a shriek, a terrified yell, and the line went dead.

Annie stared at her phone. Her throat had constricted to

almost nothing. She hit redial. The phone did nothing, then dropped the call. Figgy's phone didn't even ring.

"Bloomin' heck," she muttered.

She tried again. No response. She went to the 'Tide times discussion' group on WhatsApp, the code name for the murder chat group, and typed.

Figgy. Call me at once.

The next reply, when it came, was from Helen.

Everything okay?

Everything was seriously not okay.

The cigarette man is Figgy's neighbour. She's gone over there and now she isn't answering. I heard screaming.

Rosamund's was the next reply. *I'm going over. I'm nearest.*

Annie couldn't let Rosamund go over alone.

"OK, kids," she said, putting on a falsely cheery voice. "We're going on a trip out!"

"Yay!" declared Poppy.

"Duggee!" countered Louis, pointing at the telly.

"Emergency trip. Granny has to go and be a superhero and you're coming with."

"Yay!" Poppy repeated.

"Yay!" agreed Louis, who could see when he was outnumbered.

Getting two children into the back of a car always took longer than it should, even for a fit grandma on a mission. But soon enough, everyone was strapped into the back of Annie's car, and she over-revved the engine in her haste to get down to the seafront.

As she pulled into the car park behind the caravans, she saw Helen's dinky Fiat was already there. She'd been prepared to be the first on the scene, to leap into action, fists

CHAPTER SIXTY-SIX

flying at the assailant who had attacked Figgy. Or worse, her fertile imagination had conjured up images of discovering Figgy, still and lifeless outside her caravan.

The fact that Helen was here already was good, of course. But Annie couldn't help feeling disappointment.

"Come on, kids," she said, helping to unbuckle the pair of them. She carried Louis on her hip and Poppy ran ahead as they heard voices coming from the caravan opposite Figgy's, followed by shared laughter.

Another good sign, but hardly what she'd been expecting.

"Knock, knock, coming in," she called as she knocked on the door and entered.

The caravan was identical to Figgy's, at least in terms of layout, but the décor here was much more modern and well-maintained. On a grey plush seating area down one end sat four people: Figgy, Helen, Rosamund and a young scrawny man with a wave of blue hair.

"Oh, another one," said the blue-haired lad, handing a chipped mug of tea to Helen. "I think there's room."

CHAPTER SIXTY-SEVEN

Helen looked Annie up and down. "You're out of puff, darling."

Annie placed Louis on the floor and gave Helen a stern look. "I thought someone was dying."

"Dying?" Figgy frowned. "We're all fine."

"I heard screams. You didn't pick up your phone."

"We had a bit of drama." The young man – Braydon, was it? – squeezed a tea bag on the side of a mug for Annie as he spoke. "I don't know what your little ones would like. I've got some Red Bulls."

"They're fine," she said.

"It wasn't me screaming," Figgy told her.

"It was that wotsit," Braydon said.

Rosamund nodded, sipping at her tea. "The journalist. Jason."

He followed her nod. "Right."

"Oh, I'm glad everyone else is up to speed," Annie said, none the wiser.

"Would you little 'uns like a cup of milk?" Braydon asked

CHAPTER SIXTY-SEVEN

Poppy.

Poppy looked to Annie.

"A small one," Annie said.

"And I've got some Oreos somewhere," added Braydon.

Rosamund shuddered. "Horrible things. Taste like dust."

"They're the best biscuits ever," Figgy said.

Braydon clicked his fingers and pointed at her.

"The screaming journalist, please," said Annie, trying to hold onto her patience.

"I was coming over here," Figgy said.

"Snooping," added Braydon.

"Snooping. And Jason was in the car park taking photos of angry seagulls when Kevin decided to launch himself at him. Jason screamed. It was a proper scream, too."

Braydon grinned. "He was proper scared."

"He had to get out his pepper spray to make Kevin back off." Figgy chuckled. "That man's a bit of a coward."

"But then you vanished," said Annie, "and you weren't picking up your phone."

Helen gestured to a large bowl on a central coffee table. It was full of uncooked rice with the corner of a mobile phone sticking out of it.

"Mrs Delacroix had this bird bath water feature," Figgy said. "Pure bad luck."

"Oh," Annie said. "I see."

Braydon put cups down on the coffee table for Annie and the kids and tore off the seal from a pack of Oreos.

"And that's when I popped my head out," he said. He gazed around at them all. "Now, if I've got this right, you've declared yourselves private detectives and you're investigating Marco's death."

"Yeah, that sort of happened by accident," said Figgy.

"They thought I'd killed him at first," Rosamund added.

Helen waved a hand airily. "I was briefly accused when they found the murder weapon in my girlfriend's workshop."

"But we know they didn't do it," said Figgy.

Helen nodded. "Very gracious of you to say."

Annie frowned. "But we think it might all be to do with some dodgy cigarettes Marco was involved in."

Braydon's face tightened. "Yeah. But you're not really with the cops."

"God, no," Helen said.

"The police haven't exactly looked upon us favourably of late," Rosamund added.

Annie still wasn't entirely sure what was going on, but if her friends trusted this fellow, then she would, too. "Though, for full disclosure, my daughter is a police officer. And both my sons-in-law."

Braydon eyed her. From outside, Annie could hear the screech of seagulls. Was that Kevin again? Or all the others she'd seen on her way over?

"Er, right," Braydon said. "But if I help you out here, you're not going to turn me in?"

She eyed him. "Did you kill Marco?"

"Christ, no."

He looked convincing. "That's all right then," she said.

"And as long as you promise not to use the proceeds from the sale of dodgy cigarettes to fund drug-running, terrorism or people smuggling," added Figgy.

"I wouldn't even know how." Braydon took an Oreo, bit it in half, and pointed down the caravan. "The bedroom at the far end."

Annie walked to the bedroom, stepped through the open door and saw three large boxes on the bed. The nearest was open. Inside was the distinctive design of the Chinese cigarette packets.

"Furongwang." She returned to the living area.

"Listen," said Braydon. "I'm a delivery driver. That's all. Mostly between Exeter and Bournemouth and all places in between. Lots of companies, lots of things. Marco at the fossil shop was just one guy I delivered to. A lot more deliveries than any fossil shop rightly needed."

"You were delivering illegal cigarettes to him," Annie said.

"That's right."

"From Gillian?"

He shook his head. "I don't know who that is."

"Her cousin," Rosamund said.

"The building site," added Annie.

He nodded. "Right. That was me. I was just trying to offload some of the gear I still had in the back of my van. The police were swarming round the man's shop. I had boxes of cigarettes. The guy I pick them up from in Portsmouth didn't want them back. He made that clear."

"A guy in Portsmouth?" Annie asked.

Braydon shrugged. "I'm guessing stuff comes off a lorry or something from the port. I go over there to collect them, and then I deliver them wherever I'm told to. I don't ask questions cos I like having a job. Now Marco's dead and I'm lumbered with these boxes of cigarettes. I can hardly go flogging them round local pubs and shops."

"So, there's no link at all between the cigarettes and Gillian Hewish?" she said.

He shook his head. "Like I said, I don't know who that is."

"Damn. I thought that made sense."

She sipped the tea. It was surprisingly pleasant.

"You could just destroy the cigarettes," suggested Rosamund.

"Sorry?" Brandon said.

"Destroy them. Make a bonfire. Cigarettes are famously flammable."

Braydon smiled while offering Poppy and Louis an Oreo each. "Sorry, lady, but I need to make ends meet. D'you know how hard it is to make a living in this corner of the world? Salaries are low. That van needs a service. I don't know where I'm gonna get the money from."

There was a part of Annie that was unsympathetic. Braydon made his money as part of an international smuggling ring. But at the same time, she didn't live in the same world as young people who struggled to make ends meet.

Figgy was on her feet. She stood quite still, her hands clutching the cup. She didn't move or speak.

"You all right, Figgy-love?" Annie said.

Figgy's eyes were screwed up like she was trying to see something in the far distance.

"I think she's gone into the Matrix," Rosamund said.

"Do young people do that?" asked Helen.

Figgy's lips moved slowly. "I..."

"Yes?" said Annie.

"Use your words, darling," added Helen.

Figgy blinked rapidly. "I think I know who killed Marco."

"Yes?"

She took a hand away from her cup and flexed it as if holding something.

"I think..."

"Only thinks she knows," said Rosamund.

CHAPTER SIXTY-SEVEN

"No," said Figgy. "It's Kevin."

"Kevin killed Marco?" said Helen.

"Who's Kevin?" asked Braydon.

"A seagull," replied Annie.

Figgy looked at Helen. "No. But it's like you said, the more you feed him, the more he comes back."

"I did say that."

"And the painted stones were the answer."

"Er, they were?"

"And that's the same. The stone. The rock. The murder weapon."

"Do you understand what's going on?" Rosamund asked.

"No," admitted Annie. "I feel like I'm at one of those arty plays where everyone talks nonsense, and someone ends up in the nud in the second act."

Helen waved at her to be quiet. "Go on, Figgy. You know who killed Marco?"

Figgy stood up straight. Her expression clear. "Yes, I do."

"Well, who was it?" asked Annie.

Her gaze took them all in. "We need to go to the re-opening of Breaststrokes."

Rosamund checked her watch. "Now?"

"Yes. Now. I think the murderer will be there."

Annie gestured to her grandchildren. "We have little 'uns with us."

"They can stay with me," said Braydon.

Annie smiled. "I like you, Braydon. You've got a good heart. But I'm not leaving my grandkids with a man who might offer them a Red Bull."

"Then bring them along," said Figgy with urgency. "Come on. Let's go."

CHAPTER SIXTY-EIGHT

THE FOUR WOMEN, one man and two children headed along the beachfront path to Breaststrokes café bar. The entire front of the building was open to the promenade. Wicker sofas and café tables spilled out onto the path. Pink and blue lights pulsed in time with eighties disco music from within.

"Loud!" exclaimed Louis as they neared.

"Is it too loud, love?" Annie asked, still carrying him.

He shook his head. Beside her, Poppy threw enthusiastic fist jabs and body pumps. She had the moves, just like her granny.

"OK, Figgy," said Annie. "This is your show. Who's the killer and what are we doing about it?"

"I don't even know if they're here," said Figgy, looking around.

"Well, if we're here, I'm getting a cocktail," Helen said. "Cocktail, anyone? Cocktail?"

Rosamund nodded.

Figgy pursed her lips as they entered the bar. "I don't know what cocktails I like."

CHAPTER SIXTY-EIGHT

"Good!" said Helen. "Time for an education!"

Annie was following them through the crowd when she realised her phone was buzzing. She shifted Louis on her hip, checked that boogie-dancing Poppy was still with her, and got her phone out.

It was Dougie. She almost dropped it in her haste to answer.

"Dougie! Dougie!"

"Annie?"

"Has the baby come?" she asked. "Are they all right?"

"All fine. Long way to go apparently. Tina just wanted... Sorry, Annie. It's really loud where you are."

"Yeah. Sorry 'bout that."

"Are you in a nightclub?"

She looked around. "Not really. Sort of a café bar."

"What about Poppy? And Louis?"

She jiggled Louis. "They're with me. We're all having fun."

"But it's way past their bedtime."

She winced. "I know, I know. But they're helping their granny and we're all having a good time."

"Helping you what?"

Annie debated not telling him.

"Figgy thinks she knows who the murderer is."

"What?"

"Yeah. So, we've come down to Breaststrokes and I think she's going to find the murderer and accuse them."

"What?"

"I know. It's not your regular Friday night out but the urge seized her. I think she said it's got something to do with the seagulls."

"You can't go around accusing people of murder!"

"I'm not. Figgy is."

"No. Look. Listen... Damn, they're calling me in."

"Who? Who's calling you? Is it the baby?"

"Don't do anything stupid," said Dougie. He hung up.

Annie stared at the phone. Louis and Poppy were staring at her.

"Your daddy, your Uncle Dougie, is doing important work looking after your mums," she told them, trying to distract herself from thoughts of her daughter's labour. "He said we should all have lemonade and chips."

Louis clapped his hands. *How wonderful, to think chips and lemonade are the most marvellous things in the world.*

"Good," she said. "Let's go find some."

She moved towards the bar. The place was full. Men and women stood around chatting and sipping drinks. A stage had been set up in the back corner, possibly for a launch announcement. Annie cast about, wondering if and when cousin Gillian might show up.

She didn't see Gillian, but she was surprised to see Harper, Helen's girlfriend, apparently in the company of Rosamund's lad, Cameron. Harper seemed suited to her workshop, not to loud bars.

Helen, standing next to Annie with a bright orange cocktail in her hand, seemed equally surprised to see Harper.

"What on earth are you doing here?"

"Evening, everyone," said Annie, her arms around her diminutive entourage.

"We were just talking sculpture," said Cameron. "Hi, Figgy." He raised his bottle in a toast to Figgy.

Across the group of women, Figgy smiled at Cameron.

"Hey, Mum," he said, seeing Rosamund, who was holding another bright orange cocktail.

CHAPTER SIXTY-EIGHT

"I didn't mean 'what are *you* doing here?'" Helen said to Harper. "I meant, 'what are you doing *here*?'"

Harper gestured with her glass of coke. "This woman Gillian invited me. Wanted to talk about a piece of installation art for this place."

"Is she here?" asked Annie, looking around. She glanced at Figgy; was Gillian the murderer?

"I'm sure she's here somewhere," Harper said.

The song changed to Wham's *Wake Me Up Before You Go-Go*. Poppy was getting into her groove. Rosamund held up one hand to the little girl so they could dance together. The other hand was busy keeping her cocktail upright.

"Figgy?" said Annie. "Where are we with our murder vibes? Ready to disclose?"

Figgy didn't look ready to out a murderer. Perhaps she'd got ahead of herself, only now realising that it was one thing to play amateur sleuth and quite another to throw accusations at real human beings.

As she looked around, Annie saw a familiar figure appear at the entrance to the café bar. Detective Sergeant Nathan Strunk stood with hands on hips, surveying the space with a tense expression. His gaze latched onto Annie's and his eyebrows went up. He pointed a finger at her.

Annie pointed a questioning finger at herself.

DS Strunk nodded.

"Um, excuse me, girls," she said. "I think a policeman wants to talk to me." She started to move away then turned. "You all right watching Poppy a second?"

"Absolutely," said Rosamund, still dancing.

"Policeman?" said Figgy.

"Nothing to worry about I'm sure," said Annie. Still holding Louis, she went towards Nathan.

She had to squeeze past Jason as he tried to snap photos of the more notable attendees.

"That's it, Solomon," he said, "show the mayor your dog mess petition. That's it. Eyes wide for the camera."

The heft of Jason's satchel almost knocked Louis from her arms, but Annie wheeled around him and tottered over to DS Strunk. He wore a stern but weary expression.

"Did Dougie call you by any chance?" she asked him.

"What?"

"Dougie!"

He had chosen to stand next to a speaker by the entrance. Louis had his hands held over his ears.

"Dougie called me!" said Nathan. "He was worried you were about to do something stupid."

"Stupid? Me?"

He made a circling motion with his finger.

"All of you! He said you were still sticking your nose in police business."

"Isn't everything police business, Detective Sergeant?"

"Do not play cute with me, Mrs Abbott. Think of the upset you've already caused Tina."

Annie wanted to snap at this young man for sticking his nose into her family and her activities with her friends. But he was right.

"I promise I'm not going to do anything rash this evening," she said.

"What?"

"I'm not going to do anything rash. But I can't make promises for the others."

"What did you say?"

She took a deep breath. "I think Figgy Edmunds knows who murdered Marco Callington."

CHAPTER SIXTY-EIGHT

Just as she mentioned Figgy's name, someone cut the music.

Over on the little stage, bar manager Babs Spiro stood frozen, the microphone halfway to her mouth. She stared, open-mouthed, at Annie. Most of the crowd had turned to stare at her, too.

Down by the stage, cousin Gillian craned her neck to look at Annie. "Did you just say you know who murdered him?" she asked.

Annie took in all the faces.

"Um," she said.

CHAPTER SIXTY-NINE

"Well." Annie cleared her throat.

She felt like a little girl on stage at a school play, a whole hall of expectant faces watching her. There were only two options: crumble and flee the stage or make the stage your own and soar.

"I didn't say *I* specifically knew." She made her way toward the stage, picking a route that passed her friends. "I mean, I've put in a lot of the work. More than my fair share. But, no, I said that my friend, Figgy Edmunds, knows who killed him."

As she passed Figgy, she reached for the younger woman's hand. Figgy resisted.

"Come on."

"No."

"Come on!"

Annie stepped up onto the little stage, dragging Figgy with her. Babs, still stunned, stepped obligingly away from the microphone.

CHAPTER SIXTY-NINE

Annie smiled at the audience. Figgy, for reasons known only to herself, had decided to curtsey.

"Hi everyone." Annie gave a little wave. "I'm Annie Abbott. Long-time local resident, enthusiastic swimmer and dog walker, general all-round nuisance. This is my friend, Figgy. You might remember her from recent 'mad woman shares home with seagull' headlines."

"It didn't say I was mad," said Figgy.

"Didn't it? Anyway, we've been lucky enough to be involved with... no, lucky isn't the word. We happened to get caught up in the business surrounding Marco Callington's death, God rest his soul."

"Horrible bugger," someone called from the crowd.

"That too, it would appear." Annie squinted into the lights. "You see, what happened was, we – that's me and Figgy – found Marco's body in the front seat of Rosamund Winters' car."

"That's right, drag me into it," said Rosamund.

"Well, you come up and explain it."

Annie was surprised to see Rosamund do exactly that, orange cocktail in one hand and little Poppy Anderson in the other.

"Can I be very clear," said Rosamund to the assembled crowd, "that although he did spend a brief amount of time in my car and, yes, I did take him to the beach without realising it, he wasn't killed in my car or ultimately found there."

"No," Annie agreed. "The police found Marco's body in a wheelie bin round the back of his shops."

There were a few gasps.

"Marco's shop, Jurassic Fossils, is at the front, opposite the museum," Annie continued. "The neighbouring shops are Helen's lovely gallery and Solomon's delightful children's shop which, if you've not been, is the perfect place to buy things for your loved ones." She snuggled Louis.

There were a few loving '*aws* from the crowd. Gasps and aws – this was an audience that craved interaction.

"And good value for money despite what some members of the press would have you believe," added Solomon gruffly.

Annie ignored him. "For those that don't know, and with apologies to the squeamish, Marco was clonked on the bonce with a large fossil."

"It was later found in Harper's workshop," Figgy added, gesturing to the sculptor.

Helen was on the stage instantly. "I want to make it utterly clear that neither myself nor Harper had anything to do with the murder," she told everyone. "Despite some accusations people might have made in the heat of the moment."

"This is Helen, who owns the gallery," Rosamund said.

"We're all part of the Lyme Regis Women's Swimming Club," added Figgy.

"Not a club," said Annie.

"We swim every morning. You should join us," said Helen.

"But definitely not a club."

Jason crouched before the women on the stage and took a photo of the four of them.

Annie looked around at the people below her: Solomon, Gillian, Harper and more than a dozen others she knew from about the town.

"Figgy, why don't you tell them what you know?"

"Remember, slander is a crime," added Gillian, a twinkle in her eye.

CHAPTER SIXTY-NINE

Still standing by the entrance, DS Strunk was watching with horrified fascination.

Figgy stepped toward the microphone. "Um, I don't have any evidence."

There were immediate groans.

"But! But it's like an impressionist painting. You have to look at all the little bits and it makes sense. You see, Marco was hit over the head, probably in his shop or the alley at the back, and then the murder weapon, the rock with the fossil in it, it was found in Helen and Harper's back yard. So I guess it makes sense that the killer threw it over the wall."

"But it was in the workshop building," Rosamund pointed out.

"Yes," said Helen, "but someone had tidied up so it would be neat for when the newspaper chap came round to write his article."

Figgy nodded. "Exactly. I think that's what happened. The killer hit Marco and left him for dead, and then threw the weapon away which, when you think about it, wasn't very smart. And then the killer ran off. It was probably really early that morning because Rosamund came round later and, while she was in Helen's shop, Marco crawled or staggered into the back of Rosamund's car."

"Sounds a bit unlikely," said Babs. "Bit silly, really."

"He was concussed and dying and scared," Figgy said. "People don't do sensible things even when they're thinking straight. But that's what happened. He crawled into the front while we were all swimming and that's when he died. We found him and took him back to his shop."

"For reasons we won't go into now," said Annie. "But good solid reasons."

"But while we were there," added Figgy, taking up the thread, "the killer must have come back. They saw Marco in the car. Who knows what they thought had happened, but this was their victim. They had to get rid of him, so they hoiked him out of the car and stuffed him in a wheelie bin."

Some of the audience recoiled in disgust.

"That's how the police found him," Figgy continued. "Bashed on the head, stuffed in a bin – oh! – and with some irritation around the eyes. This all says something important."

"The person's a psycho," grunted Solomon Matheson.

"No." Figgy shook her head. "I don't think so. All those things show that the murderer was a real amateur. Bungling. Clumsy. Panicky. That no one saw them do it in the first place was just pure dumb luck. I mean, what kind of person comes back to the crime scene within an hour only to find the body sitting in someone's car? That's someone who's scared."

"I don't think anyone was scared of Marco Callington," said Solomon, puffing his chest out.

"No, I don't think you would be," agreed Figgy. "Quite the opposite."

"And what's that supposed to mean?" he demanded.

Annie laughed. "I don't think there's a person here who hasn't seen your one-man crusade against dog mess in the town this past week. I'm sure we'll get to read all about it in the next edition of the *Lyme Echo*."

Figgy nodded. "I think we'd considered Helen and you, Mr Matheson, as possible suspects. Neither of you liked what Marco was doing with his shop and both of you would have considered expanding into that space with him out of the way."

Solomon was silent.

CHAPTER SIXTY-NINE

"But to reiterate, we didn't kill him," said Helen.

Figgy looked across the crowd. "It was someone who was in the area very early that morning, before the shops were open, even before the early cafés had opened their doors."

Annie found her gaze drawn to Harper and Cameron, standing side by side near the front of the crowd.

CHAPTER SEVENTY

"There were people who had justification to hate Marco Callington," said Figgy. "I never knew him, but he seemed... unpleasant."

Rosamund scoffed. "Not half."

"But we've also discovered that he was involved in the illegal sale of smuggled cigarettes."

"Here we go." Gillian sighed, gesturing with her arms. "I've got my solicitor on speed-dial, just so you know."

"Speed-dial?" Annie asked. "What century are you from?"

Figgy held out a hand. "The cigarettes had nothing to do with you, Ms Hewish. We know that now. Sorry. Marco was getting cigarettes from some dodgy importer, in Portsmouth, we think."

"We can't reveal our sources," said Helen. Annie looked up to see young Braydon Delacroix, squirming at the centre of the crowd.

"No," Figgy said. "But we know he had them secretly imported in what were supposed to be consignments of

CHAPTER SEVENTY

fossils. That's how he was making his real money. Selling them on. Because it's difficult to make an honest living in a town like Lyme." She looked at Gillian. "To find somewhere cheap enough to live when half the properties are being sold as second homes to holidaymakers."

Gillian had her arms folded across her chest. "Building holiday homes brings jobs and money."

"To some," Annie muttered. Rumblings, some of assent, some of disagreement, were working through the crowd. The assent was mainly coming from the locals, people she recognised.

"Trying to make a living out here," said Figgy. "It isn't like life in the big cities. It's different. My new neighbour, Braydon, said that to me earlier tonight, and that's when I realised what was going on."

"Finally!" said Gillian. "Mad seagull lady is getting to the point."

"Shut your cakehole, Gillian," Annie said. "The newspaper article didn't say she was mad."

"But the seagull newspaper article *is* part of this," Figgy said.

Annie looked at her. "Is it?"

"Sort of. But also, yes, definitely. And this place." She spread her hands to indicate the bar. "You see, Marco was going to buy this place."

"In his dreams," Gillian grunted.

"He was. That's why he was down here. That's where he met Rosamund and upset her so much that she threw her drink at him."

"But didn't kill him," Rosamund inserted.

"He was going to buy the place, but suddenly he didn't have the money. He'd had money set aside to put down a deposit or whatever, but then he had to spend that on something else."

Annie suddenly understood. "The blackmailer!"

"Exactly," said Figgy.

Annie was keen to share what she'd realised. "You see, there was a note in Marco's shop. Someone had written a note saying, 'What's this worth to you?' or something like that. We thought it was about a fossil evaluation, but it wasn't. It was about the cigarette business. Someone knew Marco was doing something dodgy, so they blackmailed him."

"Now, that's a motive," said Rosamund.

Cameron put his hand up, like he was in a classroom. "Wouldn't that be a motive for Marco to kill whoever was blackmailing him?"

"Yes," agreed Figgy. "Because it's like the thing with the seagulls."

"The seagulls?"

"Yes. It's like that thing Helen said to me."

Helen looked none the wiser. "What thing?"

Figgy looked at her. "That there was no point in me trying to appease Kevin with cakes and treats. Blackmailers are never satisfied, not until you deal with them."

"I *did* say that."

"Marco was being blackmailed, and the blackmailer came back for more. I don't know how many times Marco paid them off. Maybe once, maybe more. But I think that morning, the blackmailer, who knew Marco's business inside out, had come to demand more money. Maybe they brought that note. Or they came to follow up on that note. *I know what you're up to, Marco. How much is that worth to you?*"

"Right," said Rosamund, catching on. "So, they were

talking in Marco's shop early that morning, and Marco had had enough. He snapped."

Figgy nodded. "Exactly."

"And there was a fight."

"Probably."

"And the blackmailer, panicking, hit Marco on the head with the closest thing to hand, perhaps as they were trying to run away."

"Yes," Figgy agreed.

"And then," Rosamund continued, "without thinking it through, they just threw the murder weapon over the nearest fence."

Figgy nodded. In Annie's arms, little Louis was starting to grizzle. She chucked his cheeks and pulled a face at him.

"Definitely," said Figgy. "Although they regretted that and tried to do something about it later." She paused for breath. "We now know lots of things about the murderer. They wanted money. They were greedy. And when they realised that they shouldn't have thrown the murder weapon away, they tried to do something about it."

"So, who was it?" asked Babs. "Do you know who the blackmailer is?"

"Yes," Figgy said. "But it only really became clear when Helen said that other thing."

"I'm on a roll here," said Helen. "What did I say this time?"

"John Napier's cock."

"I beg your pardon!" spat Solomon Matheson.

"It's a story about a bird who solved a crime," said Figgy. "The point is, the guilty party tried to distance themselves from the crime. Trying to act normal and innocent only served to point the finger of guilt at them."

A sea of confused faces stared up at Figgy.

"You all know me now," she said. "And why? Because of that flipping newspaper story about Kevin the seagull. Front page news. You remember?"

"Is she saying Kevin did it?" Helen whispered to Rosamund.

Rosamund was staring at Figgy, her cheeks flushed. The cocktail glass was still in her hand. "No," she said.

Annie felt she was on the cusp of understanding it all now, but she wasn't about to spoil Figgy's big moment.

"On the morning after a grisly murder in Lyme Regis," Figgy said, "the front-page news in our local paper was the fact that I've got an annoying seagull living near me. Isn't that right, Jason?"

Annie looked at Jason Mordaunt. "You said the murder didn't have enough of a local angle for the *Lyme Echo*. In fact, I remember you saying the police would probably find his death was a result of his activities beyond this town, didn't you?"

Jason lowered his camera but said nothing.

"Quite insightful, really," Annie said. "'Cos you knew about the dodgy cigarettes, didn't you?"

"He was an investigative journalist in the big city," Rosamund said.

"With big city money," added Helen.

Figgy was chewing her lip. "But he couldn't afford to replace that old Land Rover of his."

"But I need it," said Jason, his voice little more than a whisper. "Up hill and down dale..."

"And your sudden interest in Harper's work," Helen said. "That was just an excuse to poke around our yard looking for the stone you killed Marco with."

CHAPTER SEVENTY

He swallowed hard. "I never."

"This long streak of nothing, murder someone?" scoffed Solomon. "And then pick up a body and put it in a wheelie bin?"

"Oh, don't be deceived," Annie told him. "What was it you said, Jason? Self-defence lessons and weight-training. Oh!" She slapped her thigh. "The eye irritation!"

She looked at Figgy, who was nodding in encouragement.

"If you open that satchel of yours, Jason," Annie said, "will we find some pepper spray in there? Figgy saw you try to use it on Kevin earlier. I bet the police can do all manner of clever things to match that, can't they? Because when you and Marco were fighting, you used that on him."

Jason was shaking his head and clutching his bag. DS Strunk pushed his way through the crowd.

"Perhaps we could just have a chat about this at the station, Mr Mordaunt," he said.

Jason had a sickened, pale look on his face. He nodded.

"Make room!" said the detective. The crowd, muttering and peering at the accused as he was led away, parted to let them through.

Poppy tugged at Annie's waist.

She turned to her granddaughter. "Yes, poppet?"

"What's happening?"

"Well, dearest, your grandma just solved a murder mystery."

"I think *Figgy* solved a murder mystery," said Rosamund.

"We all solved a murder mystery," Helen corrected.

Figgy grinned. "Not only a swimming club but also a murder-solving club."

Annie was about to say, 'not a club'. She decided to nod instead.

"Well, aren't we bloody marvellous?" Helen exclaimed, raising her glass.

Nathan and Jason were now shadows on the promenade, fading into the dark.

"The things people do," Annie said. "Stupid pointless things, when there's... when they could be enjoying crisps and lemonade."

"Crisps and lemonade!" declared Poppy.

"Memonade!" agreed Louis and planted a wet kiss on Annie's cheek.

CHAPTER SEVENTY-ONE

"Bloody hell."

Daisy, Tina's brand-new daughter, was sleeping in the clear-sided crib beside Tina's bed.

Tina had had a number of visitors over the past twenty-four hours. Naomi and Dougie had been there for part of the labour and had returned afterwards to offer congratulations. Mike, his clothes spattered with the dried plaster and paint of his DIY job, had been with her throughout, but had been sent home to sleep by the ward team. Mike's mum had dragged herself over from Bournemouth to look briefly at the little girl and declare she was the absolute spitting image of Mike's long-departed dad.

Through all of those visits, there had been much chat about babies and polite inquiries into Tina's health.

But her conversation with DS Strunk was focused solely on Marco Callington's murder.

"Anyway," he finished, "although Mordaunt's solicitor encouraged him to give a 'no comment' throughout the interview, between the pepper spray, some partial prints in

Marco's shop, and several unexplained cash deposits into Mordaunt's bank account, we've got enough evidence for the CPS to take it to court."

"Great stuff."

"Court won't give bail so..." He brushed his hands together. "We'll see him at trial in several months' time, and we can expect the defence team to have all manner of fun and games with our investigation."

"But he'll go down?" she asked.

"Hell, yes. I'd put a hundred quid on the defence putting in a guilty plea, push the line that he was provoked, that Marco attacked first. The defence will argue that this is a one-time thing, that he has an unblemished record, maybe even try for manslaughter."

Tina glanced over at her new daughter then looked back at the DS. "He killed a man. For money."

He nodded. "He's a scumbag and the court will see it."

She smiled, then stopped herself. "Oh, God. They're not going to get my mum up in the witness box, are they?"

"Hold that thought." He made a tight-lipped expression. "She's waiting outside."

Tina's gaze flicked to the door. "I'm impressed she's held off this long."

"Oh, she's been mad desperate to come see you and the young 'un."

"But she knows I'm annoyed with her?"

The DS allowed a smile to slip out. "Have you ever owned dogs?"

She frowned. "On and off. There's always been some in the family somewhere."

He nodded. "You know that thing when a dog's done something naughty. It's eaten a hunk of beef off the kitchen

CHAPTER SEVENTY-ONE

side or ripped apart your sofa. And it knows it's done something very wrong, but it's very sorry and it loves you utterly and just wants to be with you."

"Riiight."

"You know that thing? The dog's ears are down. Big sad eyes. But at the same time, its tail is thumping a hundred times a minute and it can't stop moving round in frantic anxious circles?"

"That's my mum, is it?"

"I've honestly never seen it in a human being before. I can't work out if it's adorable or heart-breaking."

She laughed, then winced, putting a hand on her stomach. "This is my fifty-something fruitcake of a mother you're talking about."

"Hey," he said, "I'm just calling it as I see it."

Tina smiled. "Fine. Send her in."

He stood. "Good. And Tina...?"

"Yes?"

"I had a message from DI Patterson."

"Congratulations?"

"In a roundabout sort of way. She says she doesn't want to see you at a crime scene for at least the next six months. Even if your mum's involved."

"Got it." She threw him a sloppy salute.

DS Strunk left, and before the door in the side ward had a chance to swing shut, her mum walked through it.

She truly did have a sad hangdog look on her face. She stepped forward, glanced at her new grandchild and hesitated.

"You know I'm very angry with you," Tina said.

"I do." Annie held her hands together at her waist, like a contrite schoolgirl brought to speak to the headteacher.

"And do you know why I'm angry with you?"

"It's because I solved a murder when you said I shouldn't."

Tina growled. "Want to try that again?"

"I interfered with police business when I promised I wouldn't."

"You took my son and niece to a nightclub!"

"Café bar."

"Sorry?" said Tina.

"Yes. I did. I didn't mean to, but I got caught up in the moment."

"Uh-huh." Tina regarded her reckless mother. "I half expected you to say bigger girls told you to do it."

"Well... If I'm honest, Figgy was the instigator this time but... no, I did what I did. And I'm sorry."

"Yeah?"

"Yeah. I mean, yes. I am sorry. I don't mean to cause you grief and I know it must be difficult being a policewoman even in this day and age. You don't want your mum embarrassing you in front of the other coppers."

"Do you know what the worst thing about you is?" Tina said.

"It's that I'm annoying, isn't it? Yeah. Annoying. I think I'm probably annoying."

Tina seethed. "The worst thing about you is that you do all this... stuff, and you drive me nuts, and... but it's impossible to stay angry with you about it. Not for long. You are the most selfishly selfless person I've ever met and you're infuriating. But, despite all that, you're my mum and I love you."

Annie's eyes flicked up. "You love me?"

"Of course I bloody do. It's the law or something. And I

don't have another mum to love so I've got you. But, by all the gods, I do have limits, Mum."

Annie gave a solemn nod. "I understand."

"Good." The telling off was done. "Now, do you want to hug me – gently! – and come meet your granddaughter?"

Annie didn't need asking twice. She hugged Tina then crouched down by the crib.

"She's asleep," she said.

Tina suppressed a smile. "Like that's going to stop you picking her up."

Annie dipped in and picked up the tiny baby. Tina felt her heart fill up. Daisy mewled for a moment and then fell quiet again, still sleeping. Annie kissed her soft crown and sniffed it.

"You can't beat that new baby smell," she said.

"I remember it with Louis," Tina said. "You're right, though. I haven't stopped to appreciate it. I've just been too high on drugs and exhaustion."

Annie wrinkled her nose. "The exhaustion wears off after the first twenty, twenty-five years. That's why being granny's the best. All the joy. None of the pain. I've brought presents." She hesitated. "Well, they're sort of for me."

"That's a novel approach to presents." Tina reached for the gift bag Annie had put on the table.

Tina reached in and pulled out two hardback books. "Louis's journal, Daisy's journal ... What's this?"

Her mum licked her lips. "Well, I've been having a good hard think, and it occurs to me I can sometimes go overboard with the presents and stuff."

"You think?"

"I do. And they do say that experiences are much more rewarding than things."

"They do say that."

"So that's what these are for," Annie said. "It's the journal of granny stuff with my grandchildren. As much or as little as you need. You can put stuff in there. Naomi, too. I got one for Poppy. We can decide it together."

Tina squeezed her mum's arm. "I don't want to control you, Mum."

"I know that, love."

"Scratch that. I *do* want to control you, but I know I can't. No more than I can control the waves or the wind. Cos that's what you are."

"Wet and windy. Got it."

"But this is a thoughtful gesture."

"Good." Annie held Daisy close and sniffed her head again.

"It's a thoughtful gesture but... But it's never going to work. Is it?"

Annie shrugged. "Probably not. But we'll try. That's what's great about life. We get lots of chances."

CHAPTER SEVENTY-TWO

THE PAINTER, Clifford Muldoon, sat at the end of the Cobb and painted his pictures.

As far as Annie was aware, he was there every day. Which was understandable. There were sunny days and cloudy days and storm-flashing wave-crashing scary days, and they were all beautiful in their own fashion.

However, there were certain rare days when the gods of the sea and the air offered up something so perfect that you just had to be there.

This particular beautiful day was a Monday, with the beauty starting at sunrise, just before the first swimmers of the Lyme Regis Women's Swimming Club entered the sea.

As Annie tiptoed over the band of sharp pebbles by the shore, there came a panting holler and Rosamund ran past, splashed into the waves and then, less than two seconds later, did a half-dive half-flop into the water and began to swim.

Annie tried to bat away the splashes and made her way through the shallows in a much more dignified fashion.

Annie knew she wasn't a model of dignity, but you didn't have to go leaping into the sea just because it was there.

Out towards the buoys, the young Australian, Juniper, was encouraging Figgy to swim out further than she usually did. Figgy was giggling, a nervous giggle.

Annie headed out to where Helen was swimming gently along with Pammy Hampton and the twins Sally and Peg.

"Oh, here comes the new grandma," Helen said.

"Third time over," said Pammy. "I'd be happy if my Chris would give me one."

"Children are over-rated," said Sally, getting a knowing look from her sister.

"How's the newborn?" asked Helen.

Annie smiled. "Very good. Has the air of a young Danny DeVito."

"What are they going to call it?" asked Sally.

"I think it's a toss-up between YouTube and Bonjella," said Annie.

"The names today!" added Peg.

Annie looked at Helen, who returned her wink.

Beautiful day or not, they couldn't spend the whole morning in the sea. As they towelled off by the sea wall, Helen dipped into her bag and pulled out a newspaper. "Take a look at this."

"Is it another 'woman lives with seagull' story, is it?" Rosamund asked.

Helen opened the paper so they all could see.

"Any old iron?" read Figgy. "How local woman turns scrap into art."

"Not exactly the tone Harper and I would have liked," Helen said, "but it's there."

Looking over Helen's shoulder, Annie admired the

CHAPTER SEVENTY-TWO

centre-page image of Harper McCoppin in her workshop, the glow of the fire behind her, an arm resting on one of her larger dragonfly creations.

"He could have let her wipe the oil off her face," Rosamund said.

Annie wasn't so sure. "I think it makes her look ready for action."

"Sexy," added Helen.

"Hang on," said Figgy, "so Jason actually wrote the article, even though he was using it as cover to look for the murder weapon?"

"It's even stranger that the paper decided to publish a piece written by a man who's just been arrested for murder," Annie said.

"Clearly, they have no qualms about separating the creator from his crimes," said Helen. "Anyway, it's a very nice piece, don't you think? It might bring some more customers in." She tapped Rosamund's arm. "And we've sold your painting."

"*Viscera?*"

"Some buyer in the Home Counties. Going to package it up for them later today. I'll get the cash to you, soon as."

Annie gave a little clap. "Well done."

As Helen folded the copy of the *Lyme Echo* and carefully stowed it away, Rosamund said, "Well, I have news as well. Very small news but..." She took out her phone and tapped on it. "Figgy helped me set it up yesterday."

She showed them the screen. Annie could see a green and orange flower logo, the name 'Burrow' and some control buttons.

"What is it?" asked Helen.

Rosamund tapped a big round plus icon. "Heating goes

up." She tapped a big round minus icon. "Heating goes down. Finally, I'm in control."

"Oh, that's not small news at all," said Annie. "That's an important step."

"We're working on the security system next weekend," added Figgy.

"Get you, Figgy."

Figgy nodded. "My therapist has been very pleased with my recent progress. Apart from the murder stuff, obviously."

Annie blew out her lips. "The murder stuff is par for the course."

"We solve murders," said Helen.

"First rule of swimming club," agreed Rosamund. "Or is it murder club?"

"It's not a..." Annie began, then stopped.

Figgy, having got changed, stuffed her towel into her bag and made to leave.

"You fetching the coffees from the Kiosk?" Annie asked.

Figgy looked at the Kiosk and shook her head. "No coffees. Not for me. No ice cream either."

Rosamund's mouth was a circle of surprise. "Figgy swimming and not staying for coffee and ice cream?"

"No." She pointed up to the promenade where Cameron Winters waited in T-shirt and shorts. "We're on a breakout mission today."

"Breakout?" said Rosamund.

Figgy turned to her friend, her eyes sparkling. "We're going to go get a McDonald's in Dorchester."

"Not much of a mission," said Helen.

Figgy turned halfway up the beach. "And if that goes well, we're going to try wild camping on Exmoor."

Annie laughed. "Dream big, Figgy."

"Dreaming big, Annie."

Annie watched her head up to meet Cameron, then turned to look at the sea, which shimmered all along the sweeping bay, right round to distant Portland Bill.

It was most definitely a beautiful day.

We hope you enjoyed reading *The Swimming Club*. We have another mystery for you, which you can get for free as ebook or audio from our book club or you can buy in paperback. *The Missing Corpse* is a case which hinges on the most important question when it comes to cream tea: jam first, or cream? Read it for free at: rachelmclean.com/the-missing-corpse or buy the paperback from book retailers.

Happy Reading,
Rachel and Millie

READ A NOVELLA, THE MISSING CORPSE

When one of the members of the swimming club takes on a new job cleaning holiday lets, she expects her biggest challenge to be working her way through six cottages before the next guests arrive.

She doesn't expect a mystery.

Why is a picture in one of six identical cottages very slightly different to the others? Who is the mysterious woman who let herself in and cleaned before Rosamund got there? And what's that awful smell in cottage number one?

As Dorset Police investigate two murders they suspect of being connected with organised crime, Rosamund's mysteries may be more serious than she thinks. Will she and her swimming buddies be about to solve a double homicide?

Download the ebook or audiobook of *The Missing Corpse* for FREE at rachelmclean.com/the-missing-corpse or buy in paperback from book retailers.

ALSO BY RACHEL MCLEAN

The DI Zoe Finch Series – buy from book retailers.

Deadly Wishes

Deadly Choices

Deadly Desires

Deadly Terror

Deadly Reprisal

Deadly Fallout

Deadly Christmas

Deadly Origins, the FREE Zoe Finch prequel

The Dorset Crime Series – buy from book retailers.

The Corfe Castle Murders

The Clifftop Murders

The Island Murders

The Monument Murders

The Millionaire Murders

The Fossil Beach Murders

The Blue Pool Murders

The Lighthouse Murders

The Ghost Village Murders

The Poole Harbour Murders

The Chesil Beach Murders

The Beach Hut Murders

...and more to come

The McBride & Tanner Series – buy from book retailers.

Blood and Money

Death and Poetry

Power and Treachery

Secrets and History

The Cumbria Crime Series by Rachel McLean and Joel Hames – buy from book retailers.

The Harbour

The Mine

The Cairn

The Barn

The Lake

The Wood

The Port

The Marsh

ALSO BY MILLIE RAVENSWORTH

The Cozy Craft Mysteries – Buy now in ebook and paperback

The Wonderland Murders

The Painted Lobster Murders

The Sequinned Cape Murders

The Swan Dress Murders

The Tie-Dyed Kaftan Murders

The Scarecrow Murders